QUEEN OF VENGEANCE

THE KNIGHTS OF ALANA
BOOK II

AARON HODGES

Edited by Genevieve Lerner
Proofread by Sara Houston
Illustration by Joemel Requeza
Map by Michael Hodges

ABOUT THE AUTHOR

 Aaron Hodges was born in 1989 in the small town of Whakatane, New Zealand. He studied for five years at the University of Auckland, completing a Bachelors of Science in Biology and Geography, and a Masters of Environmental Engineering. After working as an environmental consultant for two years, he grew tired of office work and decided to quit his job in 2014 and see the world. One year later, he published his first novel - Stormwielder.

FOLLOW AARON HODGES...

And receive TWO FREE novels and a short story!

https://aaronhodgesauthor.com/newsletter

Book 3: Age of Gods

Book 4: Dreams of Fury

The Alfurian Chronicles

Book 1: Defiant

Book 2: Guardian

Book 3: Conquest

The Swords of Heaven and Hell

Book 1: <u>Darkstrider</u>

The Four Circles

Book 1: Help! My Wizard Mentor Had A Heart Attack And Now I'm Being Chased By A Horde Of Giant Spiders!

The Untamed Isles

The Path Awakens

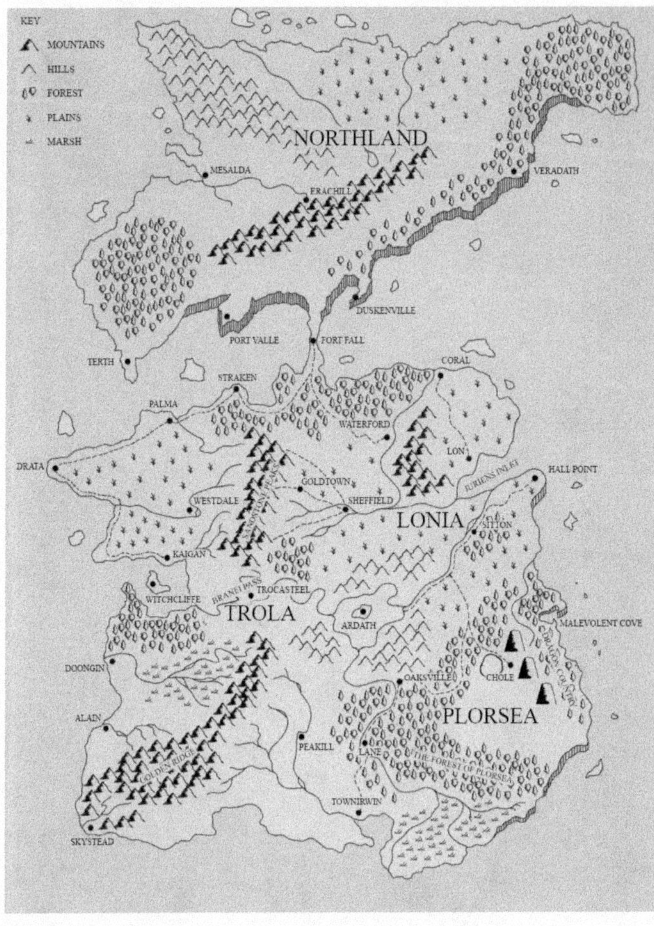

KEY
MOUNTAINS
HILLS
FOREST
PLAINS
MARSH
NORTHLAND
MESALDA
VERADATH
ERACHILL
DUSKENVILLE
PORT VALLE
FORT FALL
TERTH
CORAL
STRAKEN
PALMA
WATERFORD
DRAIA
LON
HALL POINT
GOLDTOWN
FURIOUS INLET
WESTDALE
SHEFFIELD
LONIA
SITTON
KAIGAN
BRANEI PASS
TROCASTEEL
WITCHCLIFFE
TROLA
ARDATH
MALEVOLENT COVE
DOONGIN
OAKSVILLE
CHOLE
ALAIN
PLORSEA
PEAKILL
LANE
THE FOREST OF PLORSEA
TOWNIRWIN
SKYSTEAD
GOLDEN RIDGE

PROLOGUE

Senator Isybelle strode through the narrow corridors of Lon's citadel, her heels tapping loudly on the granite floors. A breeze blew through the broad windows, carrying with it the tang of the ocean and relief from the summer heat. Red sandstone walls stretched up to the high ceilings, where spiders were busy spinning fresh cobwebs.

Muttering beneath her breath, Isybelle made a mental note to have the slaves flogged. It was enough that their ugly sandstone buildings could never compete with rival Ardath's marble palaces. There was no need to highlight Lon's poverty with uncleanliness.

A drip of perspiration slid down Isybelle's neck as she took another corner. She cursed again. Thirty years ago, she and other senators would have been followed through the citadel by slaves waving fern fronds. But King Ashoka had done away with those luxuries, claiming the Lonian crown could not afford the extravagance. Their resources had been thrown into new industries instead, seeking to transform the nation's future.

They had succeeded beyond all expectations, but Isybelle would never forgive the insult to her heritage. It was enough that the populace had lifted Ashoka, a minor noble, to the office of king. Too much that he expected his betters to impoverish themselves for his plans.

The council had tolerated him for long enough, suffering their loss of pride in silence. Until today. Now, finally, Lonia would see a return to nobility.

Ahead, armed men lined the corridor, spears held perpendicular to the floor, ready to defend the council with their lives. At her appearance, the spears rose as one and struck the tiles. A great *boom* of steel on stone echoed from the walls, announcing her arrival to those within.

The slightest hint of a smile touched Isybelle's lips as she strode the length of the corridor, her gaze fixed straight ahead. It was beneath her station to look upon fighting men —and any who caught her eye would be whipped. That was as it had been for all of her sixty years, even during those dark days when the council had existed only to serve the Tsar.

Hinges squealed as the doors to the council chamber were pushed open, and she again cursed the slaves for their negligence. An example must be made of their failure. For the first time in a generation, the Lonian council would be restored to its true glory. No infraction, however minor, could be allowed to mar this day.

Inside the chamber, a dozen men and women stood at Isybelle's appearance, their chairs scuffing gently as they were pushed back. They watched as she strode the length of the table to where her chair awaited, a slave at its side.

There she paused, savouring the moment. Long had the council waited for this day, plotting and scheming to regain their former power. Ashoka may have been incorruptible, but he'd also lacked the intelligence of his betters. In the end, he had been easily manipulated, had even married off his only daughter to buy peace for his people.

Marianne. She had played her role well as Queen of Plorsea, remaining at King Braidon's side for close to a decade. Ever dutiful to family and nation, she had accepted the arranged marriage with good grace, though she'd loathed the man from the start. That anger had driven a wedge between the girl and her father, growing into a hatred the council had been all too happy to exploit. They had only needed to wait for the right moment.

That moment had come just days ago, on the thirtieth anniversary of the Order of Alana's founding. Marianne's faith had made her predictable, and the Order's Great Sacrifice had provided the perfect spectacle to dispose of King Braidon. The carrier pigeon had arrived just last night —on the shores of Malevolent Cove, Marianne had cast down her husband and taken the Plorsean crown for herself. With Ashoka already dead, there was no one left to stand against the council.

"Let us be seated," Isybelle said finally.

"Yes, take a seat."

Isybelle froze as a voice spoke from behind her, though there had been no one there a moment ago. She made to turn, but found her body unwilling to respond to her commands. Her muscles spasmed, and against her will, Isybelle lowered herself into the mahogany chair.

"Very good," the voice came again. A woman stepped around Isybelle and approached the council table.

Isybelle's confusion turned to shock as she recognised Marianne, King Ashoka's daughter. She was not a large woman, barely five-foot-four. A floor-length black dress clung to her figure, and a fine golden crown twisted through the locks of her auburn hair. She wandered the length of the room to where the heavy wooden doors still stood open. Marianne swung them closed and dropped the locking bar into place, before facing the council.

A gasp stole from Isybelle as she found herself able to move again. She slumped in the chair, taking a second to gather herself, while the Plorsean queen sat at the other end of the table. Answering exhalations came from the other senators as they looked uncertainly from Marianne to Isybelle.

Silently, Isybelle tried to understand what was happening. Why was Marianne here, rather than taking her place on the Plorsean throne, as intended? And what strange power had she used against them?

"Thank you for seeing me on such short notice, my good senators," Marianne said quietly, her sapphire eyes boring into Isybelle from across the table. "It seems all did not go to plan in Malevolent Cove."

"No," Isybelle rasped, deciding it best to speak with the woman. Marianne would need careful handling, if Isybelle read the situation right. "But the result is the same. Your father is gone, dead for his treachery against you and our nation. Your husband, too. You are Queen of Plorsea, as we planned."

"Ay," Marianne said, leaning forward, "but for how long? My husband did not die on that beach."

"He could not have survived the reefs," Isybelle countered. Regaining her cool, she flicked a piece of dust from her sleeve, and added: "Or the dragon fire."

"We found no body," Marianne hissed.

"Ha! As far as anyone who matters is concerned, Braidon is dead. His King's Guard has been slaughtered to a man. What threat can he pose? Do not worry yourself about it, girl."

"*Queen*," Marianne answered.

"Queen of Plorsea," Isybelle said, inclining her head with a smile. "A title you have more than earned, my dear."

"And of Lonia," Marianne added.

Isybelle's smile faltered. "Perhaps you do not understand," she said, straightening in her chair. "The people, they will not accept—"

"They will accept what they are told," Marianne interrupted.

"Even so…surely you cannot hope to rule Lonia from all the way in Ardath," Isybelle ground out the words. "It is better if the council—"

"This council's duty is to follow, not to rule," Marianne said dismissively. "You exist to administer our great nation, no more. Do not forget yourself, Senator."

Isybelle sat in silence, staring at the young queen. Marianne still wore the arrogant smile on her lips, as though the whole room—indeed, the whole world—belonged to her. Remembering her father, little more than a pig farmer before the people raised him up, Isybelle's anger took hold. She shot to her feet.

"It is *you* who forget yourself, girl," she snapped, slamming her palms into the tabletop. "You are only what we have made you. Step out of line, and the council will replace you with someone who knows their place."

The young queen did not move from her seat, though the smile left her face. "What do you mean when you say you 'made me'?"

"It was *we* who put you where you are now, girl," Isybelle said. A whisper came from the other senators, but enraged, she spoke over the top of them. "*We* who made you queen to that sorry excuse for a king. If not for us, you would be *nothing*."

"Is that so?" Marianne asked, rising as well now. Her eyes flashed dangerously.

The anger went from Isybelle in a rush. Why had she said that? Their efforts to convince Ashoka to sue for peace had been a secret the council had kept for a decade. She had given it away with nigh a thought. The other senators stared at her from their seats, aghast.

But what could the girl do about it? There were two dozen soldiers outside, loyal only to the council. She opened her mouth to call them.

"I always suspected this council had a hand in my father's decision," Marianne said quietly, walking around the table towards her. "I was never anything but a pawn in your games, was I? No matter that I was barely a woman; you put me in the bed of a man I loathed, made me bear his child. It was just a game for you, a subversion, to regain your former power."

"No…I…" Despite herself, Isybelle retreated from the fury in the queen's eyes. She tripped over her chair, sending it crashing to the stone. The sound broke the spell and she shouted, "Guards!"

"They cannot hear you," Marianne said. "You are alone, Isybelle."

Isybelle sneered at the woman, waiting for the guards to come bursting into the room. Her words could not be true, and yet…no sound came from beyond the oaken doors. Fear touched her then, and she turned to the other senators.

They stared back at her, faces pale with fear. Not one of them moved to help her.

"You cannot do this!" she gasped, turning back to the queen and drawing herself up. "I forbid it! There are still more of us here than you. If you do not—"

She broke off, suddenly unable to finish the sentence. It was as though an invisible fist had gripped her by the throat, choking off her words, her breath. Isybelle fumbled at her neck, but there was nothing there, no hand to free.

"You always scoffed at the Elders and their Order," Marianne commented. "Even as a child, I remember your disdain for them. But there is power in religion, even *real* power, it seems. It just took a few bright minds to discover it."

Despite her fear, anger flared in Isybelle's chest, that her associates had so abandoned her. Her mouth opened and closed, trying to form words, but no sound came out.

"What's that?" Marianne murmured, leaning close.

The pressure relented slightly, and Isybelle spat: "It was your precious Elder's idea!"

Marianne reeled back at that, her eyes widening, and the pressure vanished from Isybelle's throat. She gasped, straining to fill her lungs as she fell to her knees.

"What?" Marianne hissed, crouching alongside her.

Isybelle suppressed a smirk. "You did not know?" She felt the balance in the room swinging back towards her. The Elders and her fellow senators be damned, she would not be hung out to dry. Looking into the queen's eyes, she offered a sigh of empathy. "I am sorry, my dear. The plan was as much the Elders' as our own, a way to open Plorsea to the Order."

Rocking back on her heels, the queen stared at Isybelle,

as though contemplating the truth of her words. "Yet it is you who would take my birthright."

"Lonia is yours!" The words left Isybelle in a rush. Though they tasted of bile, better she survived today, that she might fix this mistake on another. She straightened, brushing the creases from her satin surcoat, refusing to let the woman steal her dignity.

"I was not asking your permission," Marianne replied, her voice turning cold once more.

Isybelle faltered, taken aback by the abrupt change in her foe. "I…then what do you want of us?"

"My father is dead, my husband in the wind. Both have suffered for their hand in my fate," Marianne surmised. Her sapphire eyes turned on the council. The senator shrunk in their seats, unable to meet her gaze. "But here this council sits, thinking to rule Lonia in my stead."

"But the Elders!"

"The Elders will have their reward," Marianne snarled. "As for this council…it only seems fear its leader suffer for their crimes."

Fear wrapped its icy coils around Isybelle's gut as the queen pulled a dagger from the folds of her dress. She stumbled back. It couldn't end like this, not after all her years of planning, after suffering the indignities of poverty. This was meant to be her day of reckoning, when the council regained its power, and Lonia its nobility.

But to Isybelle's surprise, Marianne offered her the knife. Glancing from the blade to the queen, Isybelle sensed a trap and shook her head. Marianne only smiled, and as though possessed by a will of its own, Isybelle's hand took the weapon.

Marianne faced the room. The other senators sat transfixed, and Isybelle cursed their cowardice. She had done everything for them, lifted them to the heights of power, disposed of King Ashoka – and now not one lifted a finger to aid her. If she survived, they would suffer for this betrayal.

"Councillor Isybelle has confessed to the murder of King Ashoka," the queen declared, flashing Isybelle a conspiring smile. It had been Marianne herself who had arranged her father's death. "In her shame, she has taken her own life, to spare this council the horror of executing one of their own."

"*No!*" Isybelle cried, lifting a hand to beg for her life.

The dagger glinted in her slender fist and Isybelle saw her chance. Marianne's back was to her. One thrust was all it would take to free them of the madwoman. Isybelle took one trembling step. The queen looked back and their eyes met.

"Try it," Marianne said.

"*Die!*" Isybelle screamed.

Staggering forward, she raised the dagger, but a sudden, awful pain tore through her abdomen. Horror touched Isybelle as she found the dagger embedded in her own stomach. In shock she tore the blade loose and let it fall. She clutched at the wound, but blood still pulsed between her fingers. The strength fled her and she sank to the ugly sandstone floor.

Pressure touched her shoulder. She swayed, surprised to find the queen beside her. The woman's sapphire eyes smiled.

"Ah, you might have been a manipulative witch, but you had *strength*, Isabelle," Marianne whispered. "Now die, and your hateful soul with you."

The queen's touch vanished, and Isybelle slumped on her side. Voices whispered in the room as Marianne took her seat at the head of the council, but Isybelle saw no more than that. Darkness swirled across her vision and her consciousness drifted, fell away. Her last thought was of the council, of Marianne, of the Elders of Alana, and how they would all pay…

❧   I   ❧

Ocean water stung the burns on Kryssa's arms as she hauled herself onto the beach. Darkness clung to the night sky, the stars concealed by cloud. She could hardly see, was at the end of her strength, but she could not rest yet. A shout called her back into the crashing waves. She splashed through the breakers and caught Braidon by the shoulder, a second before he slipped from the arms of Caledan. The king's weight almost dragged him from her arms. She staggered, then righted herself before another wave could strike.

Caledan bent in two, gasping, but they were not safe yet. The currents had dragged them out of Malevolent Cove, but the distant glow of dragon fire still lit the horizon. Kryssa scanned the waters for Pela or Genevieve, but there was no sign of her daughter or the huntress. A tightness clutched her chest and she struggled to breathe.

"Pela!" she screamed into the darkness. "Gen!"

There was no reply and she struggled to control her panic. This could not be happening, not again. She had already lost Devon tonight, just minutes after their reunion, after he'd spoken the words she'd longed to hear all her life.

My daughter!

But the queen had killed him, as she had tried to kill Kryssa and Pela and Braidon. Kryssa had already promised the woman would pay—now she would dedicate her life to that cause.

But thoughts of revenge could wait—danger still threatened now. Clinging to Braidon with one hand, she grabbed Caledan by the shirt and dragged him back to his feet. She hardly knew the man, but her father had trusted him and so would she.

"Help me!" she shouted above the roar of breaking waves, gesturing at Braidon. "Before his bloody wife catches up with us."

Pale-faced and hollow-eyed, Caledan took hold of Braidon's other arm. The king was badly wounded, his skin cold to the touch. He had not spoken since they'd gone into the water, but as they dragged him onto the sand, a groan whispered from his lips.

Kryssa let out a sigh; he lived! She could not have born it if this had all been for nothing.

Not that she understood what exactly *was* happening.

What had Braidon, the King of Plorsea, been doing here in the first place? The others, Devon and Pela and Genevieve, had come to rescue her from the Knights of Alana, but Braidon…Kryssa had served on his King's Guard, long ago. She knew the man, and could not understand what had brought him to the black shores of Malevolent Cove.

Stumbling up the beach, they entered the treeline and carried the king several yards into the forest. There they lowered him gently to the ground. Kryssa knelt to inspect his wound.

"I'll cover our tracks," Caledan said, and vanished.

"Firewood!" she called after him.

Kryssa wondered too what the sellsword's place in all this was. She'd barely caught his name, back in the amphitheatre, but he had saved Pela from the sword of Ikar. With his help, and her father's sacrifice, they had almost escaped. But nothing could have saved them from the dragon that had fallen from the sky, capsizing their boat in its death throes. She shuddered, knowing that more of the creatures lurked in this forest.

Caledan was back within minutes, a stack of firewood in hand. He set to work lighting a small fire, using a husk of bark and dry stick to spark the wood shavings to light.

"Any sign of the Knights or the bloody Dragons?" Kryssa asked as she pulled up Braidon's shirt.

It was still too dark to see how much damage the queen had done, and she sat back, waiting for him to build up the fire.

"Dragons are on our side," Caledan said as he added a broken branch to the crackling flame. "No Knights."

Kryssa raised an eyebrow, but in the burning glow she could finally see their patient. Praying the trees would conceal the light from prying eyes, she leaned in close to inspect Braidon's wound. The king had begun to shiver, and if shock took hold, nothing they did was likely to save him. He needed to dry off, needed warmth.

With Caledan's help, they stripped Braidon of his wet clothing and laid him down close to the fire. Kryssa had seen her fair share of wounds as a King's Guard and knew a thing or two about treatment in the field, but she feared Braidon's injuries might be beyond her.

The queen had stabbed him with her rapier, leaving a small circular wound. At first inspection it did not appear serious, but who knew how much internal damage had been done. She had obviously missed his heart, but if a lung had been pierced…Braidon might drown in his own blood, and there would be nothing Kryssa could do to save him.

Placing an ear to his chest, she listened for the rattle of liquid. Braidon was barely breathing—only the slightest rise and fall of his chest revealed he lived. She closed her eyes, allowing the crackling of the fire to fade away, disengaging from the stench of smoke, the rustling of branches over-head. Concentrating on the erratic thud of Braidon's heart, the whisper of his breath, she allowed her own self to drift away.

After a few minutes, she sat back up.

"What do you think?" Caledan asked, his forehead creased.

"She has poor aim," Kryssa commented. "Thank the Gods, he might live if we can stop the bleeding and keep him warm."

She unfastened the sword from her waist and drew the blade, then paused. In the race to flee the amphitheatre she had picked it up without thinking, but now she saw it was her husband's blade. Pela had been wielding it, but had lost it in the battle with Ikar. Kryssa's eyes flickered closed. One day, she resolved to give it back to her daughter.

Then she swallowed her grief and took up Braidon's jacket. Cutting it into strips, she did her best to bind his chest tight.

"We'll need to find something to help fight infections,"

she said, sitting back on the damp earth. Her eyes slid closed as a wave of weariness swept her. "In the morning."

Caledan still stood staring down at the king. His brown eyes shone in the firelight, his black hair plastered to his scalp. Kryssa was sure she'd never seen him before, yet back in the arena he had slain Ikar with hardly a thought. Not even Devon had managed such a feat. The man was a killer, and in different circumstances she might have been cautious of him. But her father's trust did not...*had* not, come easily.

"Are you okay?" she asked into the silence.

The swordsman shook himself and offered a strained smile. "Well enough." He seated himself across the fire from her. "The name's Caledan, by the way," he murmured. "Since we weren't formally introduced back there. It's nice to finally meet you, Kryssa. You certainly don't disappoint. I didn't think anyone could stand against that giant of a Knight, after he defeated Devon."

"His name was Ikar," Kryssa replied, remembering the Knight's face at the end.

A lump lodged in her throat and she swallowed. Ikar had been many things, both kind and cruel when it took him, noble in his own way, determined to stand against what he saw as evil. Over the weeks he had held her prisoner, he had revealed his humanity in a million small gestures. But in the end, Ikar had been as much a prisoner to the Order's beliefs as she had been. And he had died for them.

"Yet you were the one who killed him," Kryssa added after a pause. "Thank you for that. I...couldn't risk my daughter's life."

She and Ikar had fought each other, but in the end the Knight had beaten her by threatening Pela's life. She'd had no choice but to surrender, though in the end it did not seem to have mattered…

A shudder ran down Kryssa's spine as she remembered the cove aflame, the waves raging across jagged reefs, the desperate fight to reach the shore, the panic as she realised Pela was missing, that Genevieve had vanished. She had lost everything in that dark place.

"I did very little," Caledan said, his eyes on the fire. "I'm…sorry I could not do more. After we went in the water…I thought I'd lost all of you." He paused, then nodded at the king. "Everyone but that deadweight, at least."

"It was brave, carrying him all that way," Kryssa offered.

"I would not have done it, if not for Devon," Caledan replied. "But…I could not ignore his last wish."

Kryssa looked away, her vision blurring. Exhaustion weighed on her shoulders and she closed her eyes. A shiver raised goosebumps on her arms, though it was hot in front of the fire.

How could she have allowed this to happen?

It was meant to be *her*. She had given herself up for dead days ago, when her last escape attempt had ended in failure and left the Elder Putar dead. She had begged Ikar to kill her, rather than continue as a pawn in the Order's game.

But he had refused, and now Devon was dead in Kryssa's place—her daughter and Genevieve as well, for all she knew.

A desperate guilt twisted her abdomen and she bent in two, the salt-soaked contents of her stomach rushing up. Groaning, she vomited into the dirt alongside the fire. The first traces of panic tugged at her. She was alone, had lost everything. For a moment she was back on the streets of her childhood, fleeing guards and dogs and slavers—always running, never safe.

Not until the day Selina and Devon had taken her in.

Sucking in a lungful of air, Kryssa sought her calm centre the way Selina had shown her, so many decades ago. She concentrated on her breath, on the slow in-out of air through her nostrils, the swelling of her chest. Blood thumped in her ears, slowing with each inhalation. A peaceful darkness rose in her mind, an empty void of calm.

Kryssa exhaled and opened her eyes.

Caledan still sat nearby, a concerned look on his face. "Are you okay?"

As Kryssa made to reply, a sharp *crack* came from the nearby trees. In an instant they were both on their feet, swords in hand. Kryssa dragged a burning brand from the fire with her left hand, and Caledan did the same. Holding the torches aloft, they scanned the shadows for beast or man.

For a second there was nothing—then the firelight caught the glimmer of blood-red scales. A giant ficus tree groaned as a taloned foot pressed against it, then toppled slowly sideways. A scream built in Kryssa's throat as it struck the earth with a muffled *thud*, but there was no time to panic, no time to do anything but stare as the Red Dragon clambered into the clearing.

It rose before them, one great blue eye watching them with frightening intelligence. The ruined remnants of its other eye still dripped blood where the crossbow bolt had struck it. Kryssa's gaze swept the rest of the creature, noticing the torn and broken scales. She swallowed, realising

the beast had encountered the weapons of the Knights—
though clearly not the explosives that had torn its brethren
from the sky.

The Knights have slain Ingytus. The dragon's words rattled
in Kryssa's skull so loudly she had to clench her jaw to keep
herself from screaming. *Others died on the sands of Malevolent
Cove. You will burn for their deaths.*

Caledan stepped between Kryssa and the beast, sword
in hand, though he could not hope to harm the creature.
"Stay back, beast," he snarled. "You made a pact, you and
your kin. We stand with the king."

The king lies dying! the dragon roared.

"He is not dead yet!"

*Ingytus was a fool to side with such feeble creatures; the pact is
void!*

"The pact stands!" Caledan shot back. His sword shim-
mered in the firelight as he pointed it at the dragon's breast,
and Kryssa wondered at his nerve. "You are bound to it, so
long as Braidon draws breath."

The dragon reared up on its hind legs, teeth bared. The
heat of its breath swept through the clearing, causing the
fire to flicker dangerously. Kryssa braced herself, preparing
for death. She could hardly believe it could end like this,
after everything she had survived.

But the dragon fire did not come, and with an awful
howl, the dragon sank back to the earth.

The pact must be fulfilled. Its voice hammered at Kryssa's
senses. *The king must drive these Knights from our land, or we will
bring our grief to your towns and cities. Betray us at your peril,
humans.*

"Braidon will complete his side of the bargain, when he
recovers," Caledan replied quickly.

The great eye stared at them, and the dragon's jaws opened and closed, as though their soft flesh were between its teeth.

So be it, finally came the reply, *but should your feeble king perish…*

The dragon left the threat unfinished. It moved off silently through the trees, obviously as desperate as they were to remain undetected by the Knights.

When it had vanished, Kryssa slumped to the ground alongside Braidon. Quickly she checked his pulse. It was weak and unsteady, though at least some colour had returned to his cheeks. Sitting back on her haunches, she looked at Caledan.

"We'd better make sure he lives," she murmured.

"Agreed," the swordsman said grimly.

❧   2   ☙

The next week dragged by at a crawl for Caledan. With the Knights and their followers sweeping up and down the coast, they had been forced to move their camp further inland. After that, the monotony soon set in. Kryssa had returned several times to scour the beaches herself, seeking signs of Pela or the huntress Genevieve, but finally she was forced to abandon the search. If their friends lived, they'd either been taken by the Order or swept elsewhere by the erratic currents of the western coast.

Caledan had given them both up for dead the first morning after the solstice, when he'd returned to the beach and looked upon the devastation left by the dragon. Burnt timbers and bodies lay scattered across the sand, washed up during the night. He could not imagine how either Pela or Genevieve could have survived the deadly waters.

Kryssa must have known it too, for she grew silent as the week progressed. Any sense of levity fell from her as she faced the cold reality of her daughter's loss. Caledan felt for her, but there was little he could say. Already he felt trapped by his friendship with Devon, by the hammerman's final words. He remembered now why he had avoided such connections—all they ever brought was pain and loss, the sacrifice of his own ambitions for the sake of others.

What madness had possessed Caledan that he'd returned to the amphitheatre rather than flee? He'd thought to help his friends, to rescue Devon and Genevieve from the clutches of the queen. But he had failed utterly. Instead, he had become minder for the ruin that was Braidon.

The fallen king might have survived the battle in Malevolent Cove, but his spirit had been destroyed by his wife's betrayal. He had woken on the first day, but had hardly moved from his bed of ferns since.

Caledan had taken to avoiding their camp during the day, preferring to range along the volcanic range in search of supplies. Kryssa had shown him a few plants that could be used to prevent infection, and he'd managed to kill a fat pigeon once with a stone. Mostly they ate berries and fruit, though Kryssa sometimes went out in the early mornings, often returning with a hare or marmot.

The sun was getting low on the horizon now and Caledan was returning to the camp, a fresh bundle of firewood tied to his back. They were encamped near a spring on the steeps of Mount Chole, still within the treeline but where the undergrowth started to thin. He wondered if Braidon would be any better this night.

As a sellsword, Caledan had spent most of his life around fighting men, but he knew little of the treatment of wounds. Braidon was lucky his King's Guard were trained in the basics of first aid, though Caledan had been surprised to learn Kryssa had once served amongst their ranks. Truly she was her father's daughter.

All the more confusing then that Kryssa had refused to teach Pela the warrior's arts—or even tell the girl about her heritage. Thinking of the naïve girl he'd first met in Skystead, Caledan wondered how Kryssa could have kept so much from her only daughter.

Then again, after seeing Kryssa's embrace with Genevieve in the amphitheatre, it was clear the woman had kept more than just the warrior's arts from Pela. A smile touched his lips as he wondered what else Pela might have missed in her youthful innocence. It quickly vanished as he remembered the girl's likely fate.

Drawing in a breath, Caledan paused on the mountainside to take stock of his surroundings. There had been no sign of the Knights or their followers for several days now, and a set of tracks he'd found heading west suggested they'd left the area. Above him, a gravel slope stretched up towards the rocky sides of the volcano, atop which a sprinkling of snow still showed from last winter.

Here and there, steam rose from hollows on the mountainside, the earth around them stained scarlet and yellow and orange. Caledan did his best to avoid those areas during his scouting, though he knew the inhabitants of nearby Chole had taken to mining the precious minerals found in the volcanic range.

Spotting a familiar landmark, Caledan entered the trees on the slope below him. He was close to camp now, and he slowly made his way into the denser forest. Away from the high slopes, the air quickly heated up, the humidity making the sweat bead on his forehead. At least with sunset nearing, the worst of the day's heat was behind him.

Voices came from the trees ahead, and pushing aside a heavy branch, he stepped into the camp.

"I don't know how she could do—" Braidon was saying, but he broke off as Caledan appeared.

Crossing the clearing, Caledan added his firewood to the stack near the fire. "Still moaning about your wife?" he asked, turning to face the king.

Braidon's face darkened, his jaw taking on a hard edge. "I loved her," he grated.

"Ay, and she made a clown out of you," Caledan replied. "Not a difficult thing to do."

The king said nothing, but his eyes shone at Caledan's words and he quickly looked away. "I was such a fool," he whispered. "Devon should have left me to die there."

The past week had helped heal the king's wounds and he could now walk short distances. But still Braidon clung to despair and self-pity, hardly lifting a finger to help while Kryssa and Caledan cooked the meals and tidied the camp. All he did was sit and complain and rage against his wife. His self-defeat made a mockery of Devon's sacrifice.

"Perhaps he should have," Caledan agreed. "I would have."

"And what is she doing now?" Braidon continued, hardly seeming to hear Caledan's words. "It's been a week. Even now she might be planning some fresh evil for Plorsea. My nation has suffered enough!"

"On that we can agree!" Caledan snorted. "Who knows, maybe she's doing a better job of it than you. The Gods know, it wouldn't be hard."

Finally his words enacted a response from Braidon. The king's head snapped up and he locked eyes with Caledan. "I did my best," he hissed. "I didn't see anyone else volunteering."

"A dimwit could have seen the Order sought power in Plorsea."

"Power, yes," Braidon replied. "But *human sacrifice*? How could I have known that?"

"I don't know," Caledan mocked, "maybe if you weren't *sleeping* with one of them, for what, eight years? *Surely* you must have noticed something when your wife started butchering the hired help?"

Braidon staggered to his feet and pointed a finger at Caledan. "How dare you speak—"

"I dare!" Caledan roared, tired of the king's self-loathing. "I dare because you do not deserve to be king. You never did, pathetic excuse for a man that you are. It was you who got us into this mess—and now you sit here wallowing, expecting us to clean it up for you, for the rest of us to save you like Devon did, and your sister before him. Well, guess what, they're all gone. There's no one left to do your dirty work for you—"

Caledan broke off as the king roared and staggered at him. Dragging his sword from its scabbard, Braidon swung it at Caledan's head, but his injuries made the king slow and Caledan leaned back, allowing the blade to cut empty air. His own blade leapt to his hand and he parried a second cut.

"Stop!" Kryssa screamed. "Or by the Gods, I'll cut you both down." She started towards them, then paused. Her hands were empty. Her scabbard and sword lay on the other side of the firepit.

"Die, *bastard!*" Braidon roared, swinging at Caledan again.

The sellsword parried, then lashed out with his boot, catching Braidon's insole and sending him crashing to the dirt. The sword spun from the king's grasp, but he scrambled across the ground and swept it back up.

"What are you waiting for? Fight back!" Braidon spat, lashing out with the blade.

Caledan knocked aside the blow and retreated. The king might have been weak, but his sword was no less dangerous and a single lucky blow could prove fatal.

"Why bother?" he retorted. "A child could defeat you."

Screaming, Braidon hurled himself forward. Caledan's sword flashed up, catching the king's blade close to the hilt and jarring it from the man's hand. Sparks flashed as it struck a rock and spun towards the fire. Caledan readied another retort—but Braidon charged emptyhanded, slamming into Caledan's midriff.

Caught unawares, the breath left Caledan's lungs in a rush. He staggered back, his foot catching on a stray root. They both fell, striking the ground together and rolling. Braidon came up on top, pinning Caledan down. The king's fist caught the sellsword in the temple and drove his head backwards into the earth.

A bright light flashed across Caledan's vision. Anger flared in his chest and he bared his teeth. The king reared back, readying another blow, but Caledan rolled to the side. His greater weight was enough to throw the weakened Braidon off-balance, toppling him sideways. A glancing blow careered off Caledan's shoulder, then he was free.

They reared up together, but Caledan was far quicker, and he hammered a left cross into the king's jaw. A punch from Braidon was easily deflected, then Caledan slammed a fist into his opponent's midriff. Braidon doubled over and collapsed to the dirt, his breath coming in strained gasps.

Rising to his feet, Caledan recovered his weapon. Leaves

crunched behind him and he spun, the blade coming up to point at Kryssa. She held Braidon's sword in one hand now, but made no move to attack.

Caledan looked back at the king. Braidon had managed to recover his breath but he remained crouching in the dirt. Their eyes met and Caledan saw the defeat in the king's blue eyes. Marianne had ruined him, cast him off and left him with nothing, not even his pride.

"Kill me," Braidon croaked. "Isn't that what you came here to do?"

It was true. Caledan had spent half his life planning Braidon's demise, plotting to get close enough to drive a sword through his heart. His sister had robbed the world of magic and so doomed Caledan's mother to a painful death, when a healer might have saved her. It was only right that Alana's family should die as well.

Caledan gripped the hilt of his sword so tight he felt the leather digging into his skin. The tip trembled as he pointed it at Braidon's throat. He had longed for this day, to finally face this man in single combat and defeat him, to take his revenge against the woman who had stolen everything from him.

The king did not move. He crouched helpless in the mud, defeated, begging for his death. In that moment, Caledan felt nothing but loathing for the pitiful creature before him. Braidon was no longer a king, not even a man. He had fallen into a pit he would never climb back out of. It would be a mercy to kill him now.

A mercy.

Caledan shuddered, lowering his sword. "You disgust me," he spat. "Pathetic creature, begging in the mud for me to end your misery. Well, you don't get to escape so easily.

You broke this nation; you can damn well stick around to fix it."

Sheathing his sword, he turned away. His eyes roamed the campsite, sharing a glance with Kryssa. He held her gaze for a long moment, realising that he could help her no longer. If he stayed with the broken king, Caledan *would* kill him. He could do no more in this forest. Kryssa could take care of herself, and he would not waste any more energy on Braidon, no matter what Devon had asked of him.

"I'm leaving," he said shortly.

"What will you do?" Kryssa asked.

Caledan started away, but he paused at the treeline, pondering the question. Finally he shook his head. "I don't know," he murmured, glancing back. "Something productive, I hope."

❧ 3 ❧

Darkness surrounded Pela, thick and suffocating, lit only by the flickering glow of a distant lantern. It seemed an age had passed since she'd last seen the sun, since she'd tasted fresh air and felt the wind on her cheeks. Overhead, the weight of a mountain pressed down on her, a thousand tonnes of rock and dirt and death that would be her tomb.

How long had she toiled now? She no longer knew, only that her arms ached and that each day she grew weaker, the flesh shrivelling from her bones, her spirit fading. The steel collar, inset with a single black gem, pressed tightly at her throat, a constant reminder of her fate.

Pela had been elated when she'd first seen the ship on the horizon. For a day she had drifted with Genevieve, clinging to the plank of wood that was their only hope. The hot sun had beaten down on them and the saltwater had drained away their strength, but finally hope had been at hand.

Only when the ship neared had they seen the black sails,

the dark-garbed men and women crowding the decks. The Baronians had hauled them from the ocean and locked them away in the bowels of the vessel. There with a half-dozen other unfortunate souls, they had been condemned, sailed upriver to Sheffield and sold as slaves. The practice was forbidden in Plorsea, and legal only for condemned criminals in Lonia. But the Lonian overseers who'd bought them had not cared about their innocence.

They had been taken from Sheffield to the mines and separated there. Pela had not seen Genevieve since, and now she no longer had the strength to worry for her friend. She had been placed in a chain gang with a dozen other unfortunate souls—some the criminals the Lonians believed them to be, others like her, taken by slavers to toil beneath the earth. It didn't matter which—those who tried to proclaim their innocence were beaten mercilessly by their captors.

Watched by an overseer, they were fed once a day, a meal of watery gruel that could scarce be considered food. At night—though there was no telling night from day in their filthy holes—they were left chained together, to sleep as best they could in the cold dirt.

The rest of the time they worked, hours upon hours uncounted, smashing the slick black rock from the walls and loading up carts, dragging them towards the surface—but never quite reaching it. When the light was but a pinprick in the distance, another crew of slaves, those trusted by the overseers, took over the barrows, loading them onto carts on a steel track and pushing them to the open air.

How Pela longed to join them. Each trip she stole a full minute to stare at that tiny light, allowing herself to dream of freedom, of returning to the outside world.

It was a hopeless dream, and soon the cruel overseer would shout and she would stagger back into the awful depths, return to the darkness and the creeping death that stole closer each day. She could feel herself wasting away, her will devoured by cold and starvation.

Her arms burned as she swung the pickaxe, but she lacked the strength to aim the tool now, and the blow missed, skittering off the paler rock she had come to know as limestone. Sparks flashed and her heart lurched. She held her breath, waiting to see if she had doomed them all. The other slaves had told her the black rock was flammable, and talked of stray sparks setting entire tunnels alight, but no fire followed, and Pela breathed a sigh of relief.

A curse came from behind her and Pela turned in time to catch the overseer's whip across her breasts. The leather tore through cloth and skin and she cried out, falling back and dropping her pick.

"Stupid witch!" the overseer screamed, lashing out again. Fire encircled Pela's wrist as the whip wrapped around her forearm. "Careless!"

Another blow followed. All Pela could do was curl into a ball and endure. Hot blood trickled across her stomach and tears beaded her eyes, but she was so dehydrated they did not fall. The overseer continued to scream, raining down blows she hardly felt, until he abruptly changed tact. His boot caught Pela in the stomach and hurled her into the wall.

The breath hissed in Pela's throat as she gasped, unable to draw breath. The overseer loomed, mining pick in hand. He tossed it at her with a sneer, and the wooden haft struck her in the forehead. Stars flashed across her vision as he snarled:

"Do that again, and I'll kill you myself."

Then he was gone, moving on to some other victim. Connected to the other slaves, the chain at her ankle tugged, a not-so-subtle hint for her to get up. All would suffer if they failed to meet the overseer's quota.

Pela crawled to her knees, wondering how much longer she could endure. The movement stirred the thick dust covering the ground and she coughed, her lungs choking in the darkness. Always the air was stale and thick with poison, so that it seemed she were breathing inside of a chimney. She could not catch her breath, no matter how hard she tried.

"Here," a kindly voice whispered.

A leather waterskin appeared in front of Pela's eyes. She straightened slowly and glanced at the speaker. It was Siden, the kindly old man who worked one chain link down, Pela's only friend in this awful place. She nodded her thanks and accepted the skin, though she took only a sip. Siden needed the water as much as her and there would be no more today, once the skin ran dry.

"You must be more careful, youngling," he whispered.

Pela nodded, though her eyes flickered closed and she swayed on her feet, barely able to keep herself upright. A hand, surprisingly firm for Siden's advanced years, gripped her by the shoulder.

"I...can barely lift it," she croaked, opening her eyes to stare at the pickaxe.

Before Siden could respond, she bent and picked it up. It was not heavy—no heavier than the sword she'd once owned. That seemed another life now, the day Devon had given Pela her father's blade. She thought herself weak then, but now she was no more than skin and bone. Even so, she gripped the pickaxe tight and forced her attention to their task.

Thick veins of black criss-crossed the tunnel walls, softer than the surrounding rock. It shone in the light of the distant lantern. Pela had learned from her fellow slaves that it burned far hotter than any wood, though she was lucky enough not to have witnessed it personally. Coal, they called it, just one of the many dangers in the death-trap that were the mines.

The fumes were another threat. There was a constant stench of rotten eggs in the tunnels, most times almost unnoticeable, but occasionally the fumes grew so strong men had been known to lose consciousness. Then the overseer would retreat up the tunnel, ordering the slaves to remain until the weakest fell, and only then allowing them to flee.

At first the constant dangers had filled Pela with terror. Eventually though, exhaustion and hunger had lessoned their sting, wearing at her until she no longer cared for her approaching death. She could not even muster fear for the overseer and his whip. Nothing could prevent the beatings, for she was so tired mistakes were a certainty. She simply endured.

Pela lifted the pick above her head and was about to strike again, when a voice called down the tunnel. Lowering the tool, she looked up, seeking daylight but seeing only darkness. Then the flickering glow of a lantern appeared around a bend in the tunnel, followed by two figures.

"Overseer Harrison!" a woman's voice echoed through the gloom. "It's your lucky day!"

"Ay?" the overseer's harsh voice called back.

Taking the opportunity to rest, Pela put down the

pickaxe and pressed up against the wall. Chains rattled as the other slaves did the same. The overseer strode past to meet the newcomers, shaking hands with the woman. There was a slightly perplexed look on his bearded face and dirt streaked his forehead—not even the overseers could escape the filth of the tunnels.

"The Order has accepted your request," the woman explained. "Their Knights are seeking fresh blood, to spread the Saviour's word to Plorsea. You are to leave immediately for your initiation. Ruebyn is here to replace you."

A young man not much older than Pela's seventeen years stepped forward and extended his hand. The overseer stared at him for half a second longer than was polite before accepting the offer. Pela could see her own thoughts mirrored in the man's beady eyes. The boy was far too young for a position of authority.

"Congratulations," Ruebyn said. "To be Knighted is a great honour. Our new queen will be glad to have your sword."

The overseer snorted. "The Knights are soldiers of the Saviour, not some traitor who thinks to rule us from Ardath."

Pela frowned, confused by the man's words. She had thought Marianne was popular in Lonia.

The boy seemed similarly confused. He glanced uncertainly at his superior, then back at Harrison. "Marianne is one of our own. The Elders and the Lonian council have both given her their blessing…"

"She is tainted," the overseer said dismissively. "Plorsean scum, we should have never made peace with them. Never mind, I will be glad to show them the true path of the Saviour."

"Yes," the woman said, stepping between them. "I thank you for your service, Harrison. You have yielded great boons for our mine." She held out her hand, and after a moment's hesitation, the overseer passed over his whip. The woman promptly deposited the cruel weapon into the boy's hands. "I can only hope young Ruebyn continues your legacy."

Pale-faced, Ruebyn looked from the whip to his superior. "Thank you, ma'am, I…I will not let you down!"

"They're yours now," she said, gesturing to Pela and the other slaves. There were twelve on their chain, the usual arrangement for each overseer. "Be sure you keep them in line. Never forget, they are criminals, and must be treated as such. Do not give them an inch, least they hang you with it." Then she was gone, their former overseer following her up the tunnel in silence.

Pela watched them go, surprised by the sudden turn of events. For a second, she felt uplifted, relieved to be free of the man who had so cruelly tortured her for all these uncounted days. As the last echoes of their footsteps faded, she looked at the young man who now controlled her life.

Ruebyn shifted nervously on his feet, his eyes flicking from the whip to his slaves. His Adam's apple bobbed up and down, and Pela realised he had no idea what he was doing. She felt a touch of empathy for him. Maybe this was his first time separated from his family, his first time away from the safety of his own home. Attempting a smile, she took a step towards him.

The whip slashed out, catching her across the face. Gasping, Pela staggered back, clutching her cheek. Hot blood seeped between her fingers—then her feet lost their footing on the uneven rocks. She crashed to the ground as the boy's voice echoed from the cavern walls, several pitches above normal:

"Stay away from me!"

Wincing, Pela pushed herself up on her elbow, her head spinning. The cut to her cheek was not deep, but like all the others it would most likely become infected. She watched the boy, expecting a fresh beating to follow, but he did not move. Eyes wide, he stared at her as though not sure what he'd just done.

A sudden anger took her, a rage she had thought long lost. It rose from the dark depths of her soul until her entire body was shaking. Pushing herself to her feet, she sneered at the boy, swaying where she stood. Her past life was a distant memory now, the fears that had once controlled her fled in the face of her exhaustion. All she could think of was the injustice of the world, that even this useless, inexperienced boy should have power over her.

"What, have you never beaten a woman before?" she hissed.

The boy gaped as though she had struck him. His eyes were wide, flicking from her to the other slaves, but they shrank back, even sweet Siden. He could not help her, no one could. She had spoken the words; there was no taking them back.

"What, are you stupid or something?" she spat when still the boy said nothing.

Raising a fist, Pela staggered at him. To her surprise, Ruebyn retreated, lifting the whip in front of him as though it were a shield. His cowardice fuelled her rage and shrieking, Pela leapt at him—but there was no strength in her legs, and instead she found herself falling. The ground rose to meet her. Light flashed across her vision as she struck.

Her sight spinning, Pela stared at the ceiling, her fury vanished as quickly as it had appeared. Darkness pressed in on her, and she could no longer tell whether it was reality or her own personal nightmare.

A face appeared through the fogs: old Siden. His forehead was creased and his lips moved, but Pela heard no sound. She sensed movement around her, felt hands grasping at her arms and legs and tried to fight them off, but her body refused to obey. A groan whispered from her lips, what remained of the shriek she had intended.

Finally, she could fight no more. Her eyes slid closed, and she sank into the kind embrace of unconsciousness.

ꞯ 4 ꞯ

Braidon sat in the darkness, listening to the slow trickling of the creek as it wound its way past the camp. He had sat there for most of the night, trapped in his ruined body as much as he was stuck in Dragon Country. Thoughts of Marianne brought an equal measure of grief and anger, but Braidon knew he was not strong enough to face her.

Once, he might have summoned the will to oppose her, to gather his followers and restore his crown, to drive Marianne and the Order of Alana from his lands. But now he was lost, his confidence eroded by a decade of failures, by his wife's betrayal, by his own folly.

And she had their son, Calybe. He was only five. Braidon shuddered to think what the woman he'd seen in Malevolent Cove would do to the boy.

He swallowed. How had it come to this? Thirty years ago, after the Tsar's death and the departure of the Gods, the Three Nations had finally been free. His reign as king should have beckoned in a new era of prosperity for Plorsea.

Instead, Trola had shuttered its borders to the outside world, ceasing all trade. Until then, Plorsea had flourished on trade between the Three Nations, situated as it was on the main trade route between Lonia and Trola. The sudden absence of the western nation had plunged Braidon's lands into crisis.

Then King Ashoka had led the Lonian army south, forcing Plorsean farmers from their land and igniting a decade-long war that had almost destroyed both nations. By the time of Braidon's marriage to the Lonian princess Marianne, both countries had been eager for peace.

Knowing Ashoka to be a kind man, if a ruthless one, Braidon had never questioned Marianne's devotion. Now he found his anger stirring at the realisation he'd been played a fool. Not even the so-called peace had been genuine. Lonia had spent the last eight years developing new weapons of war, deadly steel crossbows and terrifying explosive powder, and ships that could sail without wind or oars.

If it came to war, Plorsea would be badly outmatched. But Marianne was a shrewd woman—he knew that, at least, had not been an act. She had played her cards well, disposing of her father and husband within weeks of each other. She would be queen of both nations, without a single soldier lifting a sword.

He cursed beneath his breath.

"Can't sleep?"

Braidon was surprised to find Kryssa sitting up. Her silver eyes shone in the darkness, almost supernatural in their luminosity, and he shuddered. This was the woman he had given up his crown for, who he had crossed half the nation to save. Devon had sacrificed his last breath to see her safe, to protect his daughter.

Now Braidon was failing her, failing them all. He hung his head.

"Caledan was right," he murmured. "I'm a fool. Marianne has the Knights and her Queen's Guard behind her, and a power I cannot explain. I cannot stop her."

"Perhaps you're right," Kryssa said. Throwing off the blanket she had woven together from fern fronds, she stood. "Perhaps I should leave you here for the dragons to find."

Fear twisted Braidon's stomach into knots. "Please don't," he croaked. He was not strong enough to walk a hundred paces, let alone climb the mountain paths back to Plorsea.

"Then give me a reason to stay!" Kryssa snapped, her lips curling back in a sneer. "Show me what my father saw in you, why he died rather than leave you in your wife's tender care. Show me the man who stood against the Tsar."

Braidon lowered his eyes. "He is gone."

"Then we are all doomed," Kryssa murmured. She strode from the campsite.

He watched as the darkness swallowed her up, unable to summon the will to call her back. Then he placed his head in his hands and sobbed. All these years, he had done his best to rule Plorsea, to bring prosperity to his people. He had hated it, had loathed the bureaucracy, despaired as setback after setback saw his hope wither and die.

For the last eight years, Marianne and later their son had been his sole consolation, the only light in the darkness.

But that too had been a lie. He had nothing left to give. He was undone, broken.

I believe in you, brother.

Braidon shivered as the ghost whispered in his mind. They were his sister Alana's words, rising from the faded memories of his past. He had been a frightened child, terrified of the power that lurked within him. Magic had been a dangerous force, and those who feared it were destined to be controlled *by* it—their souls consumed, their bodies becoming host to the darkness within.

Alana had sheltered Braidon for most of his childhood, protecting him from their father's rages. Yet isolated from the world, Braidon's growth had been stunted. Only when they'd been separated had he finally flourished, overcoming his fears and mastering his magic. And finally Alana had seen the truth, that he too could be strong.

But as he'd told Kryssa, that was a long time ago. He was no longer that man. His magic was gone, his best years behind him. Perhaps Marianne was the future now, Plorsea destined to fall beneath her rule.

Braidon's mind turned back to the night of the solstice, to the great amphitheatre on the shores of Malevolent Cove. The followers of the Order had gathered in their hundreds for the Great Sacrifice, had watched as their queen attempted to burn Kryssa and Pela alive, had howled for Devon's death as the hammerman fought their champion.

Anger stirred in Braidon's stomach. If that was to be Marianne's way, Plorsea would never follow. Perhaps some of his people had been in the crowd, but many more had come from Lonia. It had been their ships that had bobbed off the coast, their Knights who had brought hatred to his land.

Their queen who had betrayed him.

He let out a long breath. Marianne thought she had defeated him, that she could betray him and he would submit without hardly a whimper. His thoughts spun. All those years of his life, wasted by the woman's treachery. Looking back, he saw now that she had been behind all his failures, that she had pulled his strings, had manipulated him all along.

Perhaps she had not chosen their marriage, but she had made a choice every day since. She had played her own game, taken her revenge, plotted her conquest.

Clenching his fists, Braidon staggered to his feet. The fight with Caledan had robbed him of the little strength he had regained, but rage gave him power. He stumbled to the stream and splashed water in his face. The cold woke him, tore him from the stupor that had gripped him since that night in the cove.

Perhaps there was no longer magic lurking within, waiting to pray upon his fear, but the emotion was no less treacherous. And he had succumbed to it, had allowed his terror to rule him.

No longer.

Braidon recalled the hatred in Marianne's eyes as she had looked upon him in Malevolent Cove. There'd been no love there, no trace of compassion. He must be the same. In that moment, Braidon's love for her died, plunged into the fiery embrace of his fury, forged into a new weapon, a hatred that would give him the strength to rise again.

He was Braidon, son of the Tsar, brother of Alana, last descendant of a line of kings stretching all the way back to the birth of the Gods.

Never again would he be defeated by despair.

A branch cracked at the edge of the clearing and he

turned to see Kryssa step back into the camp, a fresh bundle of firewood in her arms. She raised an eyebrow when she saw him standing by the creek.

"Gotten over yourself then?" she asked.

"Ay." Braidon smiled. "I think it's time we took the war to my wife."

❧ 5 ❧

ela's escape into unconsciousness did not last long. Pain soon dragged her back to reality, back to the pounding in her skull and the burning in her lungs. Tasting blood, she turned her head and spat on the floor. No one moved to help her, but she heard voices nearby.

"What's wrong with her, slave?" It was the new overseer, his voice bordering on panic. "How am I meant to do my job with only eleven of you?"

"Master, she is just a girl, and starving." Siden replied, his voice soft, beseeching. "Your predecessor saw fit to halve our rations. The girl is starving."

"I'm sure the man had good reason," the boy said.

"It was a bold decision, no doubt," Siden said, omitting his agreement. "But you are our master now."

"I am!" Ruebyn yelled. "And I want her to work!"

"She is so weak, she can barely hold a pickaxe," Siden explained patiently, "and that was before the…accident."

"She was strong enough to defy me," Ruebyn muttered,

then: "If she will not work…then she must be replaced. I cannot have a slave that won't pull their weight."

"A wise decision, Master," Siden murmured. "Her replacement would only take a few months to arrive. Your output would suffer, but no doubt it would be worth the lesson for any others who seek to avoid their duty."

There was a long pause. "What?"

Siden cleared his throat. "There is a…shortage of labour, Master."

The silence resumed. Pela did not move. Ruebyn had not noticed her awakening, and she savoured the chance to rest. For half a moment she wondered whether she might crawl away and escape, but then the chain tugged at her ankle again, chafing on her skin, and the hope shrivelled away.

"I can't fall behind the quota," he said uncertainly. "My family are relying on me to prove our worth to the queen and the Order."

"Then…perhaps there is another way?" came Siden's voice.

A strained pause followed, then: "Yes?"

Pela cracked open her eyes and found the two standing a little way up the tunnel.

Siden bowed his head. "Master, I would not presume to speak for you, but perhaps full rations could be restored. With food, we would work all the harder."

The boy's Adam's apple bobbed up and down. Wandering to one of the barrows, he took a slate tablet from a hook on the side and inspected the marks. He flicked over the contents, then looked back at the old slave.

"You currently supply ten barrows of coal per day between the twelve of you." He frowned. "Strange, according to the records I studied, that's less than expected. I thought Harrison had been performing well…I suppose the savings on food were important though, with the famine and all." The boy seemed to be muttering to himself now. "Even so…if my output increased to fifteen barrows…it might be worth the risk."

A collective whisper went through Pela's fellow slaves, though she could not tell whether it was of excitement or vexation. Either way, Siden nodded his assent.

"You will not regret this, Master!" he exclaimed.

Ruebyn's eyes widened, as though just realising he'd been talking out loud, but Siden was already shuffling towards Pela. It was too late to take back the words without Ruebyn looking foolish.

Pela sat up slowly as her friend approached, keeping her eyes averted from the overseer. She'd been beyond stupid earlier, and feeling more alert for her rest, she suddenly feared his coming retribution. There was plenty an overseer could do in this place to make her life hell, without condemning her to wherever failed slaves were sent.

Siden knelt and helped her up, but the crunch of stones announced the overseer's approach. As Pela stood, she found his hazel eyes on her. She lowered her gaze, though not before glimpsing his expression. Jaw hard and lips pursed tightly together, he looked a confused mixture of angry, confused and afraid.

"You spoke against me," he said quietly. "According to the rulebook of Itorn, that is a crime worth twenty lashes, slave."

Unable to muster the strength to resist his authority, Pela nodded dumbly. Her heart thudded weakly against her chest. Twenty lashes…in her current state, it would kill her.

Most times their last overseer had attacked in sudden fits of rage, but the punishments had ended just as quickly.

"But I struck you out of turn," Ruebyn went on. "A lesser offense, but a mistake no less. I am prepared to defer your punishment—on the presumption of your good behaviour?"

He spoke in an official tone, as though recalling the words from an old textbook, and Pela found herself wondering where this boy had come from. She inspected him more closely, her eyes long since adjusted to the dim light.

His boots were of dark leather and his clothes a fine silk, though already the pervasive dust had left its marks. Pela felt a moment's shame for the hessian rags she wore, the fabric torn in so many places that there were more holes than stars in the sky. The rough fabric chafed her sensitive skin, adding to her long list of pains.

Angrily Pela pushed aside her humiliation. Ruebyn's hair had been trimmed short in the style of the military, and she recalled the awe in his voice earlier, when he'd congratulated Overseer Harrison on his promotion. Pela doubted the boy had ever seen the Knights in action, let alone a battle, or he might not have been so excited at the thought of becoming a divine soldier.

Then she noticed the frown on Ruebyn's face and realised a full minute had passed without her speaking.

"Of course!" she all but shouted, her cheeks warming. "Master!"

The word still tripped on her tongue and she had to swallow hard to keep the bitterness from her face. The boy did not seem to notice, only offered a curt nod.

"Very well, back to work then, slave," he ordered.

"My name's Pela," she muttered without thinking, then froze, mortified.

Ruebyn stared at her a second, taken aback. Then he straightened, pulling himself up to all of his five feet and nine inches. "Do not mistake my actions for kindness, *slave*," he said officiously. "Whatever despicable crimes you have committed, you forfeited your right to a name. You are a slave and will answer to whatever I decide to call you. Do you understand?"

Pela wanted to scream at him, to tell him she was not a criminal, but one look in the boy's eyes told her Ruebyn would not listen. He had made his mind up about them the second he'd stepped foot in these tunnels. Denying her guilt would only reinforce his own beliefs. Never mind that many of her fellow slaves came from foreign villages in Northland, taken from their homes by Baronian raiders and brought here for sale.

Holding back tears, Pela nodded her assent.

"Then get back to work, *slave*," Ruebyn repeated. "There will be a second meal this evening, but I will brook no slacking until it arrives."

Pela went.

Stumbling across the uneven ground, she joined Siden at the coalface. Wordlessly he handed her the pickaxe. Stifling a sob, she took it and stepped past him before he saw the shimmering in her eyes. It scared her, how much this place had robbed her of hope, of spirit, of humanity. She was nothing now, just a body to be used until she could do no more, then discarded.

Angrily she hefted the pickaxe and swung it at the rock. The rest had restored some of her strength and this time it struck true. Imagining the black vein was Ruebyn, she struck again, and a block of coal tumbled clear. Siden picked it up and carried it to the barrow while Pela continued to vent her anger against the stone.

But in her half-starved state not even her rage could last. Slowly she faded into the dim trance that was their work, the pick rising and falling with rhythmic slowness, the pause for breath, the gathering strength, then through the whole process again. It was almost meditative, and she often found herself slipping into the trance she had once practiced in her mother's temple, fading into the darkness of *nothing*.

In that state, time passed quickly, her body working almost of its own accord, and before she knew it a bell was ringing. Shaking her head, she came back to herself—and groaned. Her arms had picked up a fresh collection of bruises from stray rocks and poor blows of the pickaxe, and a familiar ache had begun in her shoulder blades.

For a moment, Pela was confused. The bell was not usually rung until it was time to sleep. The other slaves were shuffling towards the collection of rocks where they took their meal. The chain tugged at her ankle and only then did she recall that they were to be given a second meal. She swallowed, the steel collar pressing at her throat, and tears sprang to her eyes.

She quickly wiped them away, annoyed at the display of emotion, and joined her fellow slaves. The familiar pot of broth sat between the stones. Taking up the ladle, Siden dished it out into bowls. A greasy layer had congealed on the surface of the broth and it carried the faint odour of something rotten. In another life, Pela would have turned away in disgust, but now her stomach rumbled and she gratefully accepted the bowl from her friend.

Sipping at the gruel, Pela shivered. The stuff tasted of

mould and old leather, but she had grown used to it long ago. It was hot food she longed for, for soup to warm the ice that had seeped into her core. She ate quickly, aware they could be ordered back to work at any moment, though Ruebyn was still speaking with the man who had brought the pot.

She sat up straighter as he turned away. He carried a second bundle beneath his arm as he wandered across to the circle of stones and he took a seat alongside Siden. The other slaves stared as he placed the bundle on his knees and unwrapped it.

The rich scent of roasted meat and freshly baked bread wafted across to where Pela sat. Her eyes widened as Ruebyn lifted the sandwich to his mouth. The bread gave a sharp *crunch* as he bit into it. She spied fresh salad alongside pieces of browned beef. Her mouth started to water.

Their last overseer had always taken his meal further up the tunnel, out of sight. Ruebyn obviously hadn't given a second thought to where he ate. He bit into the sandwich again, then took a book from his jacket and began to read, though it must have been difficult in the faint light.

As though suddenly realising he was being watched, Ruebyn head jerked up, his eyes locking with hers. A frown creased his forehead, then he glanced at the pot of gruel. Pela could have sworn his cheeks turned red—before his brow hardened again.

"What are you staring at, slave?" he snapped.

Pela jumped. "Sorry!" she gasped, burying her eyes in her empty bowl.

Siden chuckled and took up the pot to give her the last scraps from the bottom. The other slaves grumbled, but on the back of the second meal, offered no other complaints.

Pela nodded her thanks, though with the scent of fresh food in her nostrils, she could hardly stomach the sight of her own food.

"Eat up," Siden murmured, seating himself beside her. "Who knows how long it will last?"

Pela glanced at their new overseer again, but his attention was back on the book. "He's lucky none of us tried to jump him for it," she muttered, indicating the sandwich.

"It might even be worth it," Siden said lightly.

Chuckling for the first time in days, Pela spooned the last few scraps into her mouth and tried to ignore the taste. They had only a few more minutes before Ruebyn stood up suddenly, rewrapping the last of his sandwich in the paper parcel before clearing his throat.

"Right!" he called. "Shall we get back to it, then?"

She almost snorted at his phrasing, as if they had a choice—or that he would in any way be sharing in their toil. Not unless they counted using the whip he now kept strapped to his belt.

Instead, Pela discreetly rolled her eyes at Siden and stood. Chains rattled as the slaves returned to their stations. Pela thought they moved with slightly more vigour now, and was surprised to find herself feeling stronger than she had in in weeks.

Picking up the axe, she was just taking aim when the boy spoke from directly behind her.

"Slave!"

She jumped, a yelp slipping from her lips, and fumbled at the pickaxe—only just managing to catch it before it fell. Turning, she eyed him warily.

"Yes?"

He hesitated, looking around indiscreetly, as though

afraid someone might be watching them. But Siden and the other slaves were working further down the tunnel and their attention was on their work. He stepped in close, staring down at her.

Pela shuddered, terrified she had done something wrong. She flinched as he stretched out a hand, but the boy only touched it to her cheek, where his whip had broken the skin.

"I'm sorry…there are rules…the guidebook of Itorn," he said beneath his breath.

Pela only caught snatches of what he was saying. Before she could put them together in her mind, he shoved something into her hands. Then he was walking away, leaving her standing there in shock. She stared at the scrunched up parcel he had given her, struggling to find the courage to open it. The faint scent of bread still clung to the wrapping and she drew in a deep breath, savouring the smell. Finally she pulled open the paper, revealing the leftover portion of sandwich within.

Tears burst from Pela eyes and she sank to her knees, unable to bear the strangeness of it all a second longer.

$\mathcal{H}$ 6 $\mathcal{H}$

Another week passed before Braidon could walk any significant distance, but Kryssa was pleased with his progress. His attitude had changed since the sellsword's departure, and while a dense silence still hung over the camp, the king no longer lay in the grips of despair. Each morning Braidon would rise early to push himself through a sequence of drills and exercises that Kryssa recognised from her training in the King's Guard.

By the time Kryssa herself rose, he would have a hot cup of bush tea prepared. They had found a grove of bamboo earlier in the week and by cutting the shoots into pieces, they were able to fill the interior hollows with water and heat them over the flames. Kryssa had been cynical at first, for while Genevieve had taught her some bush craft, this was something different. But the water inside had kept the shoots from burning—at least for a few uses—and there were herbs aplenty for tea.

As the week progressed, they began to spar in the evenings, though only with sticks from the pile of firewood.

Braidon was clumsy and out of practice, slowed by his injuries, but Kryssa was impressed by his determination. There was a steely look to his eyes now, a cold resolve to recover, and she couldn't help but remember his words the night of Caledan's departure.

It's time we took the war to my wife.

It was a bold sentiment, but Kryssa could see no practical way of achieving his ends. Braidon might still live, but he had been isolated from his followers, while Marianne must have had time by now to consolidate her power in the capital.

And the queen could not have achieved her coup alone. Who else in Ardath had plotted against Braidon? To trust anyone would risk betrayal and capture. And Kryssa had no intention of ever surrendering her freedom again.

But nor could she stand by and do nothing. Pela and Gen were still missing. Kryssa could only assume the Knights had caught them. She could not bring herself to consider any other possibilities. That meant a confrontation must come, sooner or later. But first they needed to build their strength, study the ground ahead. Kryssa needed to know what had befallen her daughter and Gen, and Braidon needed to find allies.

"What about the army?" Kryssa asked as they sat by the fire on the tenth night since Caledan had departed.

Braidon sat whittling a stick on the other side of the fire. He looked up, his eyes widening. They had hardly spoken throughout the long days, and while Kryssa had been happy for the peace, it was past time they made plans.

After a moment, the king sighed. "The army was disbanded," he grunted. "Turned into local militia after the peace treaty was signed. We couldn't afford the expense of a standing army."

"Seems I missed a lot while I was in Skystead," Kryssa commented, unable to keep the anger from her voice. She was beginning to see the source of some of Caledan's frustrations.

"You disagree," Braidon stated.

"Of course."

"You think Plorsea should have been prepared for another war?" he asked. When she only stared blankly at him, he chuckled and went on. "Then I might ask why you never taught your daughter to fight? Devon told me, before…"

"Because I feared she would follow on her father's path, or my own," Kryssa murmured.

Braidon's eyes took on a distant look. "Ay, and perhaps I hoped Plorsea could finally leave its violence behind," he said. Then he blinked, and his face hardened as he came back to himself. "But I was naïve. Strive for peace, but prepare for war…that was something my father said once, I remember."

Kryssa shuddered at the mention of the Tsar, and quickly changed the topic. "The past is set. We must work with what we have. Is there anyone you trust in Ardath?"

"Only my King's Guard. No doubt Marianne has them under watch though." He paused. "And I fear what she will do with our son."

"Surely she would not harm her own child?" Kryssa said, shocked.

Braidon sat staring into the fire, but his head jerked up at her question. "How should I know?" he snapped. "She could be capable of anything, after what we saw in Malevolent Cove!"

"Then what is your plan?" Kryssa hissed. "Because there is far more than just your own son at stake here!"

The anger went from Braidon in a rush. "I don't know," he said. "I don't even know *what* she did that night. Where did her power come from, that she could hold us with only her voice?"

A shudder passed through Kryssa as she recalled the strange compulsion the queen had cast. Then she remembered Devon's voice, ringing with a strength all of his own, cutting through her words like a knife. "And how did my father free us?"

"That's easy," Braidon chuckled. "Devon always had a knack for doing the impossible!"

"Perhaps…" Kryssa replied, "or perhaps that is also where our answers lie."

Braidon did not seem to hear her. "Magic has been gone for thirty years," he murmured. "Why would it return now?"

"Yours has not reappeared?"

"No," Braidon grunted. "Though it would not help us anyway. I only ever possessed the power of illusion, to trick the watcher's eye and ear. It would not stop Marianne—and it died with the Gods."

"What about dark magic?" Kryssa asked after a moment's thought.

"Demons and their ilk perished not long after the Gods. Their power is dark and twisted, but they still needed true magic to feed it. They could not survive without the Gods." He paused for a long while, then added, "So if even a demon could not find power, where did Marianne get it?"

"From Ikar," Kryssa whispered, remembering the queen's words.

There is power in death.

"The Knight? But he was just a mortal. There were once Magickers who could transfer magic between themselves…"

"No, not his magic, his *life*," Kryssa interrupted. "Marianne told us there was power in death. She even made Pela and I wear some necklace when we were to be sacrificed—an experiment, she said. But we didn't die. It was only when Ikar…"

"*Not quite the death I wanted*," Braidon quoted his wife. "You can't think…?"

"I think Ikar was stronger than all of us," Kryssa replied. "He defeated us, had the will to stick to his convictions, despite all the evidence of the Order's corruption. They were always talking about needing a powerful sacrifice, someone worthy. Why?"

"It makes sense…in a sick kind of way," the king murmured. "The stronger the man—or woman—the stronger the power that would be taken from them."

"But not strong enough to stop my father…"

"Yes…" Braidon trailed off, his eyes returning to the fire. "Though he could barely move for the effort of holding Marianne off. I wonder…"

"What?"

The king shook his head, a frown creasing his forehead. "I'm not sure, but it feels like the answer is there. I just cannot quite fit the pieces together."

Kryssa sighed. "Either way, there is still the problem of the Knights, and the Lonian army. We need to know what we're facing."

"You're right." Braidon swore and lifted his shirt, taking a moment to inspect the wound. There was still a scab over the wound, and the flesh around it was a bright pink. "I could take weeks yet to heal. We can't afford to wait that long."

"I could go…" Kryssa started dubiously.

"No," Braidon interrupted, "Chole is the closest city to us, but it would still take five days to reach on foot. Too long for you to return if things are urgent. We'll have to go together."

Kryssa raised an eyebrow. "Are you sure?"

"No," Braidon chuckled, "but it's not like I can make things any worse."

❧ 7 ❧

P ela slammed the point of her pickaxe into the seam of
coal, then paused to sniff the air, checking for the telltale whiff of sulphur. In the last week with two meals a day,
her strength had returned, and she and the other slaves had
dug deeper than ever before. But the progress had brought
unexpected consequences, and they had encountered
several pockets of the gas that Ruebyn called "methane."

During their first encounter, the stench had been so
strong Pela's head had been spinning before she could even
put down her axe. Unlike their previous overseer, Ruebyn
had reacted instantly. His screams had echoed loudly from
the rock, ordering them up the tunnel. Pela might have
thought he'd been over-reacting, if not for the sheer terror
in this voice.

Later, he had explained that the gas was far more flammable than the coal they mined. The thought sent chills
down Pela's spine, and now she was more careful than ever.
With her energy returned, so too had her will to live, and
her terror of meeting an untimely death.

Fortunately, Ruebyn—if nothing else—was well-read on the subject of mining. He spoke often of his tutors back in Lon—famous engineers who had worked on behalf of the crown for the better part of a decade. Though the slaves rarely responded, the boy liked to talk, and Pela came to learn he was the third son of some noble family. They had sent him here to complete an indenture, to raise their worth in the eyes of the powerful who ruled Lonia.

For herself, Pela had kept her head down since their first confrontation, unwilling to risk anything that might be considered insubordination. Despite his secret act of kindness, Ruebyn had proven unfailingly proscriptive in his role as overseer, administering punishments for any transgression noted down in his precious manual.

Letting out her breath, Pela decided the rock was safe, and swung her pick again. This time it sank deep, breaking through the soft stone, and a piece of coal toppled loose. Hefting it in her arms, she carried it to the barrow and carefully added it to the load. It was only half-full, but she paused there a moment to catch her breath.

Siden joined her, a weary smile on his dusty face. "You are looking better, young Pela," he murmured, adding a large rock to her barrow.

Despite her exhaustion, Pela returned the smile. "Thanks to you," she said. "I still can't believe your nerve, convincing him to give us more food."

"A stroke of genius, I'll admit," Siden chuckled, but it faltered, turning to a hacking cough. He bent in two, eyes watering.

This time it was Pela's turn to offer her water. He accepted it with a trembling hand and took a swig.

"You're sick," Pela said, noticing the pallid colour of his skin, the purple tinge to his lips.

Returning the waterskin, Siden waved a hand as though to dismiss her words. "I'm old, it is not a new sensation," he murmured. "Come though, we had best return to our work, before the good master comes calling."

Eyeing him closely, Pela nodded, though now that her mind was working again, she realised Siden had not been well for a while. In her half-starved state she had not noticed his coughing fits, but in the last week they had come regularly, as though the cloying dust were permanently lodged in his lungs. Even while sitting, there was a wheezing to his breath, a rattling from the depths of his chest.

Lost in thought, Pela lifted her pickaxe and resumed her work. Alone again, the walls pressed in, the gloom reminding her of their fate should the tunnel collapse. She shivered, forcing her mind away from the fear, and sought instead the peaceful quiet of meditation. It helped to focus her thoughts elsewhere, to keep them from returning to all the multitude of ways she might meet her doom—burning alive, crushed beneath tonnes of rock, trapped amidst rubble, unable to move, her air slowly running out…

Pela cursed and shook herself. Her heart thudded painfully in her chest. The *clack* of steel picks on rock echoed in the darkness, a constant reminder of their doom. She sucked in a breath, concentrating her mind on the action, on the swelling of her chest, the whisper as she exhaled again.

Her heart slowed, and she continued the exercise. Each swing of her pick was matched with an exhalation, her arms operating almost by instinct, lifting, striking, again and again to the rhythm of her breath. She hardly felt the pain in her shoulders or the ache in the small of her back any longer. Her fear receded as she centred herself, and she reached for that quiet place her mother had shown her, that peaceful void where the rest of the world would fade away.

Pela longed for that escape, to leave behind the harsh realities of the world, if only for a short while. She had been practicing over the last week, but amidst the peril and pain, she had been unable to reach it. Something always contrived to bring her back. This time though, Pela sensed she was close…

It came slowly, a dim darkness that rose around her, until it seemed she floated alone on a pool of nothingness. Distantly, she sensed her body still at work—some small part of her mind directing her through the monotonous routine —but her mind was free. A sense of peace touched her, one she had not experienced for the longest time. She drifted there in the nothingness for time uncounted, for it did not seem to matter amidst the void of her inner mind.

Slowly though, Pela came to sense she was not alone in the nothingness, that some other force drifted there, something *more*. She found herself searching the endless black, though she knew nothing could be here, in her most private of places. Dismissing the sensation, she focused back in on herself.

A light flickered into life, a whiteness that seemed to spring from nowhere. It burned in her mind's eye, a candle of warmth in the black. A strange joy filled Pela, though she could not have said why. The thing was hardly more than a spark, but she was drawn to it, as though it were a part of her—as though it *were* her. Amidst the absolute black, she stretched out a tendril of her mind to touch it…

Crack.

Pela gasped as a noise in the outside world dragged her from the trance. Staggering back, she stared at the rockface she'd been mining. Her pickaxe was embedded deep in the stone, almost to the hilt. Cracks radiated outwards from her tool, growing as she stood there with mouth hanging open.

"Run!" Siden's shout came from nearby.

Dust filled the tunnel and Pela turned to run, but the chain around her ankle snapped taut and she crashed to the ground. The rocks behind her cracked and popped and she scrambled back up, fear turning her bones to jelly. With the chain still trapping her leg, she could not run.

Turning, she found Siden collapsed on the ground nearby. She cursed, searching for help, but the other slaves were further up the tunnel, the chain snaking away around a bend in the rock. They were alone. Siden managed to find a knee, but his hand was clutched at his chest and he did not seem able to move any further.

Her heart thrashing wildly, Pela staggered towards him. The shriek of breaking rock came from the wall as the cracks grew. His face pale, Siden looked up and saw her coming.

"Get back!" he screamed, but even if Pela could not have left him behind had she wanted to.

Falling to her knees beside him, she threw her arm beneath his shoulder and hauled him up. A gasp tore from her lips as Pela was reminded how weak she still was. She swayed on her feet, willing herself to move. Siden was a deadweight at her side, his breath coming in ragged gasps.

Putting one foot in front of the other, she started up the tunnel. Rocks were falling from the ceiling now. One the size of her head slammed into the ground not two feet from where she stood. If it had struck her, she would have been dead without ever knowing it.

A roar came from behind them, followed by a *boom* as the wooden support beams lining the tunnel sheared in two, bringing down an entire section. Pela staggered on, sobbing in her desperation to escape, but unable to push her beaten body at more than a hobble. They made it around the bend and found the next slave's manacle empty—Ruebyn must have freed them and fled. Furthest down the tunnel, Pela and Siden had been left to fend for themselves.

Another crash came, followed by a rush of air and dust as another section of ceiling fell. A rock struck Pela in the back of her leg, knocking her from her feet. A scream tore from her lips. It turned to a choking cough as dust filled her lungs.

"Help us!" she screamed, but it was pitch black now, the lantern swallowed by stone, the dust obscuring even the distant lights ahead.

She tried to get up, but something hard struck her in the small of her back, driving her into the floor. Clawing at the stone, she tried to crawl, desperate to live, to escape the tomb of death closing around her. The roaring came from all around now, as though she were in the middle of a land-slide, as though the entire mountain was about to fall on her.

Pain radiated from her spine, but below where she'd been struck, there was nothing. Horror rose in her throat at the thought she might be paralysed—then something sharp tore through the flesh of her thigh. A moan bubbled from her throat, where the iron collar suddenly felt warm.

Pela no longer had the strength to scream, no longer knew where Siden was, only that she had to get up. Forcing herself to her hands and knees, she crawled from the stone and dust and dark, unable to see even the tiniest speck of world, but knowing she had to go up, must follow the slope of the tunnel to safety.

Thunder filled the pitch-black, deafening her to all but the pounding of blood in her ears. She sensed rock still falling around her, felt the little stabs of pain as splinters of stone sliced her skin. In places she had to crawl just to find her way around the rubble filling the tunnel. At any moment she was sure the whole mine would collapse and bury her alive.

Then, just as Pela began to imagine that she must soon see light, that the rescuers must come for her, her foot snagged on something in the dark. She cursed, shaking her leg to free herself, and heard the telltale rattle of chains.

An awful sob rose in Pela's chest and slipped from her as a moan. In her panic she had left Siden behind, had forgotten about their shared fate and abandoned him to his death. She gripped the chain in both hand and slammed it into the ground, screaming her frustration, her guilt, her despair. It was hopeless; the steel would not yield.

She did not have the strength to return, to stagger back into the dust and dark and find her friend. There was nothing more she could do. Tears streaked her cheeks and weeping, Pela curled into a ball, to wait for the end.

The sound of breaking rock grew louder again, a creeping doom approaching through the black—until with a roar, the world came alive, and Pela knew no more.

❦ 8 ❦

Caledan slipped carefully through the press of bodies, towards the raised voices calling from the plaza. The crowd jostled around him, some doing their best to escape. Others moved forward with Caledan, perhaps drawn by a morbid sense of curiosity, though there could be little doubt as to what waited ahead.

The tall marble buildings of Ardath towered around him, their awnings worn and stained by the soot of decades, but otherwise no less grand for the passage of time. While the cobbled streets were in shadow, the narrow walls trapped the summer's heat, and the air was suffocating. Sweat dripped from Caledan's forehead, but just ahead the walls finally opened out, giving way to a plaza. A voice boomed out over the crowd, its meaning lost in the rumbling of a hundred other speakers, but Caledan didn't need to hear the words to know their intent.

He had seen it all over Plorsea on his journey from Dragon Country. In the small villages of Lane and Oaksville, the stories were all the same. The Knights of

Alana were riding in force, spreading the word of Alana, hunting the country for the blasphemous. Many of their followers had taken up the call, marching in the streets, informing on their neighbours, attacking the few Temples that remained in Plorsea, whatever they could to aid the cause.

Finally Caledan reached the open square. A brick path led around the boundary of the plaza, while in the centre, gardens had been planted in better times. Tall trees provided shade for the host of men and women drawn by the commotion, but the flowers had been trampled into the dirt by the crowd in their haste to find a view.

Caledan loosened his sword in its sheath as he stepped into the gardens. Stones crunched beneath his feet as he threaded his way between the watchers. A breeze rustled the leaves of a nearby tree. He let out a sigh as it touched his forehead, drawing away some of the heat.

Scanning his surroundings, Caledan noticed Knights stationed at intervals around the plaza. Though the heat must have been unbearable, all wore the familiar steel armour adorned with the flaming sword that was the symbol of their Order. Even their visors were down, concealing their true identities.

As Caledan watched, one of the Knights moved into the path of a spectator as he tried to leave the plaza, obviously having seen enough. A steel hand caught the man and held him tight while another Knight appeared. The captive's arms were bound behind his back as a crowd watched on, his pleas falling on deaf ears.

"Blasphemers! Traitors!"

A metallic shout drew Caledan's attention back to the centre of the plaza. There, three Knights stood with swords in hand, four prisoners on their knees before them. The prisoners' hands were similarly bound and their faces showed the purple bruises of their captivity.

The Knight in the centre raised his sword high and a roar came from the crowd. Many raised fists to the sky, though Caledan noticed even now others tried to retreat, realising too late what they had stepped into. Tightening his jaw, Caledan dropped his hand to his sword hilt, but after a moment he forced himself to release it. He was confident he could take the three Knights holding the men captive, but with their brothers lining the plaza, escape would be out of the question.

Caledan had not come to Ardath to throw his life away. He watched as the Knights stripped the clothes from the prisoners, until the four were left huddling naked on the ground. Without the use of their hands, they struggled to sit up, eyes wild as they searched the crowd for mercy.

"Darkness has crept into Plorsea!" the tallest of the Knights bellowed. "The Saviour calls for a cleansing, lest the scourge of the False Gods return to these lands."

Another roar came from the crowd. Caledan shuddered at the hatred on the faces around him. This was Braidon's doing, the result of his weakness, his failure to protect Plorsea from his own foolishness. How could he have been so blind, have ignored the darkness in the woman who lay beside him each night? If that was what love did to a man, Caledan was glad he had never felt its sting.

"The might of Alana must be renewed!" The Knight called. "The souls of the blasphemous will become her strength, when the faithful send them into her embrace. Will you do the Saviour's will?"

Caledan edged himself back and the crowd surged

forward, eager to fill the gap he had left. The sound of the gathering was like thunder echoing from the stone walls. Caledan glimpsed a man at the front of the pack lean down and scoop up a rock. He drew back his arm and Caledan quickly looked away, but he could not block out the distant *thwack* of stone striking flesh.

Picking up his pace, Caledan fought against the push of the crowd, even as more surged forward, eager to join the slaughter.

"Going somewhere, brother?"

Caledan swung around to find a Knight ahead. He swore silently and tried to side-step the man. The Knight followed, barring his path. Grinding his teeth, Caledan drew to a stop.

"Can I help you with something?"

"My brothers asked you to add your strength to the Saviour's cause."

"Maybe another day," Caledan said, offering a smile, even as a horrible scream rose above the shouts of the mob. "It's market day." He tried to get around the man again.

"I don't think so," the Knight snarled, dropping a hand to his sword.

Steel hissed against leather as he tried to draw the weapon. Realising the pretence was over, Caledan caught him by the wrist and forced the weapon back into its sheath. The Knight growled and swung out with his free hand. Caledan ducked, and still holding the man's arm, dragged him forward. The man staggered past, and twisting, Caledan launching a kick at his metallic back.

A cry rattled from the iron helmet, lost in the roar of the crowd, and the Knight flew headfirst into a tree. He crashed into the ground and started to thrash, unable to find his feet.

Men and women retreated from him, trying to understand what had happened, but Caledan was already well away, turning a corner from the plaza. He weaved quickly through the narrow streets until he reached the broad avenue that ran from the main gates to the citadel.

There he slowed, merging with the crowds, and continued his way through the city. He glimpsed several more demonstrations, but these he ignored. His worst suspicions had been confirmed. With her power affirmed by whatever she'd gained during the Great Sacrifice, Marianne had set her Knights loose across Plorsea, even on the capital itself. Those who still believed in the Old Gods—or who defied the Order's power—were being slaughtered. Something had to be done, and if Braidon was too much a coward to right his wrongs…

Caledan shook his head. What was he thinking? Just a month ago, he'd wanted nothing more than to kill the king and have his revenge. Yet when he'd finally had Braidon in his power, Caledan had spared him. Why? Because a dead man had begged him to protect the king? Caledan owed Devon nothing.

So what was he doing here, thinking to save Plorsea from the mad queen? He wasn't a hero, taken to glory, or throwing his life away on a lost cause. There was no way he could stop Marianne—to even try would guarantee his death.

Recalling that strange power she had wielded back in the cove, Caledan felt a sudden urge to flee the city. He had grown up in a time without magic. Always before he'd had the skill to face down his enemies, to match them blade to blade and conquer. But when Marianne had *commanded* him, he'd been helpless before her power. If she'd asked it, he would have taken the dagger from his belt and plunged it into his own stomach.

Finally Caledan turned a corner and was greeted by the familiar sight of the Firestone Inn. The establishment was on the rougher side of the city, but the owner was a former sellsword Caledan had fought beside in a dozen skirmishes. He had hung up his sword after the civil war, purchasing the inn from a couple retiring from the city. Caledan was confident the man could be trusted.

The wooden steps squeaked as he made his way up, announcing his approach, and the bartender thrust open the double doors before Caledan reached them. He had been a giant of a warrior in his day, wielding a twin-headed axe with enough force to carve through plate mail. But his fighting days were long over; now his beard was grey and his stomach strained against the buttons of his tunic. Even so, a grin spread across his cheeks when he saw his guest.

"Caledan!" he bellowed. "Glad to see you're still alive, I've been hearing all sorts of rumours. Come in!"

Cursing silently, Caledan cast a glance in either direction, but the cobbled street was empty, and he quickly followed his friend inside.

"Thank you, Grif," he murmured, finding himself in the dimly-lit dining room. They were alone, but he did not say more until he crossed to the bar. "I'd appreciate it if you didn't spread the news around though."

Grif chuckled. "Got yourself embroiled in something messy, have you, sellsword?"

"You might say that," Caledan replied. Seating himself on a stool, he waved for a drink.

Taking two glasses from beneath the bar, Grif poured

them each a measure of whiskey, then a second helping for good measure. He pushed the glass across the bar.

"If there's going to be trouble, I'd rather you didn't bring it to my doorstep," he said quietly. "Times are hard enough as it is."

"Agreed," Caledan muttered, "but don't worry, all going well, no one will know I'm here."

"Why *are* you here?" Grif asked. "Word is there's a bounty of your head, lad."

"World's coming to pieces, thought I should go where the action was," Caledan replied, then paused. "I saw some of the demonstrations on my way in."

Grif shuddered. "Ay. Large group of 'em rode in a couple weeks ago, joined with the little congregation in that Castle of theirs. Never caused us any trouble before now, but within a day there was talk of people being hauled away in the night. Then those Elders started giving talks around the city, claiming magic is making a return. That got a lot of folk scared."

"I can imagine," Caledan said.

After thirty years without the Gods and their gifts, people had grown used to the new world order. Magic had passed into memories, becoming a precautionary tale against the dangers of unconstrained power. Even those who still worshipped the Old Gods did so now only out of custom, knowing in their hearts those they prayed to were gone for good.

But the Order of Alana believed otherwise. The Elders had convinced their followers they must be ever vigilant against the Gods' return, had armed their Knights as their divine warriors. And now they were recruiting more followers, taking advantage of the power vacuum Braidon had left in his absence. But then, where was Marianne?

"What of the queen?" Caledan asked, his heart beating faster. Had he come to the wrong place?

"Off chasing King Braidon's killers. Last I heard, she'd had a great victory—though it came at great cost. Most of the King's Guard were lost. Can only hope she returns soon. Someone needs to take control of this mob."

"And you think Marianne is the one for the job?"

Grif frowned. "Seems she put an end to the Baronians that killed old Braidon," he said. When Caledan did not reply, he went on. "Anyway, she's the only one with the power to oppose them. There's plenty who don't like what's happening, but they're afraid of speaking out. Too many already gone missing, or been accused of this crime or another."

"And what of Lonia?"

"We were lucky. Seems their council has been busy worrying about who will rule them, now that Ashoka's dead. But I suspect whoever takes over will be eager to test their nettle against our new queen." He chuckled. "I think they'll be in for a surprise."

"You think?"

Grif only grinned. "Daughter of one king, husband to another. Must be something to her, right?"

Caledan shrugged and took another sip of his ale. Grif was right about one thing—Marianne was a worthy foe. She had played Braidon like a puppet, gathering her own followers around her, even finding a new power they had no way to match. And yet her own motives remained almost unknown.

"Dad!" a young voice burst into the dining room.

Caledan turned in time to see a boy come racing across the wooden floor. "Dad, she's here!"

A lump lodged in Caledan's throat at his words. Grif stepped out from behind the bar and scooped the boy up in his arms, his laughter ringing from the walls.

"Who's that, son?" he asked, but Caledan already knew the answer.

"The queen!" the boy exclaimed. "She's returned! They're gathering in the grand plaza now, to hear her speak. Can we go?"

"No," Caledan said, his voice hard.

Grif swung around, a frown on his face, but one look at Caledan and the words on his lips died. Rising from his chair, Caledan placed a silver shilling on the counter.

"For the ale, and a room," he murmured.

Stepping around his friend, he headed for the door. At the last minute, he glanced back. Grif still stood beside the bar, his face tight with fear. He swallowed visibly, and Caledan felt a moment's compassion.

"If I don't return by the night, give the room away," he said. "I was never here."

Then he turned and stepped back through the double doors, out into the sunlight.

❧ 9 ☙

Braidon was panting hard by the time they reached the treeline that marked the boundary of Dragon Country. The steep slope of Mount Chole stretched upwards from where he stood, all loose gravel and broken boulders. A trail wound away from them, little more than a goat track that zigzagged its way across the mountainside.

The summer sun beat down on the open scree, and Braidon wondered how he would survive such a climb. His entire body was already aching, the chest wound a constant presence, an angry throbbing that stole away his breath and left him gasping. He was in no condition to travel, let alone face whatever waited for them in Chole.

But there was no choice, and squaring his shoulders, Braidon stepped from the trees. Kryssa followed silently behind him. They had started out early, but Braidon's slow pace had already put them behind schedule. Noon was approaching and they still needed to cross the mountain range, or else face a night exposed on the open slopes.

Braidon had barely made it a dozen feet from the treeline when a sharp *crack* came from overhead. The hackles rose on his neck as a shadow fell across their path—then the Red Dragon slammed into the mountainside, sending gravel raining down around them. Braidon covered his head, wincing as a chunk of rock the size of his fist struck him. Above, the dragon turned, its amber eyes glaring down at them.

Where do you go, King?

Straightening, Braidon reached within for the will to face the creature. His weakness dragged at his confidence and his legs shook. Laughter sounded in his mind as the dragon took a step towards them, setting off a miniature landslide.

Does the mighty King seek to flee?

The beast's mockery fuelled Braidon's rage and he straightened. "I go to face our enemies, dragon!" he snarled, raising a fist. "I will hide in this forest no longer. Stay, if you wish, and hide behind your mother's skirts, but I will face my foes."

Heat washed over them as the dragon opened its enormous jaws and roared. The sound staggered Braidon and for one mortifying second, he thought his legs would give way. Then Kryssa caught him beneath the shoulder and he recovered. Together they faced down the dragon's rage.

You dare insult my people's courage?

Braidon bared his teeth. "What courage, dragon?" he shouted. "Have the Red Dragons ever shown anything but cowardice? When Archon threatened the world, where were your people? When my father came to enslave your fellows, where was the battle? Even when the lowly Knights of Alana trespass freely in your lands, you offer nigh on a whimper. No, do not talk to *me* of fleeing. At least I fight my battles."

Do you not see my scars, King? the dragon growled, its scales glittering in the noonday sun, highlighting the great tears. Its one good eye burned with untold rage. *Ingytus was not the only dragon to fight, though he was the first to fall.*

"Ay," Braidon replied, lifting his chin. "For the first time in an eon, I saw dragons fighting against the darkness. It was a glorious sight. I would see it again."

The dragon lowered its snout until the giant orb of its eye was just a few feet from them. *And what would you have of me, King?*

Braidon swallowed, hardly daring to speak the question. One memory shone bright in his mind, of a time long ago with his grandmother, when he had flown with the last Gold Dragon. But no one had ever ridden a Red. Even now he could sense the hatred radiating from the creature. Their species loathed humanity with an ancient potency. Only their desperation to be free of the Knights had given Braidon the opportunity to bargain with them. Even so, just to ask…

"Carry us to Chole," he said, before his courage failed him. The Red Dragon reared up on its hind legs with a roar, and this time Braidon saw the flames flickering deep in its throat. He continued quickly, "For I do not have the strength to cross the mountains."

The admission gave the beast pause. It stared at them a long moment, then lowered itself back to all fours. Teeth bared, its voice boomed into their minds.

The Knights have not all gone from our lands, it howled. *Some remain in our most sacred of places. A great work is underway there, a construct of stone and steel. We will not stand for it.*

Braidon bowed his head. "If I succeed in Chole, the Knights will fall. On that, you have my promise."

And what of our demand? The dragon growled. *We will settle only for Dragon Country no longer. You promised Ingytus all the lands south to the river Lane. Do you remain true to your word, King?*

A shiver lifted the hackles on Braidon's spine. He had not forgotten the promise, though it would prove costly to his people. But it had already been made, it would mean his life to go back on it now.

"Of course," Braidon said, inclining his head. "My word is sacred, and when I regain my crown your people shall have their reward."

Very well, King. The dragon flexed its claws, driving them deep into the rocky ground. *Then I will take you to Chole, though I will be forever tainted in the eyes of my people.*

"Thank you, dragon," Braidon whispered. "It shames me to ask this of you."

The great head turned away. *I am called Nidryt,* it rumbled, *and these Knights have lessened us all.*

"When did they first come here?" Braidon wondered out loud. The amphitheatre in the cove had not been built overnight.

A shiver went through the beast. *Five years past, they first appeared on our beaches. We made to drive them away, confident in our power, and many of their number died. But their weapons slew us in turn, and like our extinct cousins, my people have never been numerous.*

"I am sorry to have called you cowards," Braidon replied, ashamed despite himself.

A rumble came from the dragon's chest, laughter. *And I you, King. Now let us journey together to the Dying City.*

It stretched out a forearm. Braidon swallowed, sharing a

glance with Kryssa. The woman had been unusually silent, and her face had gone unnaturally pale.

"Ladies first?" he offered.

She swallowed visibly. "This was your idea."

Braidon let out a long breath, fear and excitement warring within. He remembered again his grandmother, Enala, and her joy sitting astride the Gold Dragon, Dahniul. It was a legacy of their family, an agreement stretching right back to King Thomas. But when Dahniul had fallen, that agreement had come to an end. Now Braidon had forged the pact anew, though with a species that would rather tear him apart than fight beside him.

He swallowed, and before his fear could stop him, climbed up onto the dragon's forearm. Weakened by his injury, he almost fell, but Kryssa's hand on his back kept him in place. The scales shook beneath him, and Braidon saw Nidryt turn his head to watch. Steadying himself, he climbed the rest of the way up the dragon's back, then grinned at Kryssa.

"Your turn!"

Kryssa swallowed visibly, her silver eyes wide. Braidon grinned. It was the first time he'd seen her frightened. He was enjoying the reversal.

"Come on, he won't bite," he said, holding out his hand.

A rumble came from Nidryt's chest and Kryssa raised an eyebrow. "I'm not sure he agrees."

Braidon chuckled. "Would you prefer to walk?"

Kryssa stood there so long Braidon thought she might do just that. But with a roll of her eyes, she leapt up quickly onto the extended forearm, then scrambled up behind him. Settling herself on the rippling scales, she looked around.

"Where do I ho—" Her question turned into a scream as the dragon leapt into the sky.

The great wings snapped open, beating the air, and Kryssa grabbed desperately at Braidon's waist. Braidon groaned as the movement disturbed his wound, but he could do nothing but hold the scales in front of him. They clung on desperately as the ground spiralled away, the soft laughter of the dragon whispering in their minds.

Wind buffeted them as Nidryt turned and made for the triple peaks. Mount Chole and its nameless siblings rose before them, jagged fingers of rock and snow, each stretching far higher than even a dragon could fly. Braidon gasped at the cold, but it did not seem to bother Nidryt. The dragon made for a pass between two of the peaks.

Braidon was not dressed for such temperatures, and he was soon shivering so violently he could hardly keep his grip on the dragon's back. Behind him, Kryssa was coping little better. Her eyes were closed and her grip on Braidon's waist was so tight he could hardly breathe. The sight restored some of his good humour though, that the woman had at least one weakness.

Behind them, the dense forest of Dragon Country stretched unbroken to the jagged western coast, but for a single blackened piece of land that the Knights had claimed as their own. He swallowed at the sight, reminded of his agreement with the dragons and the challenges awaiting him in Chole. If the Knights could wield such power here, what new terrors had they brought against his people?

A month had passed now since Braidon's apparent death. In his absence, what had become of Plorsea? He watched the approaching mountains, eager for a first glimpse of his nation. The volcanic peaks rose around them, their pale escarpments stretching up into the blue sky. Below, the earth was torn and broken, cliffs giving way to jagged slopes, and then to broad passes between the peaks. One side of the northernmost volcano had collapsed in ages past, exposing the great crater. Mounds of scarlet and yellow rock dotted the alien landscape within. Steam still seeped from the earth in places, a reminder of the violent potential of the silent mountain.

Then Braidon glimpsed movement within the crater. He leaned forward, then reeled at the sight of men and women below, swinging picks around the steaming vents, dragging carts down the jagged slope towards the faint outline of a road.

See how humanity encroaches upon our territory?

"They're Knights?" Braidon shouted over the howling wind.

No.

The dragon spoke no more, but Braidon continued to watch the people. Several looked up as they flew past, their tanned faces reflecting sudden fear. The dragon's appearance sent them racing down the slope towards the road, where several horses and wagons stood waiting. But Nidryt ignored them, and they were soon left far behind.

The volcanic range gave way to the open steeps of Chole, a vast expanse of patchy forest and sprawling grassland that stretched all the way to the Forest of Plorsea. In the time of Archon it had been desert, a deadly place filled with dark creatures that only the boldest of souls had dared to cross. Then had come the mortal Eric and his Sky magic, and the rains had been restored, returning life to the plateaus.

In his first few years as king, Braidon had feared that

magic's departure would see the desert's return. But while the summer rains had dwindled, the grasslands survived, fed every spring by glacial melt that brought streams all across the plateau alive.

Though the soils were thin and unable to sustain the traditional farming styles of the north, a nomadic group had made the lands their home. Said to have descended from Baronians, the tribes followed the wild cattle as they grazed across the plains. Braidon had found an ally there during the Lonian war, when the tribes had helped to feed his army. Idly, he wondered if he might find aid there again.

That was a thought for another day. Ahead, Chole rose from the plains, a sprawling collection of stone buildings. Most stood only two storeys tall, with narrow streets that wound in every direction, creating a maze that could confuse even the staunchest local should his attention wander.

Tall walls bordered the city, dating back to the Great Wars, before even Archon had darkened the horizons of the Three Nations. They had never fallen, not even on Archon's first coming, when the Dark Magicker had marched his armies all the way to the city gates. Even so, his defeat had almost seen the death of the city. The terrible clashing of magic between Archon and the Gods had torn the earth asunder, giving birth to the volcanic range they had just crossed, and creating the century long drought that had given rise to the nickname "the Dying City."

It was such tales that had given birth to the Order of Alana. Not even Braidon could deny the danger of wild magic, and he could well understand the fear amongst many that one day it would rise again. The Order had harnessed that fear, giving it a power they now used for their own purposes.

Nidryt circled lower, keeping close to the mountains, unwilling to expose himself to anyone watching from the city. Beyond the buildings, the waters of Lake Chole shone red in the setting sun, the lifeblood of the city. Several streams threaded their way across the plains, dwindling now with the coming of summer, but still fed by the melting snow atop the volcanoes.

The city itself had prospered over the last few decades, its inhabitants seemingly impervious to the death of magic, or war, or even the threat of another drought. They were descended from those who had remained all those years ago, when so many others had fled the Dying City, and had inherited their stoicism. In the face of adversity, the citizens of Chole stood strong, and found another way.

Perhaps Braidon would find his own answers within its ancient walls.

Pela woke to a pressure on her chest. Groaning, she tried to lift her arms to push it off, but found them trapped by cold stone. Her eyes snapped open, but they revealed only darkness. Her panic building, she sucked in a breath and coughed as dust filled her lungs. Stars flashed across her vision as her head struck solid rock above her.

"No, no, no," she gasped, a lump of terror lodging in her throat.

Her heart raced as she shifted her legs, her hands, anything she could think of. She was met by solid stone in every direction. A moan tore from her lips and terrified she started to thrash. Her fists struck the walls of her prison, but made no difference. In the pitch black she could see nothing, but she sensed the weight of the mountain pressing down on her, entombing her in the tiny hollow.

"No, please, Gods, no!"

Tears streaked her face and she kicked out. Pain stabbed through her shin as it struck something hard. Rocks groaned and the pressure on her chest increased, forcing a whisper of air from her lungs. She struggled to inhale, but could not quite catch her breath.

"Help!"

The scream was little more than a whisper, its potency stolen by the pressure, by the creeping horror of her fate. Pela wanted desperately to fill her lungs, to shout until even the dead Gods must hear her, but instead she was reduced to whimpers that turned quickly into sobs. Here was an enemy she could not fight, an obstacle she could not overcome. All she could do was lie there in the darkness and wait for death to find her.

Minutes turned to what seemed hours. There was no telling the true passage of time. Eventually Pela's panic subsided, giving way to a strange peace. She could do nothing to change her fate, and so she accepted it. Her heart slowed and her breathing eased, though the constant pressure still made it a struggle to inhale.

Time continued onwards, and her mind drifted, returning to that fateful strike. Her pickaxe had sunk deep into the rock, shattering the tunnel wall—but how? Had there been a weakness, a rotten patch of rock? But she had smelt no gas. She supposed it did not matter now.

Regret touched her at leaving Siden behind. He had been kind to her, had stood up for her when the other slaves would have left Pela to her fate. He'd deserved better than to be left alone to die. The chain was still tight around her ankle, though surely it must have been shattered by the rock fall.

Clack, clack, clack.

The sound of stones shifting was constant, though the ones around Pela had ceased to move. Listening to the noise, Pela was reminded of her own creeping fate. She stared into the darkness, wondering whether she would feel it, when the rock finally came crashing down. Would she be crushed instantly, or would the stone shift just enough to steal away the last of her breath, so that she slowly suffocated, unable to quite inhale?

Clack, clack, clack.

Pela frowned. There was a rhythmic timing to the sound now, a constant tapping. And it was not that deep groaning of rocks under pressure, but something else, almost…steel on stone?

Her heart beat faster and she tried to twist amidst her prison. Still unable to move more than a few inches, she only managed to send a cramp burning up her leg. She folded against the rock, a cry tearing from her lips.

"Wh…s…ht."

Distant words carried through the darkness and Pela could have sobbed with relief.

"Help me!" she screamed as loudly as she could manage.

The distant clacking ceased suddenly and she heard muffled voices. Unable to understand the words, she called again, though it was quieter this time, her breath not recovered from the last. The sounds resumed, the *clack-clacking* seeming faster this time.

Pela waited amidst the darkness, listening as her rescuers came closer. Soon she recognised the sound of pickaxes on stone.

They're coming for me!

She would not have thought it possible. She hadn't thought Ruebyn would care about a couple of slaves buried in the tunnels, whatever small kindnesses he had offered them. But maybe she had misjudged him, maybe he truly cared…maybe she should tell him the truth. He might be the saviour she had prayed for, might free her if he knew Pela was not truly a criminal.

Suddenly the sounds were coming from directly above her. She called out, cry of pure desperation and relief, of salvation. A stone was lifted from above her head and a light appeared, burning in the darkness. Her eyes watered but she did not look away, such was her joy.

The rest of the rock was removed and then rough hands reached into her tomb. The shackle was removed from her ankle and she was lifted out. They carried her several feet up the tunnel, and then laid her down. A lantern was held close to her face and finally Pela was forced to close her eyes.

"How does she look?" She recognised Ruebyn's voice, somewhere overhead. He sounded concerned.

"Bruised," a voice answered from beside her head. She thought it was another of the slaves.

"How bad is it?"

Firm hands patted Pela down, pressing their way down her arms and then legs. She stirred and dragged in a great breath, but only managed to moan something incomprehensible. Her chest ached, but the fresh air restored some of her strength and her eyes flickered back open.

"Hey…" she muttered.

A slave was crouched beside her. He sat back at her voice, but spoke only to Ruebyn. "Nothing broken, I don't think," he said. "Bad gash on her leg, though."

Pela remembered the rock that had slashed her leg as she'd fled, forgotten in her stone tomb. Gritting her teeth, she forced herself to sit up. Her head spun as she squinted into the glare of the lantern. A long gash stretched down her calf muscle, though it was no longer bleeding.

Ruebyn shifted closer, his jaw clenched tight. "What happened down there, slave?"

Blinking, Pela looked up at him. "The roof fell in."

Irritation showed on the overseer's face. "*Why* did it fall in?" he snapped, gesturing down the tunnel. Below, two slaves were taking turns digging out the rubble, while a third pushed a barrow past where Pela lay. "We've lost a day of work, at least!"

Pela gaped at him. "You're upset because you lost time?"

Ruebyn was apoplectic. "*Why else?*" he screamed.

Rising unsteadily to her feet, Pela looked him in the eye. "Because two *people* were trapped in there?" she said, her voice rising in pitch. "*Because my friend might be dead?*" She shook a fist and would have continued, but in that moment her strength failed and she sank back to the ground.

A strained silence followed, punctuated only by the *clack-clacking* of pickaxes—though Pela sensed even her fellows' attention on the two of them. She had done it again, lost her temper and spoken out of turn. But how could she not? Trapped in this place, doomed to one terrible death or another, better to give in to her anger than her fear.

Ruebyn stared down at her, his face a carefully-kept mask. The whip hung from his belt and his hand twitched. Pela was sure he would strike her now, that she had finally pushed him too far, but instead his hand dropped back to his side.

"You've been through a lot," he said, "and you're injured. Go to see the doctor and have that wound treated. I want you back before the night's count. I trust you will not go missing."

Pela gaped at him, unable to believe what he was saying.

Her mouth opened and closed, but in the end the only words she could get out were:

"What about Siden?"

Ruebyn blinked, flicking a glance at the rubble. It filled the tunnel from floor to ceiling. A pile of support beams had been laid alongside the waiting barrow, and the slaves were using them to prop up the ceiling again as they dug back down into the earth. Staring at the pile, Pela could hardly believe she had survived.

"I doubt…" Ruebyn began, then shook his head. His voice took on a sad tone. "By my calculations, the coal vein is another thirty feet from here. With luck, we will find him before then. If not…" He shrugged and turned away.

Pela thought to argue, but as she staggered to her feet, pain tore through her leg and forced a cry from her. The fight went from her in a rush. Ruebyn was right, there was nothing she could do for Siden. Biting her tongue, she turned away.

Starting her long trek upwards, Pela wondered whether she would make it. There would be no asking for help now. A slave was only useful so long as they could work. Even with their shortage, the Lonians would not waste much time or resources restoring a failed slave like her to health.

Then excitement touched Pela as a sudden realisation touched her. She was going up. There was only one doctor's clinic, and while she had never seen it, she knew one thing.

It was on the surface!

Her pace increased, though it remained little more than a hobble. She lifted her eyes, already looking for the distant glow of sunlight—though she was still far beneath the earth.

For a moment, Pela's mind turned to the possibility of escape. She dismissed it just as quickly. She wouldn't make it a mile in her current condition, and the punishment for runaway slaves was severe. Her arms and legs would be shattered with hammers, then she would be left in the mountains for the Felines and other animals to find. Just the thought made her shudder.

She continued on, dreams of warm sunlight on her face giving her strength. The tunnel curved upwards in a spiral, winding its way towards the distant surface. In places she had to bend over just to make it past the lower sections of the roof, but she was undaunted. Her small stature was an advantage in these cramped places—she suspected it was one of the reasons she'd been sent into the deepest sections of the mine in the first place.

Finally the tunnel widened, converging with other passages. She was overtaken several times by slaves pushing heavy barrows of rock. They gave her strange looks as they passed, though nothing was said. Less lenient overseers would whip a slave caught speaking without permission.

Another slave, burdened with a barrow of coal, had just passed Pela when she finally staggered into the great chamber where the coal was transferred into carriages for the final journey to the surface. A crew of slaves quickly took the barrow from the newcomer and loaded its contents onto a larger carriage. It must have completed their load, for the six slaves then took hold of handles on the cart and started pushing it up the steel track.

A seventh man remained behind. Though his collar still marked him as a slave, he must have held some position of respect, for he stood with arms folded and made no move to join his fellows. He watched the other slaves disappear up the tunnel, but when he turned, his eyes caught on Pela.

"You!" he shouted, a frown touching his forehead. "What are you doing here?"

Pela's legs were shaking by then, and she stood there staring at him for a long moment, unable to summon the will to speak. She sucked in a mouthful of dusty air, longing for what waited above. Bliss.

"I…Overseer Ruebyn…sending me to the infirmary."

The man stood staring at her as though he could not believe what he'd just heard, then burst abruptly into laughter. "The infirmary!" he gasped between snorts. "Of course! Shall I grab you a fresh glass of ale while we're at it?"

Pela gaped at him. "I…it's the truth."

The man's mirth vanished, his face darkening. "Scuttle back to your master, girly," he growled. "I'll not be caught slacking 'cause of some disobedient runt. Get out of here!" He took a step towards her, fist raised.

"No!" Pela shouted, standing her ground despite her injuries. "I'm going to the surface!"

"My people's the only ones gets to visit the surface," he snapped, swinging at her.

She leapt back out of his reach and her injured leg almost gave way. Staggering sideways, Pela continued to retreat, though he was forcing her back towards the tunnel she had entered by. Her boot scuffed against a rock and she scooped it up.

"I have orders," she insisted.

"Disobedient runt—" He broke off as Pela's stone struck him in the nose.

As the man clutched at his face, Pela darted forward, seeking to escape past him. But his arms swung out wildly, catching her in the forehead and knocking her off-balance. She crashed to the ground, tearing open her wound. Hot blood ran into her boot. Before she could recover, the slave staggered across and drove his foot down into her back.

"Damn witch, I'll see you hung for that!"

Blood poured from his nostrils and his face was twisted with rage. He caught Pela by the tunic and dragged her up. She cried out as her weight came on her injured leg, trying to twist away, but he held her tight. He raised a fist.

"Marcus, what are you doing?" a woman shouted.

The hackles stood up on Pela's neck as she recognised Genevieve's voice. Sudden hope swelled in her chest as she saw the huntress approaching through the gloom. Genevieve's clothes were torn and streaked by dirt, but there were no bruises on her skin. She wore the collar of a slave, the single black gem shining amidst the cold iron, but at first glance she seemed to have had an easier time than Pela. Their eyes met, but for a moment Genevieve did not seem to recognise her.

Then the woman's eyes widened and her hand went to her mouth. "Pela?" she whispered.

Groaning, Pela pulled herself free of Marcus's grip, who had frozen at Genevieve's appearance.

"Gen?" she croaked. "Is it really you?"

Genevieve pushed Marcus aside and they embraced. A dam broke within Pela as they hugged, and she sobbed quietly into her friend's shoulder, hardly able to believe Genevieve was really there. The huntress held her tight for a long moment, as though not quite able to believe it either, and then stepped back, her eyes shining with unspilt tears.

"Oh Pela," she whispered. "What have they done to you?"

"People of Ardath!" Wearing an ankle-length dress of black satin, the queen stood on a dais that had been hastily set up outside the marble courthouse. Her voice boomed out over the square, carrying to the ears of every soul in the crowd. She held her arms out to either side of her, as though to embrace her audience. "I have returned from Lon with news."

Caledan watched from amongst the throng, one man among thousands. The great square was so packed he could hardly move—even the balconies and rooftops were filled to bursting. Men and women watched her with equal parts fear and hope in their eyes. Ardath was a city afraid. The peace of the last eight years had been shattered by Braidon's disappearance, and they didn't know where to turn. They all wanted to know whether Marianne could step into the shoes of ruler.

"It grieves me to come before you today, a month after my husband's cruel murder. I thank you for your love, and your patience during these hard times. We as a nation must come to terms with this horrible tragedy." Her head dipped almost imperceptibly, and Caledan realised then that Marianne was a terrific actress. There was no hint of the raw hatred that had shone from her face back in Malevolent Cove, when she'd looked upon Braidon.

"But we must also rejoice! For though they suffered terrible casualties, the King's Guard has brought justice to our king's murderers. On the river Lane they caught the Baronian thugs, and slew them to a man. Forever will we remember those brave souls who gave their lives to avenge our king!"

A whisper went through the crowd as many lowered their eyes, placing hands to their chests. It was a gesture of faith to the Old Gods. The Knights stationed at intervals around the square made no move to intervene, though Caledan did not doubt names would be noted.

"As for our brothers in Lonia," Marianne continued, clearing her throat, "the wisdom of King Braidon and my father has been proven true. The council of Lonia has elected me as their queen. From this day forth, Lonia and Plorsea shall be as one, united in cause and action. I pray the Saviour grants me the wisdom to continue the legacy of those who came before me."

Stunned silence answered Marianne's proclamation. With Braidon's death, many had been expecting their old enemy to attack. Leaderless and with their army all but disbanded, Plorsea made an easy target. Caledan couldn't understand it—why would the council surrender their sovereignty to a monarch seated in Ardath? After the last Tsar had driven them into poverty, it went against everything their people believed.

Then with a roar, the crowd erupted into cheers. Men

and women around Caledan embraced, tears shining in their eyes as they realised this meant there would be no war. Braidon's last act had been to build a lasting peace. Perhaps Plorsea could strive again for its former glory, without the threat of violence looming on its borders.

"Alas, not all who live within our two nations are joyed by this new bond. Some seek to sow the seeds of dissent amongst our people. Just two weeks ago, a Castle in Townirwin was attacked, and two of its Elders murdered. To these few, I say you shall not prevail. I have granted the Knights of Alana the power to hunt out these dissidents, asked their Elders to cleanse this evil from our lands. In the name of the Saviour, we *shall* have peace!"

At that, the queen threw out her hands. To Caledan, the air before her seemed to shimmer. Her long auburn hair caught in the sunlight and came to life, shining as though aflame. The black dress flickered and her face lit up. A sigh went through the crowd as they looked on her, as though she might be the Saviour herself reborn.

His mouth suddenly dry, Caledan's heart beat faster, and it seemed he was seeing the queen for the first time. How could he not have seen it before? Marianne was right; she *was* the person to lead Lonia and Plorsea—even Trola, should she wish it. Who could deny her beauty, her wisdom, her *power?* Had she not hunted down the foul Baronians that had slain the king?

He swallowed at the thought. Sweat dripped from his forehead to sting his eyes. He wiped it away, aware something was not quite right. Watching Marianne, he again felt that rush of love. She was descending the steps of the dais now, offering her hands to the crowd, her whispers of comfort carrying across the square.

Caledan shook his head. It was as though a fog had attached itself to his mind. He thought again of Braidon, summoning up the anger, his rage at the king's failure…and in a rush the haze fell away. Marianne was using that strange power again—not to command this time, but to confuse, to convince the crowd she was worthy of their love.

His heart quickened as he saw the queen making her way through the press of bodies. Her Queen's Guard came behind, but Marianne was almost unprotected. Convinced of her own power, she walked freely amongst the crowd, a smile crinkling the corners of her lips.

But her spell no longer touched Caledan. Without thinking, he threaded his way through the crowd towards her. This was his chance. He knew well enough from his years stalking Braidon he would never get another opportunity like this. One quick thrust of his dagger, and Plorsea would be freed from another tyrant. He could slip away in the ensuing chaos, leave the city before anyone was the wiser.

"May the Saviour bless your family."

Marianne's voice carried over the heads of the onlookers. She was just a few yards away, so close, but the crowd was dense around her—he could not approach. Taller than most, he craned his head to watch the queen's path, trying to predict where she would go. He prayed she would not turn back to the dais.

Taking a guess, Caledan maneuvered himself into the path he hoped she would take. He held his breath as she moved closer, her progress slowed by her admirers. She stopped to talk with a mother and her newborn baby, to shake a young boy's hand, to offer a quiet word of reassurance to a one-armed veteran.

It was quite the performance, made all the stronger by

whatever spell she had cast. Even without her power Caledan might have been convinced, had he not witnessed her attempt to burn Kryssa and Pela alive.

Finally Marianne was just a few yards away. Her Guards followed close behind, but they would not be able to save her. Silently, Caledan drew the dagger from his belt and held it beneath his cloak, readying himself to spring.

The crowd parted and suddenly Marianne was standing before him. Her blue eyes shone as she looked at him and a smile touched her lips, granting warmth to her face, though he was sure it was not magic this time. He hesitated.

Then an image flashed into his mind, of the flaming arrow arcing above the waters of Malevolent Cove, of a ship burning, the scream of a falling dragon, Pela's last cry of terror. He had tried to find her in those churning waters, tried to protect her as he had before, but Braidon's weight had dragged him down into the depths of the sea. Now he was sure Pela and Genevieve were both dead. His jaw hardened into a scowl.

Marianne's eyes widened and he saw the recognition there, the realisation of what he intended to do. Her mouth opened, but he was too close for her Guards to save her, too strong to stop. His hand slipped from beneath the cloak, the dagger aimed at her heart.

"No."

Caledan gasped as his blade struck something hard and unyielding, as though an invisible suit of armour protected the queen. The impact jarred the dagger from his grip, and it clattered uselessly to the cobbles without ever touching the queen. He stared at it, unable to understand what had happened.

"Who are you?" The queen's voice was like ice. Around

them the crowd went still, as though he and Marianne were the only ones left alive in the entire square.

A pressure gripped Caledan by the throat. He tried to cry out, but the invisible fingers grew tighter and he managed only a squawk. Eyes bulging, he stared down at the demure woman. He stretched out an arm and tried to strike her down, but she stood just out of reach, and he found his feet would not obey his commands.

Then a tremor went through her face, and he caught a hint of weariness in her eyes. The grip around his throat loosened, but she stepped away before he could swing again. Around them the crowd came alive. Roaring, they surged forward. Fear touched Caledan. They would tear him apart!

"Guards!" Marianne shouted, her voice cracking. "Take him!"

A Queen's Guard leapt forward and an iron fist struck Caledan in the forehead. Red flashed across his vision. Before he could recover, strong hands caught him by the arms and forced them behind his back. The sword was torn from his belt and his feet swept out from underneath him, slamming him face-first into the cobbles.

The last of the queen's power left Caledan then. He surged against the man holding him—almost managing to throw him off. The crowd roared and he saw them pressing against a wall of Queen's Guards, trying to reach him, to tear him apart for daring to attack their beloved queen. He bucked again, desperate to escape, but a second Guard drew back his boot. Still pinned beneath the first, Caledan could not avoid the blow.

Light exploded across his vision, and then he sank into the darkness.

12

P ela stood staring at Genevieve, still not quite able to believe it was truly her. How long had it been since she'd last seen the huntress, since they had been separated, since these dark tunnels had become Pela's life? She could hardly keep the tears from falling.

Finally, Pela realised she had not answered her friend's question. "I'm fine," she whispered, surreptitiously wiping her eyes. "What…what about you?"

Genevieve face was a picture of shock, and Pela realised how she must look. She hadn't seen herself in a mirror for weeks, but bloodied and bruised and half-starved, covered in coal dust with the clothes rotting on her back, she must be a sight. Pela's cheeks grew warm, the collar pressing uncomfortably against her throat.

"Are you sure?" Genevieve asked, ignoring Pela's question.

Swallowing, Pela flicked a glance at the head-slave that had attacked her, then lowered her eyes. Despite the joy of their reunion, Genevieve could change nothing. If Pela spoke out, she would only have to face the repercussions later. She nodded quickly.

"I have to go to the infirmary," she said, gesturing at her leg. The wound had opened again and a trail of blood was congealing on her leg. "There was a cave-in."

"Then come with me," Genevieve replied quickly, casting an angry glare at Marcus. She must have a higher position amongst the slaves than him, for he shrank away from her. "I'm heading up myself. I was just dealing with a rat infestation in the latrines."

"There are latrines?" The words slipped from Pela before she could stop them. Genevieve's mouth fell open and Pela quickly went on. "I'm…much further down the tunnels."

A mask slipped over Genevieve's face and Pela knew the huntress was struggling to hide her pity. But in the end Genevieve said nothing, only let out a long breath, and gestured to the tunnel leading to the surface.

"Come on," she said softly. "I'll take you."

Pela nodded and the huntress took the lead. Despite the encounter with Marcus, Pela had at least rested from the long climb, and she managed a reasonable pace for the first hundred feet. Soon, however, the exhaustion returned, and they slowed. Genevieve filled the silence with her own story.

"When they found out I was a hunter, they put me to work bringing in meat to supplement their supplies," she explained as they walked. "There's plenty of game in these mountains—deer and goat, and marmot on bad days."

"Why didn't you run away?" Pela whispered, trying to preserve her breath.

"I'm always accompanied by a couple of their own hunters, though calling them that is generous. They couldn't catch a rabbit with a broken leg. No wonder they needed me."

"Lucky," Pela puffed, pausing to suck in a lungful of air. "You don't know what it's like…down here every day. We sleep where we work, eat and do our business. There's no escape, and only the dim lanterns for light." She looked up as she spoke, her heart beating faster at the glimmer of light amidst the black. It was daytime.

Genevieve lost some of her colour as Pela caught up. "I…only spent a couple of days down there," she said, and her voice cracked. "I cannot imagine…Pela, I promise I'm going to get us out of this. We'll find a way back to Kryssa, I swear."

Pela said nothing, only nodded. She knew the truth. It lurked behind the whites of Genevieve's eyes, whatever her reassurances. The huntress was brave and strong and determined, but she had no magic. She could not perform miracles, and not even Devon could have rescued them from this nightmare of a place.

"It's okay," Pela whispered, resting a hand on the woman's elbow. "This isn't your fault, Gen."

"I…" Genevieve's voice faded, but she swallowed and went on. "I won't give up. I'll protect you."

Pela chuckled, though the act made her chest ache. "That's what everyone says," she said, smiling despite herself, "but I'm not a girl anymore. I can look after myself. Protect yourself, Gen. It's all either of us can do now."

Silence fell between them and they continued their steady march up the tunnel, though Pela went more and more slowly. Her eyes began to water as the light grew brighter, but she could not look away. Sunlight speared through the tunnel, setting the swirling dust aflame. A weight seemed to lift from Pela's shoulders, as though the light itself were magic, possessed of a power of its own.

It also burned, and by the time they reached the surface, Pela's eyes were watering so badly she could barely see. Red dots danced across her vision and she held a hand against her face to shield her eyes—though as they emerged onto the mountainside, she realised it was a cloudy day.

A pain began in the back of Pela's skull and fingers of despair wrapped around her mind. After so long in the darkness, would her eyes ever readjust to the light? What was the point of going on if she could never see a blue sky again?

Even so, she forced herself to at least take one look at her surroundings. The stark red slopes of the Sandstone Mountains fell away beneath them, down to the river lands far below, where the plains of Lonia stretched all the way to the ocean. She could not see that far though, and within a few seconds the glare forced Pela to cover her eyes.

At least the air was fresh, the cool breeze carrying with it the scent of alpine grass and livestock. A roughshod town sat just below the entrance to the mine, which was little more than a black hole in the side of the mountain. Steel wheels squealed on their tracks as the slaves tramped past with their carriage, returning to the darkness. Pela heard them muttering as they passed, but did not open her eyes.

"This way," Genevieve said gently, taking her hand. "Come on, I'll lead you. It's not far."

Pela swallowed, horrified at her own weakness, but there was nothing she could do but allow the huntress to lead her. The slope was broken and she staggered several times, her feet tripped by unseen obstacles. Genevieve caught her each time, hauling her back up, and after a few minutes Pela sensed they were inside a building.

It was still bright when she opened her eyes, but with the door closed she could manage in the gloom. The room itself was sparsely furnished but for a dozen stretchers, many of them occupied by the sick or injured—though none of the patients sported the collar of a slave.

Movement came from the other end of the room as a man entered from another door and paused beside one of the stretchers. He held a notepad in one hand and mumbled to himself as he made marks on the paper. He did not notice them until Genevieve loudly cleared her throat.

"Oh!" the man exclaimed, jumping half a foot in the air and spinning towards them. "I didn't see you there! How can I help you?"

Pela said nothing, only stood staring in disbelief at the man. She had not recognised his clothing in the gloom, but now that he faced them, the fiery sword on his robes was clearly visible. It marked him as an Elder of the Order, as one of the men who'd kidnapped Pela's mother, who had seen her life torn apart and her freedom taken.

Pela's rage flickered into life, and she fought the urge to launch herself at the man. It would be so easy, here alone but for the sick and the injured. And he was old, his face lined and hair long and white. His kindly eyes did not fool her, not after everything she'd seen these last few months. He could not stop her, not once her hands were around his frail neck…

"Elder Lewis, I have a new charge for you," Genevieve said, gesturing to Pela. "She was caught in a collapsed tunnel. Her overseer wanted you to patch her up."

"A slave!" Lewis exclaimed, striding forward. His face

registered surprise. "Are you sure...which overseer was this?"

"Overseer Ruebyn," Pela snapped.

She took a step towards the man, but before she could make any more untoward threats, Genevieve snatched her by the arm and dragged her back. They shared a glance, and while the huntress said nothing, Pela caught the warning in her eyes.

Behave!

Grinding her teeth, Pela nodded. Genevieve gave her arm a final squeeze, then turned to face the Elder again.

"Special circumstances, you understand," she said, flashing the man a smile. "She has a nasty gash, but I'm sure your talents will have her back to work in no time."

Still frowning, the Elder wandered closer. "Yes, yes," he murmured, his eyes sweeping Pela up and down. "Your leg, I see. Nasty indeed. You can walk though? Of course—otherwise you would not be here, no?" He chuckled at his own joke, then gestured to a bench that ran along one wall. "Jump up there then, so I can take a look."

Pela looked from the Elder to Genevieve, not quite sure what to make of it all, but her friend only shrugged.

"I'd best be going," she said, offering Lewis another smile. "I trust you will both be okay?" she continued, flashing Pela a pointed look.

Pela rolled her eyes, but when Genevieve did not look away, she nodded her ascent.

"Yes, yes, of course!" Lewis said, none the wiser to their unspoken communication. "I can hardly feed myself, can I, looking after all these sorry souls! Would you bring back some mutton, Genevieve? The goat does not agree with my stomach."

"I'll see what I can do, Lewis," the huntress replied. "But the sheep live high up near the snowline, and they don't let me roam that far very often."

The Elder sighed, but then his eyes brightened. "I will put in a request! If the game is there, I'm sure they will not refuse."

"Very good," Genevieve murmured. She stepped towards the door, then glanced back, her eyes catching on Pela. "Goodbye, then."

Pela swallowed, struggling to dislodge the lump that had suddenly formed in her throat. "Bye," she whispered.

Then the huntress was gone, leaving her alone with the Elder and his patients. For a moment he stood staring after Genevieve. He gave his head a shake, and was all business again.

"Very well, what do we have here, young…sorry, I don't believe I got your name?"

Pela blinked. "What?"

"Your name, ma'am, you do have one, don't you?" Lewis asked, more slowly this time, as though speaking to a simpleton. "I can hardly just call you 'girl.'"

"Pela," Pela whispered, before she could think better of it.

After so many days answering to "slave," as though she were no more than a tool to be used, her name felt strange in her mouth. It was good to speak it, to remind herself she truly existed, that she had a past—and might still have a future.

Only a second later did she realise it might have been a mistake, that she might be recognised as the same Pela who had escaped the Great Sacrifice all those weeks ago. But Lewis only smiled.

"Very good, young Pela," he said. "Now, if you'd be so good as to lie on your stomach, I can inspect that wound."

Pela obeyed, though the metal bench was cold and her clothes offered little insulation. A shiver went through her as the Elder prodded the wound in her hamstring. Clenching her teeth, she muffled a groan, but Lewis must have felt her tense, for he released her at once.

"This won't do," he muttered to himself. "Wait one minute."

He disappeared back through the door at the end of the room, returning a few minutes later with a glass in hand. Copper coloured liquid sloshed within, and when he put it in front of her face, Pela caught the scent of alcohol.

"I'm afraid I have nothing stronger than my own whiskey," he said with a smile, "but it'll at least take the edge off the pain."

In truth, every part of Pela ached. Her leg was just one more pain added to her collection, but she wasn't about to refuse his offer. Taking the glass from his hands, she swallowed its contents in a single gulp—then coughed as the fiery liquid burned its way down her throat. Lewis chuckled and patted her on the back until she recovered. Then she lay back down, and he began his inspection anew.

"Not so deep," he muttered, and Pela felt his fingers prodding the wound again, "stones and dirt though…have to be cleaned…risk infection…painful."

Pela swallowed, her eyes watering despite the whiskey. She breathed a sigh of relief when he stood up. They shared a glance, and she glimpsed sadness in his eyes.

"You were the only one in the collapse?" he asked softly.

Grief closed over Pela's throat as she remembered

Siden, trapped or dead beneath all that rock. Wordlessly, she shook her head.

"I'm sorry," Lewis whispered, placing a hand on her shoulder. "I wish I could help more, with your kind. I do not know what crimes you committed to find yourself here, but you are still human. I fear my people forget our own humanity sometimes, that we drift too far from the path of the Saviour. We need more overseers like this Ruebyn of yours."

Stunned by his words, Pela could only manage a nod as Lewis returned to the back room. What he'd said made no sense. In Malevolent Cove, dozens of his fellow Elders had watched in ecstasy as Pela and her mother were tied to the mast of a ship and set alight as part of their Great Sacrifice. Only Genevieve's intervention had saved them.

But she saw none of that same fervour in Lewis. She watched him with fresh eyes as he returned, wondering what kind of man he truly was, to speak of kindness while wearing the robes of an Elder.

"This is going to hurt," Lewis said as he walked up. He held another glass of whiskey in one hand, a bottle of clear liquid and rag in the other. "You'd better take this."

Pela took the offered glass and swallowed it as quickly as the first. Her vision swam as she lay back down—she'd hardly drunk more than a sip of ale before today, and the spirits went straight to her head. This time when the Elder's fingers prodded her leg again, she giggled.

"Cold!" Pela gasped.

"I'll take that as a sign the whiskey is helping," Lewis replied.

Chuckling, he soaked the rag in the clear liquid from the bottle. Pela stilled as she caught the raw stench of alcohol, far stronger than before. She opened her mouth to ask what he was doing, but Lewis gripped her by the leg and wiped the cloth through her wound before she could sit up.

A gasp tore from Pela. It as though her leg had been aflame. She writhed against the bench, but the Elder's grip was like iron around her ankle and she could not tear her leg free. Panting, she clung to the steel table leg. Another scream escaped her before she snapped her mouth closed. Teeth clenched, she closed her eyes and endured.

Seemingly an eon later, Lewis stepped back with a grunt. "It's done!"

Relief washed through Pela. She opened her eyes and her vision spun, but when she looked down she saw he had spoken the truth. The dirt and stones were gone from her wound. Pushing down the nausea in her stomach, she sat up. Smiling, Lewis offered her another glass.

"Take your time with this one," he chuckled. "The worst is behind us."

Her hand trembling, Pela accepted his offering. She took a sip as he retrieved a tub of cream and bandages, and began to dress her wound.

"So how long have you been here, young Pela?" Lewis asked as he worked.

"Not long," she croaked, her eyes flickering closed. The cream was cool on her leg, smothering some of the fire from the cleaning. She took another sip, and found she quite enjoyed the taste of the whiskey. "A month?"

"You must have committed a great crime, to have ended up here so young?"

"Only the crime of being Plorsean," she replied offhandedly.

His hands froze on her leg. For a moment, Pela did not

notice the change that had come over him, but when she finally looked down, he was crouched, staring up at her. She frowned.

"What?"

Lewis rose slowly to his feet, his face grave. "What do you mean, 'the crime of being Plorsean'?"

Pela's heart lodged in her throat. Why had she said that? She had seen slaves beaten for denying their crimes. Even Ruebyn had threatened her just for telling him she had a name. For the briefest of seconds she had forgotten Lewis was the enemy, but his reaction now revealed his true allegiance.

"I…" She trailed off, unable to think of a lie that would convince him.

"Pela, if you are innocent…I can help you," he whispered.

"*What?*" The question burst from Pela in a rush.

Lewis rested a hand on her shoulder. "Tell me."

And despite herself, Pela did—everything that had happened to her since the Baronians had plucked her from the ocean. Of the time before that, she said only that her ship had gone down in a storm. She did not mention Genevieve, in case she was making a terrible mistake trusting Lewis. The liquor made the words come easily, though several times she stumbled over her own tongue in her rush to get the story out.

By the time she was finished, the hour was late and the sun was beginning to set through the windows. The red light hurt her eyes and she had to close them again, though a headache soon began in the back of her skull anyway.

"I am so sorry, young Pela," Lewis whispered.

He embraced her, and despite herself Pela hugged him back, though she had run out of tears long ago.

"I promise you," he said, pulling back finally, "I will get to the bottom of this."

"Thank you," she whispered, unable to express the depths of her gratitude.

"For now though, we must go on as though nothing has changed," he continued. "For if what you say is true, there will be those who wish to conceal the truth."

"You mean…?" Pela whispered, the hope crumbling in her chest. She couldn't say the words, lest she make them true.

"I am afraid so," Lewis said gently. Taking her hand, he lifted her to her feet. "For now, young Pela, you must go back to your overseer. You must go back into the mine."

13

"Halt!"

A woman's voice echoed from the shadows of the guard booth nested in the walls of Chole, bringing Kryssa to a stop. Braidon staggered on for another half-moment, until her hand whipped out to catch him. That jerked him out of his stupor and he looked around, eyes widening beneath the shadow of his hood.

The awful dragon had deposited them in the foothills half a day's walk from Chole, and they'd spent the last six hours tramping across the jagged terrain in a desperate attempt to reach the city before nightfall. While they were no longer desert, the summer sun had still been hot on the plateau, sucking the moisture from the air and the strength from their tiring limbs. The scant cover provided by the occasional patch of trees had been welcome, as was the end of their journey. But night had fallen an hour ago, and Kryssa feared the guards would not grant them entrance. There were still dark things that lurked out on these plains.

"My friend is unwell," Kryssa called.

It was not a lie. Though his injuries were outwardly healed, they still sapped at Braidon's strength. Only by sheer determination had he made it this far, and no one who looked at him would deny his illness. He swayed on his feet, eyes distant again, and she knew his mind was elsewhere.

"Gates are closed," came the gruff reply from the guardhouse. "Come back in the morning."

Kryssa could not see the woman through the narrow slot in the stone, but she wasn't going to be deterred so easily. "Please, we need a doctor!"

Shadows shifted behind the stone window, then a lantern flickered into life. A man's face appeared, looking out at them.

"Lass is telling the truth, Nicoyl!" he cried.

"Like hell," the woman guard muttered.

Even so, after a moment there was a rattle of metal and a squeal of hinges as a smaller door set into the wooden gates swung open. A woman stepped through wearing chainmail and a scarlet cloak—the same kind worn by all Plorsean warriors in service to the crown. Kryssa swallowed at the memories it stirred—she had once been adorned in the same fashion, though her cloak had been marked with the golden embroidery of the King's Guard.

"Please," Kryssa said, spreading her empty hands, "it's just the two of us. We'll do no harm."

"Inns will all be closed at this hour," the woman replied coldly.

"Nonsense, Nicoyl," the second guard cut in as he followed her out the gate. He was far larger than his counterpart, and held his spear loosely at his side. Striding across to stand beside the woman, he grinned at Kryssa. "There'll be space at the Bolthole, probably the Foxglove as well."

"Quiet, Dominic," Nicoyl snapped. She flashed him a glare and Kryssa couldn't help but smile, though it disappeared before the woman's eyes returned to her. "Now, what are the two of you doing, arriving in the city at such an hour?"

Kryssa patted Braidon on the back. "As I said, my friend here was injured. Hurt himself crossing the plateau and we fell behind schedule. Lucky we made it at all!"

The suspicion in the woman's eyes did not change. "These are hardly the times for casual trips across country. You came from the south, you said?"

"Oh, enough of this, Nicoyl!" the second guard interrupted. "Can't you see the man's dead on his feet? Looks like he's about to keel over. Come on, I know a doctor who'll take a look at you at this hour. You think you can hold down the fort while I'm gone, Nicoyl?"

The woman could only watch, stunned, as Dominic ushered them forward. He had them both halfway through the gate before the she managed to reply.

"Dominic, don't you dare leave me here alone again!" she screamed. Striding after them, she slammed the door closed and threw down the crossbar. "I swear by the Saviour I'll report you this time!"

Already halfway down the street with Braidon in tow, Dominic waved a hand. "Don't worry, I'll be back before you know it!"

Kryssa hurried after him, though she cast a quick look over her shoulder as she went, pitying the woman. But her misfortune was their benefit, and Kryssa breathed easier when they turned the corner and entered the maze that was Chole's winding streets.

"Sorry about Nicoyl," Dominic was saying when she

caught up with him. "Stickler for the rules, that one. And a follower of the Order to boot. Been hearing some terrible rumours about their lot these last few weeks—glad there's not so many of her kind here in Chole. Can't handle the heat, them Knights of theirs."

"What *has* been going on?" Braidon panted as they turned another corner. "We've been on the road a while, and haven't had much news."

"I bet you haven't," the guard murmured, "Your Majesty."

And suddenly Dominic was down on one knee in front of Braidon, head bowed. For a second they both stood there gaping, then Kryssa grabbed the man by the shoulders and dragged him back to his feet.

"*Enough of that!*" she hissed, casting her eyes around for watchers, but they were alone in the narrow streets. During its years of drought, Chole had developed an unsavoury reputation, forcing its residents indoors after sunset. While it was now one of the safer cities in Plorsea, the habit remained ingrained in its citizens.

Dominic chuckled at their panic and started off again as though nothing out of the ordinary had happened.

"How did you know me?" Braidon asked a block later, when they were sure no one was following.

"Knew you both the second I looked out of the guardhouse!" Dominic exclaimed. "Though I'm not surprised you don't remember me, except maybe from notoriety. Had a problem with the drink, once upon a time. Can't blame ya, really, kicking me out of the recruits for ya Guard."

"Oh!" Kryssa said, surprised.

She studied his features more closely when they passed the next street lantern. His hair and beard were closely cropped, black but for where a few strands of white were beginning to show, and his eyes were a cool grey. He certainly carried more weight than anyone who had ever served with the King's Guard, but then, Dominic had not said how long it had been since his discharge.

She could not pick his face, but then that was not unusual. She had served alongside hundreds during her ten years with the Plorsean army, and could not remember every soldier she'd met.

"Well, if you can help me now, I'll see you have whatever position you desire!" Braidon said as the shadows pressed in around them.

Dominic only chuckled. "Helping a dead man, that'll be a new one. I guess the official story was a tad overblown," he said, then added, "But no, I deserved what I got. Best thing that ever happened to me, really. Quit the drink and made a new life here in Chole. Never looked back, well, not till I saw our rightful king standing outside my gate."

"Thank you," Braidon said, and from his tone he meant it. "It seems I don't have many friends left these days."

"And where *are* you taking us, Dominic?" Kryssa asked, her suspicions not so easily swayed.

They must have been passing through a sparsely populated section of the city, for the street lanterns were less frequent now, leaving many of the intersections unlit. Kryssa cast a glance over her shoulder, but the streets remained deserted. Most of the buildings were single story here, built of stone taken from the foothills of Golden Ridge. But those quarries had run dry long ago, and here and there she spotted newer houses, recognizable by the irregular volcanic stones that had been mortared together to form their walls. Heavy wooden shutters barred the windows, blacking out even the faintest hint of light from within.

"My house, of course!" Dominic replied. "We're not far now."

Kryssa loosened her sword in its scabbard. With Braidon barely on his feet, their defence would fall to her if Dominic betrayed them. The guard seemed to be no more than he appeared—a former soldier wanting to aid his king—but Kryssa had learned not to trust anyone when it came to protecting Braidon. Not even his wife, it seemed.

"Must be quite the story," Dominic was saying, "with the queen taking your throne and all. And the Lonian one at that! All some secret plan of yours, I guess?" He chuckled to himself. "Or perhaps not, lookin' at the state of ya."

"What was that about the queen?" Braidon said sharply.

"You really are out of touch!" Dominic exclaimed. "Your wife went straight to Lon after her victory over the Baronians that ah, apparently *didn't* murder you? Anyways, she spoke with the Lonian council, convinced them to make her queen there, too. To have been a fly on the wall during that conversation, ay?"

"That must have been after the Cove," Braidon croaked to Kryssa.

"And I bet I can guess how she managed to convince them," Kryssa said, pursing her lips. "It's even worse than we thought."

"Wait, what was that about the Baronians?" Braidon asked. "Devon said she went after them with my King's Guard, but they weren't with Marianne when…I saw her last."

"Oh!" Dominic fell silent then, his face becoming a mask of sadness. "You haven't heard about that either?"

Braidon's hand snapped out and caught the man by the wrist, dragging him to a stop. "*What?*" he hissed. "What did she do to them?"

Kryssa pressed closer, her heart palpitating in her chest. Though she had retired almost two decades ago, there was a kinship amongst the Guard, both past and present. They were the most elite fighting unit of Plorsea, the king's last defence against betrayal. The best of them competed in a tournament every three years, to test their skills and challenge for the right of King's Champion—the best of the best. While Kryssa herself had never attained that honour, she had been close on several occasions.

"They're gone," Dominic whispered, his eyes wide. "They died to the last, fighting the Baronians. The Queen's Guard finished off what was left of the scum, or so your wife tells it."

"No," Braidon gasped.

He staggered back, his legs collapsing beneath him. Kryssa moved quickly, catching him beneath the shoulder and hauling him back up, though she was reeling as well. Faces flashed before her mind, men and women she knew still served in the Guard—gone now forever.

It didn't seem possible—and yet now she realised it made perfect sense. Caledan had told her that Pela's safety had been entrusted to the King's Guard, when they'd set out on their hunt for the Baronians. And yet, a week later, her daughter had been tied to the mast alongside her. Kryssa had hardly spared a thought for her former comrades this past month, but she realised now they would never have surrendered Pela so long as a single Guard remained standing.

Finally Braidon managed to get his feet back underneath him. Releasing him, Kryssa took a step back. Teeth bared, Braidon straightened. In the poorly-lit streets, he was almost unrecognisable. Raw hatred was etched into every line of his face, and his eyes glowed with an unspeakable rage.

"Take us to your home, Dominic," he ordered, his voice showing no hint of weakness now. "We have a war to win."

$\maltese$ 14 $\maltese$

Caledan woke with a start, aware something was wrong, but unable to quite recall what. He opened his eyes and found himself in a richly furnished room. Woollen carpets covered the floors and a massive tapestry took up an entire wall, depicting the view from a mountain-top, of a green land of forests and grasslands and rivers, stretching away to a distant lake. There was an island in the centre of the lake, the gold and marble spires of a city rising from its clifftops. It could only be Ardath. In the image, shadows stretched from the mountains across the entire land —everywhere except the great city, which seemed to glow with a light all of its own.

Allowing his gaze to roam, Caledan took in an empty hearth and a pair of glass doors leading out to a balcony. A small mahogany desk had been placed near the doorway. He started, finally noticing the woman seated there. Fountain pen in hand, Marianne's features were set, her attention concentrated on the papers lying scattered across the desk.

His mind working slowly, Caledan stared at the queen,

trying to recall how he had come to be there. Images flickered in his mind—his dagger thrusting for Marianne's heart, the sudden paralysis, then pain as a Guard struck him, and fear as the crowd bayed for his death.

Shuddering, Caledan made to rise—and only then discovered he'd been bound hand and foot to the chair. He growled, straining against his bindings, and the chair tilted wildly to the side. His anger turned to fright and he leaned the other way, trying desperately to balance himself. It was too little too late, and he toppled to the floor with a crash.

Laughter carried to Caledan's ears as he thrashed against his bonds. He swore loudly, then to his surprise, the ropes gave way. Tearing himself loose from the chair, he struggled to his feet and faced the queen.

A broad sofa lay between them, but she had not moved from the desk. Her eyes danced as she watched him, lips turned upwards in mirth. Roaring, he leapt across the sofa and dove at her…

…only to find himself flung into the sofa by an invisible force. His head whipped back, striking the wooden support behind the cushions. Light flashed across his vision as he slumped against the couch. Groaning, he tried to rise, but finding himself off-balance, toppled sideways instead.

"You should be more careful, sellsword," Marianne observed, leaning back in her chair. "My doctors inform me it is unhealthy to take so many blows to the head."

Caledan looked up from the sofa. The queen drummed her fingers against the desk, one eyebrow raised as though waiting for an answer. She showed no fear that he was free, though Caledan had seen no Guards—in fact, they seemed to be alone.

"What am I doing here?" he growled.

Marianne smiled. "You don't remember?" You tried to kill me in the Grand Plaza."

Rubbing his head, Caledan scowled at her. "I remember *that*," he said. "How did you stop me?"

"Practice and skill," Marianne replied, and for a second her eyes appeared to glow. "Your name is Caledan, no?"

"How…?"

"You have been out for hours—time enough for me to do some research. You are a sellsword, I am told?"

Caledan nodded, and clenched his teeth as the pain in the back of his skull redoubled. His stomach swirled and it took an effort of will not to throw up on the queen's sofa. Normally he might have elaborated with a few of his exploits, but the strangeness of the encounter had robbed him of words.

"And quite proficient, if the stories are true," Marianne added. "Well, just as you have spent your entire life honing your skills with the blade, so too have I spent the last eight years studying the secrets of the mind and body. Ever since I discovered what the Elders had uncovered."

"Magic, you mean?" Caledan asked.

The queen shrugged. "To your limited understanding, yes it would appear as such, though this power bears little resemblance to the gift passed to humanity by the False Gods."

Caledan only grunted. He had no idea what she was talking about.

Marianne smiled. "I can see the distinction does not interest a man of your profession." She stood and wandered around the desk. "So tell me, sellsword, why would a sellsword of your skill so debase himself, serving the cause of the beggar king?"

"Who says I work for Braidon?" Caledan snapped.

"The Saviour forgive me if I am mistaken, but did I not see you carrying away my *beloved* husband in Malevolent Cove?"

"Devon bade me protect him," Caledan scowled. "But I would never serve Braidon."

"I see." Marianne took a seat on her desk. "But Devon is dead. I made sure of it. Does that mean then, that you sought to kill me of your own accord?"

Caledan grinned despite himself. "Is that so surprising? It's only fair, isn't it, after *you* tried to kill *me?*"

To his surprise, Marianne threw back her head and howled with laughter. Clapping her hands, she hopped off the desk and threw herself down on the couch beside him. Caledan stared at the queen, wondering whether she was mad. She was so close to him now, he could have reached out and snapped her tiny neck.

Her eyes shone as she watched him though, and Caledan sensed he did not have the power to touch her. He relaxed into the sofa, deciding it was better to hear her out than to throw away whatever goodwill he seemed to have earned.

"It was you who killed Ikar, wasn't it?" she asked suddenly, the smile falling from her face. "He was my friend once, you know, before he became a Knight."

Caledan swallowed, his blood suddenly running cold. He sensed it would be a mistake to lie, and yet to tell the truth… "I did," he croaked. "To…save my friends."

"Ah yes, Kryssa and her daughter, Pela. I was saddened to involve the girl. Had I known my dear husband still lived, I would have moved mountains to find him, to have him take her place." Her eyes flashed. "I take it he is still alive?"

"He lives," Caledan agreed.

"I don't suppose you'd like to tell me where he's hiding?" the queen asked. A shadow darkened her face and the fire appeared in her eyes again, burning with a terrible intensity.

Caledan swallowed, suddenly unable to look her in the eye. His ears popped, as though a great pressure were building in the room, but he forced himself to speak. "I would rather not. He's with…a friend."

"So others survived as well." The pressure vanished as quickly as it had appeared, and when Caledan looked at the queen she was just a woman again. "No matter," she said. "They will reveal themselves in time. But what of you then, sellsword? Why come here to murder me? Surely you could not have been so arrogant to think you would succeed?"

"I was close enough!" Caledan retorted, his pride dented by her words. He half rose from the couch, but a look from Marianne sat him back down.

The queen flicked a hand. "You are skilled, I grant you that. And I expended too much of my strength on the crowd. You must be strong-willed, to have resisted my influence. I had mastered *that* skill long before Malevolent Cove."

Caledan narrowed his eyes. "You took something from that Knight, from Ikar, didn't you?"

Marianne shrugged. "Ikar was a faithful servant once, but his allegiances had shifted. He served the Order, not me." She smiled. "And I needed his life force after I was thwarted by your friends."

"I didn't think there was a difference between you and the Order."

A *click* came from the outer door before the queen could

answer. She rose from the sofa as a high-pitched voice called from outside:

"Mama!"

Caledan started as a young boy, no older than five, came racing across the room. Marianne stepped around the couch and dropped to one knee to wrap him in her arms. His laughter echoed from the high ceilings as she ruffled his curly black hair, so like his father's.

"Calybe, what are you doing out of your lessons? Your teacher will be in a fit of worry!"

"I was bored, Mama!" the boy cried. "And...the other children, they said something bad had happened to you!"

"Did they?" Marianne's face shone as she held him out at arm's length. "And what do you think?"

The little boy frowned, his blue eyes becoming serious as he looked her up and down. A grin stretched his plump cheeks. "You're okay!"

"I am." Marianne hugged him again, and the boy giggled. "Now run along back to your classes, Calybe, before your teacher comes looking for you!"

"Okay, Mama!"

The boy darted from the room without a backwards glance, his tiny feet slapping loudly on the stone floors. Rising, Marianne turned towards Caledan again. The smile fell from her face, the light in her eyes turning dark.

"There are many things you do not understand, sellsword."

❧ 15 ❧

Three days passed before they found Siden's body. Pela stood in silence as the slaves carried his body from the rubble and dropped him unceremoniously to the ground. A cry tore from Pela at the sight, and dropping her pick, she shoved her way past them and fell to her knees beside him.

Taking his cold hand in hers, she held it to her chest, wishing she could go back, that she'd had the strength to carry him clear. She didn't understand why, but he was dead because of her. Ruebyn claimed there must have been a weakness in the rock, a natural impurity that had collapsed their supports, but she knew the truth. *Something* had happened while she'd meditated, before the tunnel had collapsed, but she was too afraid to reach for it again.

Now her last hope that Siden might still live had been crushed. His body lay before her, bruised and broken, his pale eyes open but unseeing. She closed them as gently as she could, sensing the accusation there, a reflection of her own guilt. There was no way of telling whether he had suffered. Remembering her own torment, lying trapped in the darkness, she prayed death had come quickly for her friend.

"Pela."

She flinched as a hand settled on her shoulder. Swallowing, she turned to Ruebyn, waiting for the reprimand, but for once it did not come. His eyes were sad as he looked at Siden's body.

"He was a wise man," he said, "and a good worker. He will be missed."

Anger touched Pela and she came to her feet. "His name was Siden," she snapped. "And he was more than just a *worker*. He was a *person*, a good man."

Ruebyn shrank before her rage, his eyes growing wide, but he quickly took control of himself. His shock turned to anger and he tore the whip from his belt, shaking its coiled loops in her face.

"You forget yourself, *slave*," he growled, "and his death changes nothing. He was still a slave. He surrendered his personhood when he committed his crimes. *Just like you.*"

"I didn't!" Pela screamed, shoving him. "I'm innocent!"

Staggering back from the blow, Ruebyn gaped, his eyes flickering between Pela's face and his chest as though she had stabbed him. Then the meaning of her words seeped in, and he bared his teeth.

"Innocent?" he asked, his voice dangerously quiet.

Pela's whole body shook with pent-up fury. For the last three days she had kept her silence, waiting on the hope that Lewis had offered. But as time trickled by, her hope had withered. The sight of Siden dead amidst the rubble had burned away the last of it, and she realised now that no one was coming to help her, that no one cared. No doubt the

Elder had been playing some jest, toying with her innocence. What a fool she had been!

But no longer.

"I am Pela from Plorsea, and a free woman, by the laws of your land!" she snarled.

A violent *crack* came from Ruebyn's whip as it struck empty air, an unspoken threat. Pela flinched but stood her ground. She refused to be cowed any longer, to crouch and cower in the darkness and wait for someone else to save her. It was time for her to plead her own case, and be damned with the consequences.

"I'm innocent," she grated, baring her teeth.

Ruebyn stared her down, the leather whip clutched tightly in one hand. His shoulders rose and fell as he sucked in a great breath. Too late Pela realised he was preparing himself, gathering his courage to do what he must. The whip snapped out, catching Pela in the side of the head. Pain slashed through her ear, but momentum carried the whip on, and the length of leather wrapped taught around her throat.

She gasped and staggered back, only for the whip to bring her up short. Her ear throbbed, each beat of her heart sending agony burning through her skull. Only the metal collar had protected her throat from being torn.

Jerking his wrist, Ruebyn dragged her forward. Flickering lights obscured Pela's vision and her feet tripped over an unseen rock, sending her crashing to the ground. Ruebyn yanked again on the whip, and it slipped free of her collar. Jaw clenched, eyes wide and lip trembling, he readied himself for another blow.

"Overseer Ruebyn!"

A voice carried to them from further down the tunnel.

Ruebyn swung around, his eyes widening as a slave strode up. The man paused in front of the overseer, his eyes flicking to Pela for half a second.

"Yes, slave?" Ruebyn snapped. He seemed impatient, but as Pela dragged herself to her knees, he curled the whip back in on itself and clipped it to his belt.

"Sir!" the slave said, clearing his throat. "I…err, believe we have found the cause of the collapse."

Ruebyn's eyes had returned to Pela, and he answered almost absently, "What is it?"

"Another cave, sir." The slave paused. "It's…you had better come take a look."

The entire side of Pela's face was aflame and hot blood was running from her ear. With a trembling hand, she tried to feel the damage, but the pain redoubled at her touch. She cried out again and found Ruebyn's eyes on her. His lips were parted and for a second, horror registered in his eyes.

Then he jerked his head around, returning his attention to the slave. "Show me."

The man nodded and they retreated down the tunnel, leaving Pela alone in the dirt. Sobbing to herself, Pela pulled herself up, determined not to be defeated. Even so, her strength almost failed, and Ruebyn was disappearing round the freshly excavated bend in the tunnel by the time she found her feet.

Standing in the shadows, Pela cursed the boy with every vile word she knew. Their whispers carried to her from around the bend, and with a start Pela realised she was alone. Her head whipped around, checking, but it was true. The rest of the slaves were down the tunnel with Ruebyn. Her heart began to race. The chain around her ankle that had connected her to the others was gone, broken in the collapse. Ruebyn was still waiting for a replacement. This was her chance!

She started up towards the surface, adrenaline giving her strength. The tunnel rose steeply here, winding around in a sharp spiral that only allowed her to see ten yards ahead. But before she had made it a dozen feet, the whisper of voices came from ahead, followed by the soft rattle of metal.

Pela froze, cursing beneath her breath. Quickly she scanned her mind for an excuse that would allow her to pass whoever was approaching. Her gaze was drawn back to where Siden's body still lay, forgotten by his former comrades. She swallowed. His death had left Ruebyn's team a slave down; perhaps Pela could convince them she had been sent to request a replacement.

It was a frail excuse, but it was all she had. An escape attempt had next to no hope of succeeding anyway, but she was tired of waiting. Gathering her nerves, Pela continued. The voices grew louder and she wondered who would be venturing into these dark depths, what they wanted.

Abruptly the tunnel straightened out. Pela searched the darkness for the owners of the voices. A lantern must have burnt out, for the tunnel was cast in shadow ahead, and for a moment she saw nothing. Then a distant light flickered on metal, and she saw who was approaching.

Ice filled Pela's stomach. Before she could think, she turned and fled back the way she'd come. A voice called after her, but she did not stop, though it was Lewis who had spoken. He walked at the head of two Knights, their armour shining like dull mirrors in the darkness. Despite the Elder's earlier kindness, Pela sensed the Knights did not come with good intentions.

A crash of metal sounded as the Knights started to run. In their heavy armour, they would not catch her, not even in her weakened state. But there was only one tunnel in this part of the mine, so deep beneath the surface, and it ended in rubble. She was trapped.

Then Pela remembered what her fellow slave had said—that they had uncovered a cave. Could there be another exit from the mine? It was her only hope, though Ruebyn and the rest of her chain gang were waiting there. At least they were not armed with broadswords; she might just be able to slip past, if she was quick.

She staggered down the tunnel at twice the rate she'd gone up, only slowing at the final bend when Siden's body came into view. Guilt touched her again, but there was no time to pause now, and she stumbled past. The shouts of the Knights had fallen quiet, but from ahead she could hear the voices of Ruebyn and the slaves.

Light flickered as they came into view. Pela's strength was at its end now and she slowed to a walk, hoping Ruebyn wouldn't notice anything out of place. He glanced up at her appearance, and she saw a spasm twist his face. His hands shook as he clenched them, then forced them down until his arms were rigid. He nodded as she walked up.

"Slave," he said, "glad you could finally join us."

Pela ignored him. Her eyes were fixed on the tunnel wall. Though two of the slaves held lanterns, there was a shadow on the rock, a great patch of darkness that seemed to resist the light. A shiver started in her scalp and raced down her spine as she crept closer, unable to tear her gaze away. It was only when Ruebyn held out his hand to bar her path that she understood what it was.

"Careful," he whispered, his hazel eyes catching hers. "We don't know how far down it goes."

A lump lodged in Pela's throat and she did not try to resist his tug. The slave had spoken the truth—there was a cave, but not like anything Pela had imagined. A few feet from where she stood, the floor of the tunnel gave way to emptiness. She knew now what her pickaxe had struck—a great emptiness beyond the seemingly solid rock, a cavern that extended who knew how far into the earth.

Absently, Pela bent and picked up a stone. Ruebyn watched in silence as she tossed it over the side. They waited a long time, but it was as though the rock had vanished into a void. She never heard it strike the bottom.

"Stop!"

Pela spun as a metallic voice came from up the tunnel. The two Knights rattled into view, broadswords in hand. A vice closed around her chest as they approached, slowing now that they could see she was trapped. Movement came from behind them as Lewis came into view, his robes now dirt-streaked and his face ashen. When he saw her standing between Ruebyn and the other slaves, his eyes widened and sadness twisted his features. Panting, he stumbled to a stop.

In that moment, Pela realised he had not betrayed her after all. She had done this to herself. She had spoken about her past, and now her crimes against the Order had finally caught up with her. Not even Lewis could save her now. Meeting his gaze, she nodded her thanks.

"Pela of Skystead," the Knight in the lead growled. "You're to come with us."

Pela tensed her fists, readying herself for one last battle. She would not let them take her again, would not let them make her a spectacle for their followers. No, better she die here, in the darkness, than to suffer their cruelty a second longer.

"What's this all about?" Ruebyn said, stepping between her and the Knights.

Shocked, Pela gaped at him. The Knights were not so impressed. "Out of the way, fool," the leader spat.

Ruebyn's eyes widened at the insult and he drew himself up. "Excuse me?" he snapped. "I would have expected more manners from a Knight. Now, the girl is in my possession. She will go nowhere without my permission."

The Knights stopped before him, their faces concealed by cold steel. "You dare stand in the path of the Saviour's justice, boy?"

"The Saviour's justice?" Doubt crept into Ruebyn's eyes. "What are you talking about? She has already been sentenced—is that not why she's here?"

"This Plorsean brat murdered an Elder in cold blood," the first of the Knights growled. "Only death can pay for such a crime, so that her life may serve the *Saviour*."

The colour fled Ruebyn's face. He stood there in stunned silence, looking from the newcomers to Pela, his mouth hanging open. "Wh-what?" he finally managed.

"Enough of this!" the second of the Knights roared. "Let the traitor share the same fate as the Plorsean traitor."

Pushing past his comrade, he swung the broadsword at Ruebyn. Pela cried out as the blade flashed and Ruebyn staggered back, clutching at his chest. Without thinking she caught him before he fell. He sagged in her arms, his weight almost dragging Pela from her feet. The slaves leapt away and the lantern light danced across the tunnel. By its light she saw blood on Ruebyn's fingers.

Stones crunched as the Knight advanced, sword raised.

Pela stumbled back, trying to keep the distance between them.

"She protects him!" the Knight snarled. "The coward has betrayed us for his consort!"

"Filthy beast," the second agreed. He moved to bar any escape up the tunnel. Beyond, Lewis still stood, one hand against the wall as though his legs alone could not keep him upright. Cackling, the Knight went on, "Your wisdom saw through their act, Watkyn. The honour of their cleansing is yours."

"Gladly," the Knight facing them growled.

"Get back!" Pela shrieked, struggling beneath Ruebyn's weight.

She should have dropped him. She was at the end of her strength, and her ear still throbbed where the whip had struck her. But she could not bring herself to abandon him. However misguided they might have been, the Knights had struck him down because of her. She could not bear another life on her conscience—not even Ruebyn's.

He groaned in her arms, hand clenched tight against his chest to stem the bleeding. She dragged him with her, though there was nowhere to go. Her stomach churned as she glanced over her shoulder. The darkness loomed. Dust swirled down from above, burning gold in the flickering light, so that it almost seemed that the opening to nowhere were magic. But beyond the light, the void beckoned.

A terrible cold touched Pela as she stepped up to the edge. Stones tumbled down into the cavern, rattling from its sides, then...*nothing*. The Knight cackled, the crunch of his footsteps approaching. He knew they had nowhere to go. Pela flinched as he darted forward with his sword, teetering on the edge. But it was only a feint. Laughter rattled from the ceiling, hammering at Pela. Her body a mess of pain, she swayed on her feet.

The Knights had her cornered, beaten. Ruebyn panted into her chest, his weight hard on her shoulder. Pela could not see how bad his injuries were, but his blood had stained her clothes. She feared he might perish at any moment.

"Come, little girl," the Knight taunted. "Give yourself up, and we may spare your lover's life—if my blade has not already killed him."

"The Elders will be pleased to have you," the second Knight said. "You caused our Order great shame at the Cove. That must be put right."

Anger gave Pela strength, and she scooped up a rock. "Screw your Elders!" she screamed, hurling the rock with all her strength.

The first Knight ducked, but there was a satisfying *clang* as it struck the second in the helmet. Despite the heavy armour, the blow staggered him. Roaring his rage, the first leapt, mailed fist extended. Pela's stomach twisted and instinctively she leapt back with Ruebyn—into nothing!

Suddenly there was no ground beneath her feet. She fell through the icy darkness, the void rising to swallow her up. A desperate hand clutched at her clothes—and she realised the Knight had followed her over the side. Her scream echoed off unseen walls, then with a great *crash,* she struck water.

16

Braidon and Kryssa spent the next week hidden in the house of Dominic. Braidon grew more restless with each passing day, frustrated by his continued weakness, and increasingly worried by the rumours arriving from across Plorsea. Travellers spoke of Knights hunting down the followers of the Old Gods—even to the capital itself.

Despite what he'd seen with his own eyes, Braidon still struggled to understand how Marianne could have unleashed such evil against her adoptive nation. But then, she'd happily slaughtered the King's Guard for her cause, though they had dedicated themselves to protecting both their lives.

Fortunately, while Chole had a Castle of its own dedicated to the Order, its followers were not numerous in the city and so far its Knights had kept to themselves. But it would only be a matter of time before they too joined the cause.

Braidon had taken to rousing early each morning to exercise, seeking desperately to regain his former strength.

Dominic's house boasted a large open courtyard with a fountain in its centre, and Braidon would spend an hour before dawn practicing the sword patterns his grandmother had taught him in his youth. His wound still pained him, a dull ache that would not go away, but he could rest no longer, not with Marianne out there, hell-bent on destroying his nation.

Stopping her had become an obsession for Braidon. Caledan had bade him to fix his own mistakes, and he intended to do just that. No longer would he look to others to protect him, to make the hard decisions. He had been betrayed too many times, and his friends had paid the price.

As he trained, he imagined each of his fallen comrades. Devon was first, his face pale as Marianne struck him down. Then Genevieve and Pela, disappearing beneath the waves of Malevolent Cove, and his Guards, Rylle and Salver and Aldyn and so many others, cut down by Marianne's treachery.

With each face his anger grew. He wanted to scream, to shout and rage at his wife, to demand to know how she could have thrown away everything they had built.

And at his core, there was that terrible fear: that she had their son. Calybe had been the light of their lives, but Braidon doubted even that memory now. Marianne had casually murdered hundreds—what did she care for the life of one child, even her own?

He shuddered to think what she might do. And so the fear and rage drove him on, pushing him through the weakness. He was resolved to do everything in his power to stop her. Each morning the rising sun found him a little stronger than the day before.

A week after their arrival, it found him in the courtyard

cutting wood. The summers were short in Chole and the wood rounds needed to be chopped and sorted before the first winter snowfall. The exercise was painstaking and difficult, but there was an art to it, one Devon had shown him long ago. He'd been just a boy then, caught up in a battle between the greats, but Devon had always treated him as an equal.

Sadness touched Braidon and he paused for breath, remember the smiling hammerman and his penchant for calling all he met "sonny." That had been Devon's way, he supposed. It didn't matter who you were—sailor or scholar or soldier—he treated all the same.

It was difficult to believe the hammerman was truly gone. Any moment, Braidon expected the giant warrior to come walking into the courtyard, a broad grin on his bearded face. Surely not even death could keep Devon from a fight.

But after so many years of battling, of striving against impossible odds, it seemed right that Devon could finally rest. Braidon just prayed he had the strength to finish the fight Devon had started.

Clouds darkened the sky as the morning grew later. Soon a light rain began to fall and Braidon decided he'd done enough for the day. He buried his axe in a wood round and headed inside. At the door he paused at a small shrine to the Three Gods, little more than a wooden platform with three candles. Dominic's wife, Janylle, must have lit them while Braidon was outside. Closing his eyes, Braidon sent a brief prayer to the long-departed deities.

The action turned Braidon's mind to his sister. These past weeks he had found himself missing Alana more than he had in years. *She* would not have spent weeks sulking in the forest, hiding from her responsibilities. Alana had never backed down from a fight; she would not be daunted by the frightening new power Marianne had discovered.

"What should I do, sis?" he whispered to himself.

Angrily, he shook his head. Already his resolve was faltering, giving way to the self-doubt that had crippled him his entire life. He straightened his shoulders and turned his back on the shrine. This was his fight and he would find his own way to win. He had to.

Braidon wiped his feet on the doormat and followed the scent of spiced eggs into the kitchen. Kryssa was sitting at the small table, while Janylle stood at the bench chopping carrots. Dominic was already on duty at the city gates, not due back until the afternoon. Janylle smiled as Braidon approached the woodstove and lifted the lid on the frying pan. The smell of turmeric and paprika wafted in his nostrils, making his eyes water, and he quickly replaced the lid.

"Take a seat, Braidon," Janylle insisted, waving him away. "You're on dishes, remember?"

Chuckling, Braidon obeyed. He'd tried to cook them a meal only once, and had been banished from using the stove ever since.

Kryssa raised an eyebrow as he sat. "How goes the training?"

"Well enough," Braidon sighed, "but it needs to be more. *I* need to do more."

"Have you thought any more on what happened in the Cove?" Kryssa asked, sitting forward in her chair.

Braidon waved a hand. "Of course. All I can figure is that Marianne stole the life force from Ikar as he lay dying.

There were Magickers once who did the same thing with magic. My father, for one," he finished bitterly.

"Marianne mentioned the Tsar!" Kryssa exclaimed. "When she gave us the necklaces."

"It's not a pleasant thought," Braidon said with a shake of his head, "stealing another's life force to grant yourself power. Marianne could be ruthless, but I never guessed…"

"She fooled everyone, Braidon," Kryssa offered.

He only shrugged. "Anyway, even if our theory is right, it takes us no closer to a way to match her."

"No," Kryssa sighed, the excitement leaving her face.

"Breakfast time!" Janylle interrupted, placing a steaming mug and plate in front of Kryssa.

She had scrambled the eggs with tomatoes and spices, giving them a rich red colouring, while the hot drink smelt of cardamom and ginger. Milky brown in colour, it was known by the locals as *chai* and had a rich spiced flavour.

"What, still no coffee?" Kryssa asked mournfully.

Braidon accepted his breakfast with a grin. Kryssa had been asking the same question all week. Coming from Skystead, she was used to coffee being cheap and easily accessible, but Chole was a long way from the main trade route south, and only the rich could afford it here. Fortunately for Braidon, he had never developed a taste for the bitter drink.

Janylle offered an apologetic smile. "Afraid it can't be had for any amount of money just now," she said, "with the troubles we've been having since your friend here decided to abdicate."

Braidon winced, though it was a timely reminder of his responsibilities. He took a sip of chai and began to eat. His thoughts turned back to what Kryssa had said, about Marianne taking inspiration from his father. Braidon could not reveal himself until he knew exactly what they were up against in Marianne and her allies.

It was the Knights of Alana he most feared. He wished he'd never let them gain a foothold in Plorsea. But he had underestimated the void left when the Gods had fallen. Without magic, without Antonia, Jurrien and Darius to unite them, the world had fallen into disarray.

The Order had taken full advantage, offering their followers a new purpose—to aid Alana in her eternal battle against the False Gods. Once revered across the land, the Three Gods had become the enemy, tyrants who had enslaved the world with their magic.

And Braidon's own sister, once feared for her role as the Tsar's enforcer, had become their holy Saviour, the one who had freed the world from the False Gods. According to the Elders, she fought for them still, keeping the Gods at bay. And she needed her followers to be strong, so that their strength became her strength, to keep the horror of magic from returning.

It was a worthy tale, Braidon couldn't help but think, but he had been present when the Gods had fallen, when his sister had lost her life. He knew the truth. The Elders had spun the stories to suit themselves, to forge a new power, to bring their Order to life.

But amidst the falsehood, they had obviously discovered one truth: Marianne could not have found her new power alone. It was linked to the Elders and their awful rituals, he sensed. And while their new power did not have the same bite as old magic, it remained dangerous. Marianne had taken something from Ikar and used it to *command* them. She had even altered her rapier, somehow allowing it to cut through Devon's hammer.

Braidon wondered if he might do the same. The thought made his heart quicken. There had been a time when he could conjure illusions so perfect none could tell truth from reality. His grandmother, one of the most powerful Magickers of the age, had trained him to master his emotions, and by extension, his magic. In the end, his power had helped he and his sister to defeat their father.

But that was thirty years ago now, those powers long gone. And while Braidon still longed for the thrill, for the rush of magic burning in his veins, he knew it would never return.

"Where will you go, Janylle, if there is fighting?" Kryssa asked.

Braidon jerked back to the present at the sound of his friend's voice. Finishing his last bite, he rose and carried his dishes to the cast-iron sink. He filled it with hot water from a pot on the stove and began on the dishes, while Janylle answered Kryssa's question.

"Where *can* we go?" Janylle whispered. "Trola is barred to all. Lonia is the source of our problems, though they're quickly spreading across Plorsea. If it comes to it, I would go to Northland, but…I fear now that Dominic has found you, Braidon, he will want to fight.

Braidon sighed. "I wish I could refuse him, Janylle. But I am desperate. Plorsea needs every fighter we can find."

"Do not worry, *My King*," Janylle said, her voice lacking its usual warmth. "I'm sure you'll find plenty still willing to die for your crown."

"I didn't mean…" Braidon started, but when he turned to face her, the woman had already left the room.

Kryssa met his gaze instead. "That was tactful."

Braidon scowled. "It's the truth. Marianne has every

advantage—an army, followers, a secret power. We have nothing! No one!"

"And yet Janylle freely opened her door to you, though it would be worth her life if the queen found us here. Now you're asking for her husband's life as well. It's too much."

"*Nothing* is too much!" Braidon exclaimed, slamming a fist into the counter. "Don't you understand? Marianne will destroy everything with her greed! Or have you not been listening to the stories? Her Knights are pillaging the countryside, slaughtering innocents for no reason other than who they send their prayers to. What else would you have me do?"

Kryssa could not match the fire in Braidon's eyes and she looked away. "I don't know, Braidon," she murmured. "Remember what we talked about in the forest? About a perfect world? Maybe I believe in that vision more than I realised. I know we cannot turn away from this fight— though every fibre of my being screams for me to abandon you to search for Gen and Pela. But even I cannot bring myself to ask the same of others."

A sigh slipped from Braidon and the anger went from him in a rush. He lowered himself into the seat alongside Kryssa. "I'm sorry," he said, "it is easy…to forget. I pray to whatever remains of the Gods for both our families. But their fate is bound to Plorsea, and we can cling to childish notions of peace no longer. We must fight if we ever want to see our loved ones again."

Their eyes met across the table and for a moment it seemed Kryssa might argue further. Then a *click* came from the front door. They were both on their feet in an instant, hands on sword hilts. They shared another glance, and then Kryssa slipped silently from the kitchen into the corridor. She returned a second later, Dominic following behind her.

He still wore his guard uniform, and a glance out the window revealed it was not yet even midday. The rain had grown heavier and water was beginning to pool in the street. Braidon frowned at the man, his blood running cold. Dominic was puffing and his face was red, as though he had run all the way from the gatehouse. Stumbling into the kitchen, he bent in two for a moment, catching his breath.

"Dominic, what is it?" Braidon cried finally, unable to take the waiting. Had something happened?

Dominic straightened, sweat dripping from his forehead. "It's the Knights," he gasped. "A new squad just rode in, from Lonia. They say they've come to cleanse the followers of the Old Gods. They're marching on the Temple of Antonia—now!"

17

Kryssa's heart beat faster as she followed Braidon through the winding streets of Chole. The rain was falling hard now, the sky dark overhead. Dominic led the way, reminding her of his wife's fear, that he would lose his life following Braidon's cause. But he was their only chance of reaching the temple in time. Chole was a maze, and while she occasionally caught a glimpse of the triple spires of the Earth Temple rising above the rooftops, they could have never found it without him.

At least it was within the city. Unlike Skystead, many in Chole still openly worshipped the Three Gods, even maintaining the Temple of the Earth. Though all knew the Gods and their magic had departed from the world, their memory was ingrained in the very stones of Chole. Magic might have once doomed the city, but it had been magic too that saved it, restoring the rains and returning life to the desert.

Perhaps that was why the Knights of Alana had not acted until now. While they had followers in the city, they were not numerous, and the dozen Knights who garrisoned their Castle would have been badly outnumbered if they'd acted against the temple. But according to Dominic, another twenty had arrived in the city not an hour ago—enough to cow a crowd of unarmed civilians.

"Braidon, what are we going to do?" she asked as they rushed through the narrow streets.

"I have a plan," Braidon replied shortly. He did not look back, and she almost missed his added, "I think."

She cursed inwardly. What could Braidon do against so many? He might have recovered much of his strength, but twenty Knights against the three of them was impossible odds, even for her father.

Thunder crashed above as Kryssa caught the first cry of voices from ahead. Rain lashed down and the streets were beginning to flood,. Water gushed around Kryssa's boots as the gutters overfilled. Movement came from nearby doorways as people stepped out into the streets with arms outstretched. Kryssa only cursed. Rain was a rare blessing for the citizens of Chole, but it made their progress difficult.

They were soaked to the skin by the time they turned the last corner and found themselves standing before the Earth Temple. Dedicated to the Goddess Antonia, its triple spires rose high above their heads, while below, a long series of steps led up to the oaken gates. Marble pillars lined the way, beckoning the faithful to their worship.

Today though, the temple's visitors did not come to meditate. The Knights of Alana stood like statues facing the steps, rain streaming in rivulets down their armour. Lightning flashed overhead, and for a second Kryssa wondered if the Storm God, Jurrien, would return to strike them down. The boom of thunder followed before fading away, leaving the Knights untouched. She knew then they were alone, that it was up to them to stop these men.

"What are they waiting for?" she cried over the roar of the storm.

They stood in the narrow street, still unnoticed by the Knights, but it could not last.

Dominic pointed at the doorway to temple. "Them."

Kryssa followed his finger and saw with a start that the Knights were opposed. A dozen men and women stood at top of the marble stairs, arms linked to bar their enemies' passage. Many wore the green robes of Earth Priests, others the clothes of citizens. Terror shone from the faces of all. There was not a weapon amongst them, but still they stood unwavering against the steel of the Knights. Kryssa's heart swelled at their bravery.

Then fear touched her as a Knight's voice rose above the pouring rain. "Step aside, blasphemers," he cried. "We do not come for you today, only to destroy the lair of the Goddess, so that this city might be free of her taint."

"Not this time," Braidon hissed, starting across the street towards them.

Kryssa cursed, afraid Braidon's anger was going to get them all killed. They had no plan, no way to fight twenty Knights by themselves. But it was too late to argue. Dominic was already at the king's side, and loosening her sword in its sheath, Kryssa hurried to catch up.

"Turn back, foul Knights!" a faint voice carried from above.

Laughter came from the Knights as one lifted his sword. "If you will not flee, you will burn with your Goddess."

"You hold no power in Chole!" the voice spoke again. "Turn back, or may the Gods strike you down!"

"Our Saviour banished your Gods long ago," came the laughing reply. "Now we have come to drive your kind from these lands." There was a crash of metal as they started up the stairs.

"Stop!" Braidon bellowed, his voice ringing from the walls of the temple.

Kryssa's stomach tied itself in knots as the Knights looked back and saw the three figures challenging them. The sight gave them pause, but only for a moment—then the laughter returned, rattling strangely from the iron helmets.

"What have we here?" a Knight called. "The champions of the Gods?"

"A champion of the people," Braidon shouted. He threw back his hood and the rain washed down his face. "I am Braidon, the rightful king of Plorsea!"

Kryssa cursed beneath her breath and edged closer to Braidon. If it came down to a fight, they could not allow the Knights to separate them, or they would be cut down in seconds. Not that they stood a chance regardless. Kryssa gripped the hilt of her sword tight, wishing she'd followed her instincts and gone seeking her daughter. She didn't want to throw away her life, not after fighting so hard to win it back.

Silence answered Braidon's declaration. Coming from Lonia, the Knights did not recognise Braidon, and in the thread-worn tunic and pants, he looked nothing like a king. After a moment the laughter came again, though this time there was no warmth in the sound. Slowly the Knights started back down the steps.

"King Braidon is dead," their leader said, "and should stay that way. You are obviously mad, poor man, and a blasphemer to stand with these sorry souls. But fear not, we will cleanse you of that evil. Along with this foul temple."

Steel rasped on leather as twenty swords emerged into the gloom. Lightning flickered again and Kryssa held her breath, calling upon Jurrien to strike them down, but still there was no answer. She sighed, a self-disparaging smile touching her lips. She knew better than anyone that the Gods were dead—her own adopted mother had witnessed that sad day.

Yet Kryssa couldn't help but look to them for guidance in her darkest moments. It was a childish habit, born from her days as a street urchin, when the Gods had been her only source of hope. Even now it gave her comfort, to think they might still exist somewhere, beyond knowing, beyond life. That they heard her prayers, and sympathised.

"The temple of Antonia has stood here for a thousand years," Braidon retorted. "The Three Gods are welcome in Plorsea. You are not."

"The False Gods are sacrilege," the leader of the Knights screamed over a boom of thunder. "It is our duty to wipe them from the Three Nations, on behalf of the Saviour."

"You do not speak for my sister," Braidon hissed, his voice was taut with rage. "I have heard enough. Begone from my nation, foul Knights."

The Knights exchanged glances, but the three of them stood alone against their twenty. Steel thumped on stone as they started forward as one. Kryssa cursed and drew her sword. Her hair was tied back, but water streamed down her face, obscuring her vision. She wiped it away with her free hand, wondering how the Knights were coping in their helmets and breastplates.

"Aim for their armpits, groin and throat," she said to Dominic. "That's where their armour is weakest."

Still wearing the uniform of the city guard, Dominic nodded and hefted his spear. She could see his face beneath the half-helm, sensed his fear. But at least his weapon had reach—Kryssa would have to avoid their broadswords to get within striking range. She still wielded Derryn's—Pela's— short sword, and while it was light to hand, it could not pierce the heavy plate mail.

Then Braidon stepped in front of them, one hand raised to stay them. "No," he growled, though whether it was to the Knights or his comrades, Kryssa could not have said.

Either way, she was too shocked to disobey. Kryssa and Dominic stood staring after the king as he strode towards the Knights, his sword still in its sheath. The hairs lifted on Kryssa's neck as the rain swirled about Braidon. Wind came howling down the street, buffeting them so hard that she stumbled, but the king walked on.

Reaching the bottom of the stairs, the Knights paused at the sight of the lone man approaching. Kryssa read the confusion in their hesitation. She felt it too. What madness had possessed Braidon? Slowly the Knights spread out in a semicircle to surround him, ready to strike. Above them on the steps of the temple, the priests and citizens guarding them temple watched on.

Kryssa stared at Braidon, willing him to draw his sword, but he stood with his eyes closed, as though he were no more bothered by the Knights than a passing cloud. Swearing beneath her breath, Kryssa lifted her sword, preparing to go to his aid. Whatever madness he was attempting had obviously failed. She started towards him…

Boom.

A cry tore from Kryssa as lightning arced from the sky and struck the king. The air itself shook with the crashing of thunder. She staggered back, tossing her sword aside in terror that she would be next. Behind her, Dominic screamed and threw himself on the ground, his spear going skittering across the cobbled street. She stumbled towards the guard, unwilling to look back, to see what awful fate had befallen Braidon.

Screams came from the direction of the temple and she imagined the Knights scattering in terror. She had prayed to Jurrien for lightning, but the storm had missed its mark, had struck the king instead. The air hissed and crackled with the terrible energy. Kryssa hoped at least some of the Knights had been killed as well.

She had to know. Gathering her courage, Kryssa glanced back. Her heart lurched in her chest at the sight that met her. She stumbled to a stop, unable to believe, to understand. Braidon still stood where he had before, seemingly untouched by the storm. Lightning flickered in the street, its brilliant light dancing across the king's arms, gathering in his palms.

The Knights fell back, unmanned by the appearance of this new magic. Their screams were echoed by others nearby, as those who had heard the confrontation fled back to their homes. Even Dominic scrambled to his feet and took off running down the street. Decades had passed since anyone had witnessed such a sight, enough time for magic to become the unknown, something to be feared.

Kryssa could only stare in disbelief. Where had Braidon found such power? They had spoken of Marianne's powers, but this was far greater than what the queen had revealed in Malevolent Cove. Hope swelled in her chest, that maybe they could succeed after all, maybe they could win.

The Knights had realised it too, and they fell back as one, as though fearing the Gods themselves had returned to smite them. Even their leader fled, but one alone stood his ground. Kryssa thought he was too afraid to flee. Then he lifted his blade and pointed it at Braidon.

"You are truly Braidon?" the Knight gasped, as though fighting just to breathe.

Braidon laughed. The lightning in his hands flashed and thunder rolled from the stone walls. Screams came from the nearby buildings and the rest of the Knights hurled aside their blades and scrambled back.

"I am!" Braidon's voice rose above the thunder.

"Good," the Knight hissed. He seemed to resolve something in his mind, and straightening, he took a step towards the king. "Then this is nothing but illusion!"

The breath caught in Kryssa's throat. The Knight was right! She had only been a young girl during the days of magic, but Braidon had admitted it to her himself, that his power had only ever been to construction illusion. However Braidon had managed to recover his magic, the Knight had seen through his trick.

Hearing the man's words, the other Knights hesitated, though none dared return to support him. The sight of Braidon's power was too strange, too unknown for them to confront. Instead, they waited to learn what would happen.

Braidon refused to back down. A smile twisted his lips as he pointed a finger at the Knight. The blue fire lit his face, casting it in light and shadow.

"Are you sure, sir Knight?" he asked.

Drawing himself up, the man pointed his sword. "I am Sir Harrison, and I am sure!" He roared—and charged.

A finger of lightning leapt to meet him. Crackling and hissing, it swallowed the Knight up in its light, a brilliant glow that forced all but the bravest to look away. A deafening *boom* crashed over the street. Kryssa stared into the conflagration, thinking the Knight had been right, that Braidon's bluff had been called.

Then an awful scream pierced the thunder, a shriek of agony that went on and on. The lightning flickered, returning to Braidon's hands with another *boom*. Shadows danced across Kryssa's vision and for a second she could not see what had become of the Knight. Then her sight returned and a gasp slipped from her throat.

Braidon's lightning had left the Knight's armour aglow, the steel plating turned molten in its intensity. Kryssa slapped a hand to her mouth as a muffled cry came from behind the scarlet visor. It turned to a gurgle, fading to nothing as the life was seared from the unknown Knight.

The cold eyes of the king turned on the other Knights, aglow with power, the lightning still flickering in his hands.

"Go from here," he roared, "or die like your fellow!"

The Knights did not need to be told twice. They fled, racing down the street as fast as their heavy armour would allow. Braidon waited until they vanished around a corner before turning and striding up the steps towards the temple.

Still in shock, Kryssa took several moments to go after him. He was moving quickly, but as he neared the top of the steps she saw him stagger. At the entrance to the temple he paused, and the priests and citizens parted to allow him entrance. Kryssa caught him there. Dominic still had not returned, but at least he was safe. Together they stepped into the shelter of the temple.

Only then did Kryssa catch the king by the shoulder. "Braidon!" she said, then words failed her; all she could manage was a single: "*How?*"

Braidon turned towards her, and she gasped—his face had lost all colour. The king was as grey as he'd been when she'd dragged him from the waters of Malevolent Cove. It was as though the very life had been drained from him. Swaying on his feet, he offered a fleeting grin.

"Told you I had a plan," he said.

Then his eyes rolled back into his skull and he crumpled to the stone floor.

$\mathscr{H}$ 18 $\mathscr{H}$

Darkness. Water all around. Ruebyn's weight dragging her down. An icy cold seeping into her bones…

Pela jerked as an iron hand grasped her by the ankle. A scream burst from her lips, bubbling in the silent depths. She kicked out in desperation, feeling herself sinking, desperate to free herself of the Knight. Her boot connected with something solid, and the pressure was gone. Distantly she heard a reverberation, of a panicked man falling forever into the darkness.

But she'd lost her grip on Ruebyn. She could not leave him behind, not after failing Siden. Pela waved her arms and connected with his shirt. She grabbed him and kicked out for the surface. Her lungs burned and her strength was all but gone. Desperation drove her on, the awful craving for oxygen.

All around her was pitch black. There was no telling how far they had sunk, no way of knowing they were even rising. The surface could be a hundred yards above, or one, and she would never know. But growing up in Skystead, Pela had never been far from the water. She was a strong swimmer. All she could do was keep on, keep kicking, and pray to all the Gods…

A splash marked the sudden return of sound as Pela broke the surface. Gulping in great lungfuls of air, she hauled Ruebyn up and turned him on his back. He was cold as ice and for all she knew he'd already bled to death. There was no way of telling. She spun around and around, searching for light, but could not even see the tunnel above.

How far had they fallen? And where were they now? She needed to get out of the water. Her body was already shaking, and soon the water would suck the last of the warmth from her. Pela strained her eyes, seeking out some glimmer that might offer hope, a way out. But there was nothing, only the impenetrable black—

There!

It was just a glimpse, the slightest spark, so faint she might have imagined it. But there were no other options. She struck out through the water, dragging Ruebyn with her. Her strength, already robbed by the battle above, faded every second, leached away by the icy cold. She could sense the abyss lurking below, the infinite depths waiting to claim them both. Fully clothed in steel, the Knight had never stood a chance, but they might, if only she could find the edge. But her every gasp, every desperate splash, seemed to be swallowed up by the void, as though the chamber might stretch out forever.

But that was impossible. They were under a mountain.

It has to end somewhere.

Pela tried to reassure herself, but in the icy darkness, despair clung to her and she found her mind drifting. What would it be like to sink beneath the surface and know no more? Would her soul be able to escape this place, or would even her spirit be trapped here, forever?

The fear built in her chest, a primal, animal thing that screamed for her to run and never stop. She picked up speed, desperate to escape the pool. She even considered releasing Ruebyn and letting him sink into the depths. What did she care for him? She owed him nothing, after how he had treated her. He was probably already dead, his weight a burden she did not need to carry. And yet she kept on with him, unable to let go.

When she finally found the bank, it came as such a surprise that Pela shouted out loud—then cursed and started to sink. She'd blindly slammed her free hand into a rock and now she could barely keep them both afloat. Ruebyn started to slip from her grasp and she had to claw desperately at the rock to keep them both from slipping beneath the surface.

Fortunately, the lip of rock was not high, and half-dragging, half-crawling, she managed to pull herself and Ruebyn from the water. There she collapsed to the ground, gasping and sobbing while her entire body shook, barely able to believe she'd survived, that she'd escaped.

The air was still cold, but at least it was better than the water. Lifting herself up, she put a hand to Ruebyn. Her heart sank at the ruddy cold of his skin, but she would not give him up for dead yet. She reached for him, accidentally hit him in the face, then moved her fingers down to his chest. She was sure she would find a great gaping wound, but after a long moment of searching, she could only find a narrow cut that ran across his ribs.

Breath hissed between her teeth as she sat back on her

haunches. The Knight's blade had barely nicked him. The impact with the water must have knocked him out, but the wound was certainly not mortal. Moving her fingers to his neck, she reassured herself that he still had a pulse.

She smiled despite herself. At least his life was not on her conscience. And poor though his company might be, she was not alone.

Lying down on the stone, she wrapped her arms around her chest in a vain effort to keep warm. A shiver wracked her and she cursed. The darkness pressed in, impenetrable, and unable to take it any longer, she closed her eyes.

The fear came creeping back, that she would be trapped down there forever. If she could not find a way out, how long would it take to perish in this place? Days? Weeks? Months?

Weariness pressed on her, the exertion of the past few hours catching up. Though she was damp and freezing, she could not resist the call of sleep. Her mind drifted into dreams of summer skies and open mountain fields…

Pela woke sometime later, unable to tell how much time had passed. The darkness was unchanged. Silence still enveloped the cavern. She was warmer though—she'd rolled up against Ruebyn in her sleep. With a start, she shoved him away, and he woke.

"What the…where…*what the hell?*" his voice shouted in the darkness, followed by a *crack* as he struck some unseen projection of rock. A string of curses followed.

"Ruebyn, calm down!" she hissed, reaching out a hand to him. There was no telling whether anyone was still listening for life in the tunnel.

"Slave, what have you done?" he growled. His fist struck her hand and she flinched back.

"Nothing!" she snapped. "This was your precious Knights, *remember?*"

There was a long pause, and she hoped he *did* remember what had happened above.

"That…that was a dream, surely?" he murmured. She heard him patting himself down. "I dreamt they murdered me…No, you've done something—treacherous witch!"

"It was barely a scratch," Pela said, her voice dripping scorn. "And the only thing I did was save your stupid life. More than you deserve, after what you did to me."

"After…" Ruebyn trailed off. Unable to see his face, she could not tell his reaction, but after a moment, he continued in a sullen tone, "You defied—"

Pela struck him in the face. She barely connected, her blow glancing off his chin, but even so she heard him scramble back.

"You attacked me!" he gasped. "That's a death sentence."

Pela would have hit him again, but he was too far away now. She laughed in his face instead. "I'm already under a death sentence. Weren't you listening up there? The Order wants me dead."

"A mistake, surely…" Ruebyn murmured. "Stupid thugs. You don't even weigh ten stone, how could *you* have killed an Elder?"

His disdain for her ability stung. Pela drew herself up. "It wasn't hard," she hissed. "I stabbed the bastard in the back, and he died like anyone else. And if you don't shut up, you'll be next!"

Ruebyn fell silent at that, and after a moment Pela sighed, thinking she'd frightened him. "I—"

"*You killed an Elder!*" he shrieked, his voice taut with rage. "They'll burn you for that!"

Pela's anger rose in answer to his. "They already tried," she sneered. "Besides, if I burn, you're going to burn with me now! Or didn't you hear? They think we're lovers."

"Fools," Ruebyn gasped. "I'll take you back and explain…"

"Like hell," Pela snarled. "I'm not going anywhere with you."

A stunned silence answered her declaration, then: "But…you have to!"

Pela's laughter floated up into the darkness. "I don't have to do anything. I'm free now, and I'm not giving that up for anyone. You can do what you want, but I'm not going back."

As she spoke, Pela felt a pang of guilt. She had left Genevieve behind, to suffer alone. But she had spoken the truth—she would never return to the torments of the mine. She would rather die.

"But…I can't go back without you! They'll…" He trailed off, as though unable to speak the words.

"Kill you. Torture you. Send you to the mines?" Pela snapped.

Ruebyn said nothing, and in the silence she sensed his despair. Guilt touched her then. With all his learning and his noble upbringing, it was easy to forget the overseer was little more than a boy. He was as naïve to the world as she had been just a few short months ago.

Pela sighed. "I'm sorry I dragged you into this, Ruebyn, I am. I didn't mean too. But you're right: you can't go back."

It was a long time before Ruebyn answered. "Then what do you propose we do?"

"Find a way out of this cavern, for starters," Pela replied. Tentatively she reached out and patted him on the shoulder. "Come on, we're in this together now. Take care, there's a big pool of water back there, I've only just started to get dry. I'm sure I saw light this way." She tugged him in the direction she was indicating.

"Thank the Saviour," Ruebyn whispered.

"I doubt Alana had anything to do with it," Pela muttered.

"What would you know about the great Alana, murderer?"

Pela whirled at him. "Me? Oh, I don't know. How about the fact my uncle was *Devon*, someone who actually *knew* her!"

There was a stunned silence, then: "Your uncle is the *Consort of Alana?*"

"Was," Pela said sharply. She started off again, taking care with each footstep to ensure there was earth in front of her. In the pitch-black, it would be easy to fall into a pit they could never climb back out of. "Your precious queen killed him."

"I don't understand any of this," Ruebyn whispered after a while. "Marianne is your queen as much as ours."

Pela snorted. "*That* was what confused you? She only took the crown by trying to have her husband murdered."

"None of this makes any sense," Ruebyn groaned.

"Then don't worry your pretty little head about it," Pela snapped. "Now keep it down, I'm trying to concentrate."

To her surprise, he obeyed. They continued through the

cavern, their boots squelching with each step. Pela's had been close to falling apart before going into the water; they were disintegrating beneath her now. She prayed they would hold together a little while longer, at least until she could get safely away.

Ahead, the light seemed to grow, but as they neared, Pela began to suspect it was not the surface at all. She slowed, suddenly fearing they were heading back towards part of the mine, and Ruebyn walked straight into her back. She cursed and stumbled forward—but the ground was not where it should have been.

Pela started to fall, only for her boots to strike rock several feet down. The surface was slippery, taking her feet straight out from underneath her, and she fell painfully on her backside. Then water was gushing around her and she was sliding down the smooth stone, picking up speed.

Ruebyn's cries chased after her and she realised he had fallen as well. There was nothing she could do for him. She dug in her heels but the rock was slick and she raced on towards some unknown end.

The slide ended in an abrupt *splash*. Pela gasped as the icy water embraced her, though this time it was no deeper than her knees. A cry came from behind her, followed by a second splash as Ruebyn tumbled into the shallow pool. He thrashed about, still shouting at the top of his voice, before finally realising he wasn't sinking. Stilling, he whipped his head around, eyes wide.

"Gah!" He spat out water.

At the same moment, Pela realised she could *see* him. She swung around, heart suddenly racing as she raised her fists. If they were back in the mine…

A gasp whispered from her lips. She'd been right about

the light not coming from the surface, but it wasn't manmade either. Overhead, a thousand pinpricks glowed on the low ceiling, each like a tiny star in the night sky. If she hadn't known they were underground, she might have thought it *was* the sky.

"What are they?" she whispered, still staring at the lights.

They filled the whole cavern, leading away into the dark depths, following the path of an underground stream. Each was so faint it could not have illuminated even a finger, but together, the thousand tiny stars cast enough light to reveal the cavern around them. The cascade down which they'd fallen stretched up behind them, its waters dancing over milky white rock. The creek ran from an opening above, beyond which the cavern was like a black hole in the night sky.

"They're glow worms," Ruebyn answered quietly. "They live in the darkness, near water. They use their glowing tails to attract insects."

"Magic," Pela whispered

"No—" he started, but she waved him to silence.

From where they stood, the stream continued through a canyon of silver rock. Stalagmites rose from the earth like daggers, reaching for the ceiling where their opposites hung. The magic lights continued around a bend in the cavern and out of sight.

They stood together in silence for a while longer, taking in the glory, the wonder. Pela wondered if they were the first humans to have ever set eyes on this place. Then she thought of the awful, ugly coal mines somewhere above, and decided it was a blessing that this secret place remained untouched.

Finally Pela stirred, realising the cold was slowing draining the feeling from her legs. Rousing herself, she turned to her unwilling companion.

"Come on, Ruebyn" she murmured. "Let's see if this stream leads us outside."

$$\text{🙙}\quad 19 \quad \text{🙘}$$

Caledan gritted his teeth and strained against the chains binding his wrists. The shackles cut into his flesh and the bolt attaching the chain to the wall wobbled slightly, but did not come loose. Finally he slumped panting against the stone, though the wrist chains kept him from sitting. He had stood there for more than a day so bound, and now his whole body ached.

The dungeon was far beneath the citadel and the air was like ice, his breath misting before his face. The steel shackles burned his skin and he still wore the same clothes he'd been taken in, more suited to the summer heat. Marianne had disposed of him here after her questioning, and he had no idea how long she planned to keep him. Would she leave him forgotten in the tiny cell to rot? Or would she drag him back out one day soon, to be executed in a display to her followers?

Either way, he had no doubts about his fate. Even if he could escape the shackles, the heavy iron door to his cell would not be opened by anything but the key. Silence seemed to permeate the very air; not a whisper or scream reached him from outside. His offence had earned him a place of honour in the dungeons and he was alone on this level, far below where they kept the common criminals.

His only light came from a candle in the corner. He watched the tiny flame as it flickered, the candlestick growing shorter with every drip that ran down its side. It was burning low now.

Movement came from the corner as a rat emerged from its hiding place. It crept across the cell towards Caledan—until he shouted and stomped his feet. The vermin vanished back into its bolthole—only to return a few minutes later.

Caledan shuddered as he imagined the tiny teeth feasting on his wasting flesh. Did Marianne plan to feed him? Since she had left him here, no one had come, and his stomach roiled with hunger. How long would it take for starvation to kill him?

The candle flickered again. The stub was burning just above the pool of wax in the plate. He swallowed, wondering what would become of him in the darkness, what mad creature the queen would find when they finally hauled him out.

The meeting with the queen was his only source of hope. The strangeness of the encounter, her talk of his motives, and Braidon, had left him confused. And there had been no fear in her eyes, no worry that he was a threat to her. Why, then, had she brought him to her apartments? And why had she then sent him here, like a toy she was suddenly tired of?

She had certainly seemed a different woman than the Marianne he had met on the sands of Malevolent Cove. There she had been indomitable, crushing any enemy who stood before her, equal parts hatred and rage in her eyes. Yet in front of her son she had been kind, maybe even shown love.

Clang.

Caledan's head snapped up as something sounded from the corridor outside. The breath caught in his throat. Had the time for his execution already come? Or had they finally decided to feed him?

Footsteps sounded beyond his iron door and light shone from the crack beneath. He strained against his bindings one last time, desperate to free himself, to give himself a chance. But the chains held him fast.

A *bang* came from his door as the locking mechanism was opened, followed by the squeal of rusty hinges. The brilliant light of a lantern spilled inside, momentarily blinding Caledan, and he was forced to look away as four silhouettes stepped into his cell.

"So this is the assassin?" a man asked, his voice echoing loudly in the stone confines.

"The sellsword," Marianne answered.

Caledan's heart quickened as he saw Marianne standing nearby, a familiar face at her side. It was the young Elder from Townirwin, though Caledan had never learned the man's name. He had also been in Malevolent Cove, so must have some standing within the Order's hierarchy. A Knight stood at the man's shoulder, while one of the Queen's Guard shadowed Marianne.

"Doesn't look like much," the Elder murmured.

With a grin, he drove a fist into Caledan's midriff. Unable to pull away, Caledan tensed, but the weight behind the Elder's blow still forced the breath from his lungs. Gasping, Caledan lost his footing and fell sideways. The chains rattled as they caught him and held him up, tearing at his flesh.

Stifling a groan, Caledan straightened. "You punch like a child," he spat.

The Elder did not rise to the bait. "There is strength in this one. I will enjoy taking his life force."

"He was sent by Braidon, Servo," Marianne murmured, her tone reprimanding. "Though you insist the man is no threat, he continues to interfere."

Servo waved a hand. "It matters not. The sellsword failed, didn't he? This only shows Braidon's weakness, that he must resort to such underhanded dealings."

"He is the rightful ruler of Plorsea, whatever we might claim. So long as Braidon lives, he remains a threat."

"To you," Servo murmured.

"To all of us," Marianne snapped. "Or do you think Braidon would forgive the Order so easily, should he rise again?

"To all of us, of course," Servo agreed. "Though Braidon would find that what we have unleashed is difficult to undo."

Marianne's lips twisted into a scowl. "Yes, though I must say, I find your methods distasteful, Servo," she said, folding her arms. "Perhaps you could educate me, but I cannot see what point these cleansings serve, not when so many take place without an Elder present. Such waste! Or have you shared the secret knowledge with your Knights now?"

"Of course not!" Servo hissed. "That knowledge is sacred."

Marianne rolled her eyes. "Then why the killings? I thought you were a logical man, Servo. What point do they serve, other than to turn the people against us?"

"The blasphemous must be cleansed to serve the Saviour!"

"Truly?" Marianne's voice took on an awed tone. "These cleansings are to aid Alana in her eternal battle?"

"So it is writ—"

Marianne threw back her head and howled. "Please, spare me, Servo. You do not expect me to still believe that tosh? I was married to the woman's brother. There was nothing special about him—quite the opposite. Why would it be different for the sister? No, the Order gave me comfort when I was a child, but I am a woman now. Do not spout your stories to me."

Servo's face had grown dark as Marianne spoke. Now he stepped in close, casting her in shadow. "Careful, My Queen," he growled. "I have stood for years with my brothers on the side of the light, casting back the darkness of the False Gods. It is time for your adopted peoples to join that fight—or perish. No longer can Plorsea enjoy the privilege of freedom without the sacrifice. The Saviour demands they have a hand in these cleansings, so that all are bound to our cause, so that they may never return to their False Gods."

"I see," Marianne smiled. "And if I forbid it?"

"That would be a very bad idea, *My Queen*," Servo said, his voice barely a whisper.

"These deaths do not serve my purpose," Marianne insisted.

"They serve *mine*," the Elder growled.

"Then you had best do what you promised," the queen snapped. "I want Braidon dead, not sending assassins to my city!"

Servo laughed. "Then you should have done it yourself.

Perhaps it is your resolve that must be questioned. After all, you had him in your power. So many years as his wife… maybe you grew to love him?"

"I am no one's wife," Marianne replied sharply. "Not now, and never again."

"My apologies," Servo replied, though the smile on his face suggested otherwise. He took a step closer, so that he towered over the tiny queen. "Though *never* is a long time."

Marianne's ice-cold eyes did not flinch away, and when she spoke, her voice barely rose above a whisper. "Does that trouble you, Elder?"

"Not overly much," Servo said simply. "I am sure your mind will change one day, when confronted with the *right* suitor."

The queen did not move so much as a finger, but suddenly Servo folded in two, as though struck by a blow to the stomach. He staggered backwards and crumpled to the ground. Steel hissed on leather as swords flew from their sheaths. The Knight and Queen's Guard stepped between Marianne and Servo, their blades pointed at the queen's throat.

Caledan stared, shocked by the turn of events. Marianne did not seem surprised, though her eyes burned with rage. "Kildren," she said, looking at her Guard, who still pointed his sword at her. "You're dismissed."

The man only smiled. "The Saviour was ever my master, Marianne. You cannot—"

He broke off as Marianne waved a hand. A sharp *crack* came from the man's neck. The colour drained from his face and he crumpled to the floor without a sound. He lay there unmoving, eyes fixed on the ceiling, forever unseeing.

Silence followed, then Servo began to laugh. Groaning,

he lifted himself from where he'd fallen and stepped over the dead man.

"Such fire!" he gasped, waving his Knight back.

A scowl twisted Marianne's face and she raised her hand again, but this time something gave her pause.

The Elder smirked. "That's right, My Queen," he hissed. "You might have collected some small degree of power in Malevolent Cove, but do not forget who offered you that gift."

"Oh, I do not forget," Marianne snarled. "But I refuse to be manipulated any longer. Isybelle told me what you did before she died, about the role the Order played in arranging my marriage to Braidon."

Servo studied her for a long time, as though contemplating a fly trapped between his fingers. His hazel eyes shone in the lantern light. The tension built, an almost palpable pressure that hung over the room, as if a silent battle were being fought between them. Caledan could sense something gathering, a swirling power that throbbed at his temples.

Finally it was Servo who broke, his eyes flicking away, though he did not seem overly perturbed. Still smiling, he wandered to where Caledan hung from his chains. Keeping his gaze averted from Marianne, he spoke in a calm voice:

"You have gathered more power than I had thought." His eyes were dark as they looked on Caledan. "Perhaps I made a mistake, offering you our knowledge."

"I swore revenge on all those who had a hand in my marriage," Marianne replied. "My father, the council, you and your Elders, you took an innocent girl and made her your puppet. You robbed me of my life—why should I spare you?"

"I'll admit, we did not expect you to act against the Lonian council." Servo faced the queen. "That was a bold stroke, proclaiming yourself queen of both nations."

"They had outlived their usefulness. As, it seems, have you."

Marianne clenched her hand into a fist and Servo staggered, clutching at his chest. Faster than Caledan would have believed possible, the Knight leapt at Marianne, broadsword raised to strike her down. She spun, redirecting her attack, and the Knight slammed to a halt, his blade just inches from her face. Her blue eyes bored into the man and his plate mail groaned—then caved inwards as though struck an awful blow.

A wheezing groan whispered from behind the iron visor. Steel rattled on stone as the sword slipped from the Knight's hands. Then his feet went out from underneath him and he crashed to the ground. Marianne stood staring down at him for a moment, then returned her attention to Servo.

The Elder had regained his feet. He stood alone now, but remained unperturbed.

"You must tell me, Marianne, where you found such power," he murmured. "We gave you only one life in Malevolent Cove, but you have stolen far more than that."

Marianne smirked. "Your way is not the only way, Servo," she said. "But I will tell you nothing. Are you ready to meet your precious Saviour?"

To Caledan's surprise, Servo laughed. "Oh, it would be a delight, but alas, I do not think today shall be the day."

"Oh?" Marianne hissed.

"No." Servo's voice took on a steely tone as his gaze roamed the cell, pausing on each of his fallen men. "It is a shame to lose such worthy followers. I shall pray that the

Saviour welcomes them into her sacred army. But I have many more servants, while you stand alone." He paused, his eyes returning to Marianne. "Tell me, how goes little Calybe's lessons, My Queen?"

Caledan's heart lurched at the man's words, recalling the innocent boy that had come running into Marianne's apartment. For a second, Marianne wavered, her eyes betraying her fear. Then the mask settled back into place.

"Leave him out of this, Servo," she growled.

The Elder straightened, clutching his arms behind his back. "Oh, the boy will remain safe enough—so long as you behave, *My Queen*," he replied, his voice cold now. "But should you ever forget your *duty* again, well…I cannot make any promises. Now, I think we are done here, yes?"

He watched Marianne for a second, then laughed and walked past her out into the corridor, taking the lantern with him. His footsteps faded away, until finally there was silence.

The breath left Marianne in a rush and she sank to her knees. Head bowed, she sucked in great mouthfuls of air, as though she had just run a great race. Time stretched out, the only sound the soft whispers of the queen's sobs.

Caledan stared at her, lips parted as though to speak, but he was unable to put words to what he'd just witnessed. Seeing the rawness of her grief, he found himself wanting to go to her, though they were bitter enemies.

Finally the queen grew silent, and lifting a hand to her face, she wiped away the tears. Rising, she turned to look at Caledan. The grief was gone, her face a perfect mask of composure once more, though he could see the rage burning in her crystal eyes.

"Now you understand?" she whispered.

❧ 20 ❧

It was night when Pela and Ruebyn finally stumbled from the cave back into the world, and at first Pela did not even realise they'd escaped their rocky tomb. The tall cliffs of a canyon rose to either side of them and the night was clear, the pinpricks of stars so similar to the glow worms that her exhausted mind did not recognise the change.

Then Ruebyn grabbed her, his face alive with excitement. "We're free!" he exclaimed, hugging her in his excitement.

Blinking, Pela struggled to understand what he was saying. "We did it?" she asked, then finally noticed the brilliance of the full moon shining above. Her mouth fell open, then: "We did it!" Despite herself, she hugged Ruebyn back, unable to believe it was true.

Then she released him and sank to the ground, weeping at the joy of it. *She was free!* No one in the mine knew she was alive, no one was coming after her. She could have howled her triumph from the mountaintops—if she'd had the strength to manage more than a slow shuffle.

"What is it?" Ruebyn asked, uncertainty replacing his happiness.

Seeing his confusion, Pela wondered how he could not know, how he could not realise what this meant for her, to be free of the darkness, to have her life back. But then Ruebyn understood little but what his books and teachers had taught him—nothing of the real world. She shook her head.

"Nothing," she said, rising. "And everything. I'm free."

The smile slipped from his face at her words and he took a step back. That Pela could understand. She was free, but her victory had cost the boy everything. The distance restored between them, he swallowed. She knew what he was going to say before he said it.

"I should take you back, and beg for their forgiveness."

Pela smiled, good-humoured despite his words. Nothing could take away her happiness now—certainly not Ruebyn. "I can see three problems with your plan." She started off along the narrow canyon before he could reply.

"What?" he shouted, running to catch up with her.

"One," Pela said, counting on her fingers, "I won't go willingly, and I doubt you have the strength to carry me."

She glanced over her shoulder at him, waiting for a reply, but he said nothing, and she went on.

"Two—you don't know how to get back to the mines."

"I could find my way," he snapped.

"Really?" Pela asked, raising one eyebrow. "Where do you think we are?"

He paused, his eyes flickering across the night sky. Then he pointed at one of the cliffs. "That way is east."

Pela was impressed, though she kept her face carefully neutral. "Well and good, but have you ever travelled in the mountains? Do you know which gullies are passable, which are dead ends? What would you eat, and how will you stay warm at night?"

"It's summer," Ruebyn retorted. "How hard can it be?" But even as he spoke, a cold breeze blew through the canyon. Their clothes were still damp from the stream and he quickly wrapped his arms around his chest.

Pela chuckled. "It's the *end* of summer. Or is it autumn already?"

"See, you don't know any better than me!"

"I lost track of time down there," Pela snapped. "And I grew up in Skystead." When Ruebyn only offered a blank look, she sighed and explained. "It's a small town in Plorsea, wedged between the mountains and a fjord. My mother and grandmother and I spent many nights camped in the mountains when I was young. I even went by myself a few times, when I was older and our inn was empty."

"Your family ran an inn?" Ruebyn sounded surprised.

"Yes," Pela said gruffly, "but that's besides the point. You'd starve or freeze to death long before you found your way out of these mountains.

Ruebyn fell silent at that and they continued, the only sound the crunching of stones beneath their boots. Pela surveyed their surroundings as they walked. The overseer wasn't the only one who could read the stars, and it seemed the canyon was winding north. Better than east, though she would have to find a pass west over the mountains eventually. Without any means of removing her collar, she could not return to Lonia without being recognized as a slave, though that was the fastest way home to Skystead.

Her only other option was to seek refuge in Trola—but that too might prove fatal. The nation's borders had been closed for decades and they did not take kindly to interlopers. Once Trola had been the jewel of the Three Nations, but their army and many of their cities had been crushed by the Tsar. Impoverished as they were, surely they would not turn Pela away, not when they learned of her plight.

"What was the third reason?"

Pela started and almost fell, her foot slipping in the loose gravel. They were still following the stream that had led them from the cave, its babbling waters winding slowly through the narrow gorge. She frowned at Ruebyn, not understanding, and he rephrased his question.

"You said there were three problems with my plan."

It still took her a moment to recall what he meant. She chuckled. "Your Knights are many things, but forgiving is not one of them. It might have been an accident, but you still helped cause the death of one of them. They would kill you for that alone."

Ruebyn scowled. "What would you know, slave?"

His words struck Pela like a blow and she staggered to a stop. Slowly she turned to face him, a terrible rage building within her. She wanted to hit him, to beat him as he had beaten her. Her ear still ached where his whip had struck. Unconsciously she lifted a hand to it, then flinched away as she touched the swollen flesh.

"My name is Pela," she snarled, "and if you ever call me a slave again…" She took a step towards him, leaving the threat unfinished.

Ruebyn scrambled back, and losing his footing, crashed to the ground. His mouth hung open in a great O and he lay staring up at her, shocked by the outburst. Pela leaned in close, fists clenched so tight she felt the nails cutting into her palms.

"And I'm never going back, not for anyone."

But even as she spoke the words, Genevieve's face flashed into her mind. Quickly she turned away before Ruebyn saw the panic in her eyes. She had not told Lewis about the huntress…but what if Lewis or the surviving Knight figured out their connection? For a moment, Pela wavered.

Then memories of her time beneath the earth came rushing back, the constant cold, the dust and dirt and danger, the darkness. Her gaze lifted to the clifftops at the thought, seeking to reassure herself. There was a distant glow to the sky and she realised the dawn must be nearing. She sucked in a breath, watching the light, and grew calm once more.

No, she could not go back, not even for Genevieve. The huntress could look after herself. Pela started off again, her mind turning to the future. For the first time in an age, she wondered who else had survived the Cove. She could not imagine Caledan succumbing to the currents, but Braidon had been in a terrible way when the boat capsized. As for Kryssa…Pela could not bear to think of her mother's fate. And if she had survived, Pela would have to tell her about Genevieve. The thought was not a pleasant one, and she quickly forced her mind back to the present.

Boots crunched on stone as Ruebyn started to follow her again. Pela turned to scream at him to go away, but the words died on her lips. The boy's face was a picture of abject misery, his eyes downcast and his cheeks lined with sorrow. She sighed. He might know how to read directions from the stars, but he was helpless out in these mountains.

"What is it like, where you're from?" she asked, wanting to understand him better.

"Loud, busy," he answered immediately. "The streets are always packed, people are always going somewhere. I hated it. But my teachers always came to our house. The courtyard was my favourite place to study at this time of year." His voice took on a dreamy tone. "We have a fountain that runs in the summer. At sunset the light turns its waters red —a trick the architects designed when they were building the house. Though it only works for a month."

Pela snorted. "What a waste of time."

"Yes, I imagine someone as uncultured as yourself would think so," Ruebyn replied in a haughty tone.

Laughing, Pela climbed over a cluster of boulders blocking their passage. The stream threaded its way beneath them and emerged on the other side, making the climb down difficult. Pela managed it, but a splash came from behind her as Ruebyn landed one boot in the water. He cursed, and she giggled despite herself.

"So why did you come to the mines then?" she asked. "If you enjoyed your little courtyard so much?"

Ruebyn's face grew tight. "Duty. The Order is a rising power in Lonia, especially now, with our new queen ruling from Plorsea. My parents sent me to the mines to court their favour. I'm to be a Knight one day…" He trailed off, and swallowed visibly before continuing. "Though now…my family will surely disown me, or our name will forever be tarnished."

His voice was thick with despair and Pela sighed. "Maybe you'll get lucky?" she offered. "Braidon could win. Then you'd be a hero, for rescuing me."

"Your king is dead," Ruebyn replied. "Surely even *you* must have heard that?"

Pela rolled her eyes. "Were you not listening to anything

I said back there?" When Ruebyn only gave a blank look, she scowled. "I said Marianne *tried* to kill her husband. But she failed. Braidon is alive, or at least I pray to the Gods he's still alive. He was with my mother, and she's…full of surprises."

There was a long, disbelieving silence. "You truly are mad," Ruebyn said finally.

Pela ground her teeth, but it was obvious the conversation was going nowhere and she let the topic drop. They pressed on for another hour as the sun brightened the horizon, only stopping once when they crossed a set of animal tracks. There were only a few, in a patch of sand near the stream, imprints of a giant paw. The sight made Pela's blood run cold and they quickly moved on, eager to leave the creature's territory behind.

Pela's legs were aching by the time the canyon finally opened out into a broad gulley. The stream raced ahead, merging with a larger river threading its way down the mountain. Large gravels covered the entire three hundred feet width of the valley. In places the river split around islands of patchy vegetation, forming half a dozen channels that would make a crossing difficult.

A second cliff on the other side rose even higher than the canyon from which they'd just emerged, leaving them only two paths to choose from. Pela looked upriver, finally seeing the challenge that lay ahead. Sunlight touched the western mountains, turning their snow-capped peaks a fiery red and causing her eyes to water. They rose ten thousand feet overhead or more, impassable to all but the most experienced of climbers. But there would be a pass, some way through—she had only to find it.

Pain lanced through her temples and Pela was forced to

look away. Her eyes were burning and she cursed, remembering the debilitating pain of her last trip to the surface. The light was growing rapidly now and she could barely keep her eyes open. She started upriver, desperate to find shelter before it became too bright for her to see. Ruebyn followed her in silence.

Thankfully, clouds rolled in with the break of day and Pela managed another hour before she could go no further. Finding a narrow opening in the cliff, she crept inside and settled in the shadows, hardly caring if Ruebyn followed. Stars swirled cross her vision and the headache was a constant now.

Jagged stones filled the crevice and Pela cursed as one tore through her boots. She sank to the ground anyway, wracked by pain and so exhausted she could not take another step. The rocks were cold but with the heat growing outside, she savoured their touch against her skin. Laying her head against her arm, she stayed there for a while, catching her breath.

Finally the aching from her boots became too great and she sat back up. Removing the offending items, she tossed them aside and sank her head onto her arms again. Rock crunched as nearby, Ruebyn tried to make himself comfortable.

It didn't take long for the heat Pela had built up during the walk to dissipate. Her clothes remained damp despite the morning's warmth, and after half an hour she was shivering. Ruebyn crouched nearby, his eyes distant, as though pondering some puzzle in his mind. Every so often a tremor would wrack him, though to his credit he did not complain.

Pela gritted her teeth, wondering whether they should continue. But just a glance outside made her eyes burn. The clouds had lifted and the gravel outside their tiny cave was aglow with sunlight. It was so bright it hurt to look in the direction of the entrance, even with her eyes closed. She would be as blind and helpless as a newborn kitten outside their measly shelter.

Cursing, she turned away. They were horribly unprepared for a trip through the mountains, even in summer. Still weak from starvation and poorly clothed, they would be lucky to survive another night.

"So…" Pela jumped as Ruebyn spoke into the silence. She swung to look at him and he froze, mouth hanging open. But when she said nothing, he managed to swallow his fear and continued, "Pela…did you really kill an Elder?"

She sighed. Outside the wind howled down the valley and fingers of ice seeped into their cave, making her shiver. The cold of night clung to the stone and she longed to crawl outside and bathe in the sun's heat. But she remained, fearful of its intensity. She turned Ruebyn's question over in her mind.

"Yes, Rueben," she said finally. "Though he was the only person I have ever killed."

"Why?" he whispered, his face twisted by a frown.

Pela laughed. His face was an open book, and she knew he truly could not imagine why someone would commit such a deed.

"Because he was trying to murder my mother," she replied. "For worshiping the Three Gods."

"False Gods," Ruebyn corrected, though there was no force behind it. His eyebrows knitted together and he added, "There are some in the Order who believe such…cleansings are necessary."

"My mother and her friends never hurt anyone," Pela

murmured. "They only went to pay their respects. They were happy—*I* was happy. Then your Elders and their Knights came, with their swords and their hatred, and changed everything. You think I am the monster, for killing one of your precious Elders, but I never wanted any part of this. I am only what they forced me to become."

Ruebyn had no answer to that. He sat rolling a rock between his fingers, eyes downcast, lips pursed. After a while Pela realised he was not going to respond at all. She lay back down, exhaustion weighing on her like an anchor. It was still up for debate whether she could trust the former overseer, but nor could she remain awake for another second. Her eyes fluttered closed, and she slept…

When she woke, Pela was glad to find that her clothes had dried and the sun was dipping towards the distant horizon. Finding her eyes were coping a little better, she allowed herself to hope they could adjust to the real world again.

Ruebyn lay asleep nearby, mouth hanging open and giving the occasional grunt. A smile touched her lips. Like this, she could almost imagine him as an innocent young man, rather than the young noble that had called her a slave. It was a shame she had to wake him.

Pela replaced her crumbling boots and kicked him lightly in the shins. He woke with a start, eyes swinging wildly in his skull as he raised his fists. Seeing her standing over him, the fright faded.

"What is it?" he grumbled, rubbing sleep from his eyes.

"Time to go," she murmured, gesturing outside. "If you're lucky I might find us something to eat."

It would be tough at this time of year, but she had spotted some brambles amongst the vegetation dotting the gulley, and hoped there might still be some late berries. It was too warm to find trout in the streams, but if they were lucky the salmon might still be running.

The thought reminded her of the paw print they'd spotted earlier and she left Ruebyn to get ready, wanting to scout out the way ahead. The Mountain Felines near Skystead rarely approached humans, but the Sandstone Peaks were wild and few people ever set foot here. The creatures might not be possessed of the same fear. Outside, she saw no sign of a large animal, but that meant little with such a creature. One might be lurking a few feet away, concealed by its camouflage, and she would not know until it was upon her.

"Where *are* we going?" Ruebyn asked as he joined her outside.

"Someplace safe," Pela murmured, not wanting to delve into her plan. It would be hard enough to make the journey to Trola without Ruebyn knowing their destination. Given that their odds in the western nation weren't a lot better than in Lonia, she thought it best to keep the former overseer in the dark for as long as possible.

Ruebyn said nothing. Pela took his silence as anger and faced him, but the boy was not looking at her. Her heart lurched as she followed his gaze downriver and saw movement. Quickly she grabbed Ruebyn and dragged him back against the cliff face.

"How did they find us?" she hissed.

"The Elders have their ways," Ruebyn said miserably.

21

Braidon woke to a pounding in his head and pain shooting through every inch of his body. It began in the base of his skull and radiated outwards, lighting his entire being aflame. His stomach lurched and before he could stop himself, he rolled onto his side and vomited.

Laughter greeted him, but when he tried to open his eyes, the light burned directly into the back of his skull. He quickly closed them again. Groaning, he lay his head back down. There was cold stone beneath him and he sighed as it took some of the fire from his skull.

"Where am I?" he asked, knuckling his temples.

"Inside the Earth Temple," Kryssa replied. "After you passed out, I thought it was probably best if the whole city didn't see you incapacitated."

"Did it work?" he asked.

His mind was hazy, his memory of what had happened outside the temple little more than a blur. He recalled the Knight's challenge, his sudden fear at being called out, then cold anger, the determination to do the impossible. After that, nothing.

"By 'work', do you mean burn the Knight to death?" Kryssa asked, her normally cool tone touched with awe. "If so, then yes, it worked."

Braidon tried opening his eyes again. This time he found it slightly more bearable. Carefully he pushed himself up—then cried out as pain sliced his forearms. His strength gave out and he collapsed back onto the stone bench. He lay staring up at the blue sky, struggling to catch his breath. It was a moment before he realised the strangeness of where he was.

They weren't quite as inside the temple as Kryssa had led him to believe. Around them was a garden of soft green plants and blooming flowers, orchids and roses and a dozen other varieties he did not know. A bird chirped from the branches of a nearby tree and the air carried the rich, earthly scent of the forest. It was warmer too, as though they were cut off from the world, in some hidden refuge.

Sitting up more carefully this time, he massaged the muscles in his arms. With the better vantage point he saw they were in a broad courtyard enclosed on all sides by marble walls. Windows dotted the stone, and he glimpsed men and women wandering past them in the green robes of Earth Priests. The three spires of the temple stabbed skywards in a triangle overhead, and from the position of the sun, Braidon guessed it was nearing noon.

He frowned. What had happened to the storm? And had it not been afternoon when they'd come? He turned to Kryssa, his heart beating faster.

"How long was I asleep?" he asked.

"A day," Kryssa replied. "Don't worry, no one knows.

The priests are good at keeping secrets. Though word of your feat outside has definitely gotten out."

"Why do you say that?"

"Oh, you'll see," Kryssa said ominously.

Braidon was feeling a little better now, though in truth he was surprised he was alive at all. He'd pushed himself too far, though it had been impossible to know before he attempted it. At least he'd started small, or he would already be dead.

Kryssa sat on another bench opposite Braidon, her gaze fixed on where he sat. His vomit had fallen amongst the roses and he felt a touch of embarrassment. Then his anger returned, that he'd been forced to go so far, to take such a risk. He pushed himself to his feet, but his legs were not ready and he staggered several steps before Kryssa caught him.

Lowering him to the bench alongside her, she leaned close, as though she might learn his secrets in the depths of his eyes.

"How did you do it?" she whispered finally, sitting back.

Braidon felt a thrill as he recalled what he had discovered, the power he'd tapped. It had been so simple, in the end, little different than accessing the magic he'd once wielded. Though what he'd done had been a forbidden thing then, so dangerous only the desperate or foolish would consider it.

"The same way Marianne found her power," he replied, "only without using someone else's life force."

Kryssa frowned, pondering his response. It took a moment for his words to seep in, but finally her eyes widened with understanding.

"You used your *own* life force?" she whispered. "Isn't that…"

"Dangerous?" Braidon croaked. "Extremely. Could I have some water?"

Rising, Kryssa waved to a passing priest. Words whispered between them and he disappeared, returning a minute later with a jug and plate of dried fruits. Braidon downed the entire thing in one gulp, then placed it beside him with a sigh. The food quickly followed. The water cooled his throat and eased the pounding in his head, while the sustenance cleared his mind.

"It…was still a better option than using another's life force." He shuddered at the thought.

"Agreed!" Kryssa replied. "Though…I still don't understand, how could you create true lightning, if with all your power as a Magicker, you could only make illusions?

Braidon smiled. "My *magic* came from the Light Element. It allowed me manipulate energies to create illusions. But it was not my *magic* that summoned the lightning. My own life force created it, not some gift from the Gods. Though, I'll admit, it *was* an illusion until the Knight challenged me."

"Oh?" Kryssa asked.

"My life force is like a candle before a forest fire compared to the magic I had before. Its energy is limited, and I wanted to avoid exhausting myself. So I created the illusion of lightning. But when the Knight called me out, I was forced to make it real. And that almost killed me. I should not have used so much energy…but it is a new skill. I didn't realize it would drain me so quickly."

"Wait…" Kryssa murmured, "but if this was possible all along, why did no one ever think of it?"

"Because we were taught *never* to use our life force as power," Braidon replied. "Another second back there, and I would have killed myself with the lightning."

"But then…" Kryssa's eyes became great circles in her face. "That must mean anyone could do the same as you?"

"Yes," Braidon replied. "With practice and meditation, this is a power everyone could use. Though I fear those who are not careful, who lack discipline, may end up destroying themselves with the effort."

"A gift for all," Kryssa whispered.

"Ay, and one the Elders have sought to keep from their own people. So much for the world being equal beneath the Saviour."

Kryssa snorted and started to turn away, then swung back again. "That must be why they hate us!" she gasped.

Braidon frowned. "Sorry?"

"You said this new power requires meditation. Followers of the Three Gods still practice the old ways. Sooner or later, someone was bound to stumble upon this discovery."

"You're right," Braidon exclaimed, then: "And while they were hunting down believers, they were also finding a way around their own limitations. By stealing another's life force in the moment of their death, they could cast as many spells as they wanted without costing themselves anything."

The smile slipped from Kryssa's face. "And that means we're still not powerful enough to face the queen. With their Knights loose across Plorsea, who knows how many innocents they've murdered and turned into power?"

"Yes, we must be careful. Now, what is happening outside?"

Kryssa smiled at that. "You'd better come see," she said, rising and offering Braidon her hand.

He took it and she led him from the courtyard into the corridors of the temple. Several priests were walking past, but they stopped when they saw him, their mouths falling open. Braidon nodded and followed Kryssa, their whispers chasing after him.

Movement came from ahead and Dominic appeared from around a corner. The man had obviously returned home to refresh himself, for his chainmail was shining as though recently polished and he appeared well-rested. He snapped a salute at their approach.

Braidon chuckled and clapped him on the shoulder. "None of that, Dominic," he said. "You helped me when I had no one…err, almost no one. I won't forget it."

Nodding, Dominic fell in with them. "Thank you, sir," he blurted out, then: "They're waiting for you, sir!"

"Who?"

The man looked confused. "Everyone, sir."

That's going to get wearing, Braidon thought with a sigh, before realizing what the guard had said. He looked at Kryssa to demand an answer, but she laughed before he could get the question out.

"Relax!" she gasped. "Come on."

She shoved him ahead, where two priests were just pushing open the doors of the temple. The hinges moved without a whisper and sunlight burst into the corridor. Braidon's heart started to race. Not knowing what waited outside, he paused on the threshold, but another gesture from Kryssa sent him forward.

A roar greeted him and Braidon reached for his sword, thinking they were under attack. Then he realised he was alone at the top of the temple steps. The sound came from below. A crowd packed the narrow street so tightly they could barely move.

Braidon stumbled forward another step, his legs still weak, and a sudden silence fell. The hairs on his neck stood on end and he realised every eye in the street was upon him. Marble columns lined the stairwell, leading down to where the crowd waited—waited for him to speak!

He sucked in a great breath and stepped up to the top of the steps. Opening his mouth, he searched for words to offer them, but they refused to come. Then his eyes were drawn out over the surrounding rooftops, across the city to where another building rose from the dust of Chole.

The stone walls of the Order's Castle lurked like a shadow on the horizon, a distant threat, a promise of violence. He had won the first battle, but within those walls waited the Elders and their Knights. They would know what power he had used, knew he'd been bluffing. If a second Knight had challenged him, Braidon would have failed.

His heart beat faster as he turned to the crowd. The Order would come for him soon and he did not have the strength to stop them. But those below did. They were the army he had prayed for, the strength he needed to topple Marianne. He clenched his fists, thinking of how she had dismissed him, the contempt in her eyes as she'd looked at him. But he would show her, would take back what was his, would make the world right again.

And it would start with Chole.

"My people!" he cried, his voice echoing down the street. "Your king has returned!"

Whispers rose to greet his announcement and Braidon smiled. He let their confusion go on for a while longer, and then raised his hands. The silence was instant.

"I know you have questions. Fear not, they will be answered in time. But know this—my wife is a traitor. Marianne tried to have me murdered, so that she might take my throne. Now she sells us to her Lonian masters, would let their Knights march into your great city and burn your temple. She would take away our heritage, our history and beliefs. I will not allow it!"

A roar met his words as the crowd lifted their arms in salute. Braidon stood poised on the edge of the steps, listening to their shouts, allowing them to build themselves into a frenzy. Then he spoke again.

"The Order demands your obedience, demands you bow down to their Saviour. They would rob us of our freedom, would cast down the Gods that served us faithfully for so many centuries and replace them with a lie. Well I say, we will not stand for it! Follow me, good people of Chole, and we will cast down their Castle and drive their foul Knights back from whence they came!"

The voices of the crowd were deafening now, rumbling up from the street like an earthquake. Braidon's heart soared. He had his army. Together they would march on the Castle and drive the Knights from Chole, make the city safe from their evil. Then let Marianne try and stop him. An army could starve on the arid plains around Chole, and while the walls were old, they were solid, rebuilt during his father's reign.

Braidon dragged his sword from its sheath and thrust it into the air. "Follow me, for Plorsea!"

22

Pela and Ruebyn walked all night, the way lit only by the stars and the soft glow of the moon, but there was no losing their pursuers. The flicker of their torches was a constant presence, far below but always there, always threatening. Pela had no idea how they'd been found so quickly, how they even knew she was alive. All she understood was the sickly feeling of despair in her gut, the fear of being caught again, of being dragged back into the dark.

She'd been surprised when Ruebyn continued with her. There had been a moment when she'd thought he would betray her, but in the end his sense of self-preservation was greater than duty, and they'd set off upriver in silence.

Pela led them up the gulley for hours, following the whispering waters of the river. She was afraid to leave the open ground, for while they might lose their pursuers in one of the narrow canyons that opened in the cliffs every few hundred feet, they might just as easily meet a dead end and be trapped. Even in the broad gulley they had trouble. Several times they were forced to cross one of the smaller river channels when their way was barred by a cluster of boulders or a high bank of earth. The lack of light slowed their progress, but there was no help for that.

As the night progressed, Pela sensed their pursuers drawing closer. She was sure they hadn't been spotted yet, but when daylight came it would only be a matter of time before they were caught. If they continued in the light—*if* she could continue—they would be seen. Then their pursuers would know exactly how close they were, and hunt them all the more desperately. In Pela's exhausted state, they would be overhauled within hours.

But nor could they find a place to hide, for the hunters were following their tracks.

Their only hope were the winding mountain paths. That meant leaving the broad gulley and entering the maze of canyons.

Ruebyn stumbled along beside her now, his face a mask of misery, arms wrapped around his chest. It was colder this night, and no matter how hard they trekked, the icy air leached the warmth from them. The wind howled down from the mountain peaks, carrying with it the promise of winter. Out on the riverbed there was no shelter and each blast was like a thousand tiny needles striking Pela's skin.

As the moon closed on midnight and the torches remained stubbornly on their trail, Pela finally made the decision. A dark opening in the cliffs beckoned ahead, and she altered their course. They forded a narrow stream, not even bothering to remove their boots, and tramped up to the canyon.

Pela studied the entrance as they approached. It spanned twenty yards and appeared to narrow further inside. Enough to keep the worst of the wind from them.

The cliffs on either side were not so much vertical as steeply sloping—in daylight she might have even been able to climb them. Below, the ground was dark and she could see little but the sheen of water against the far cliff.

"We're going in?" Ruebyn asked.

"We don't have a choice," Pela replied. "We have to lose them before daylight."

"How far does it go?"

"How would I know?" Pela snapped.

She moved inside without looking back. Gravel crunched beneath her feet, but in several places it turned suddenly to sand, sinking her boots to the ankle. She swore. They would need to be more careful not to leave tracks, or they'd never lose the hunters.

"It could end in a hundred yards, or several miles," Pela explained a few minutes later, feeling guilty for yelling. "There's no way to tell."

"Oh," Ruebyn replied, his voice taut. She could tell he was trying to mask his fear. "Do you really think we can outrun them?"

Pela glanced back. Ruebyn was watching her with a mixture of hope and awe, that she might be able to lead them to safety. A smile touched her lips.

"I may have...overstated my abilities slightly, earlier," she admitted, "but so long as we're alive, we have a chance. My grandmother always said that."

Ruebyn offered a grunt that might have been agreement, and she laughed. "She was a very positive person. Something about the Goddess Antonia saving her life when she was younger?"

"The...that's blasphemy!" Stones rattled as Ruebyn staggered to a stop.

She glanced over her shoulder and raised an eyebrow. "It's the truth. Devon was there, and Braidon—your precious Saviour too, actually. Maybe if we survive, you could ask Braidon the truth about his sister, and what happened that day."

"I have nothing to say to your king, even were he actually alive," Ruebyn grated. "Thanks to him, Lonia is a poor shadow of its former glory. His father's taxes drove our farmers off their land, leaving their crops to rot while our people starved."

"Braidon is not the Tsar," Pela replied, "and don't forget, it was *his* sister that freed us all from their father's grasp."

"Why do you think the Order of Alana was born in Lonia?" Ruebyn shot back. "We do not forget. Alana's sacrifice redeemed her past, freeing us from the Tsar and the False Gods both. But her brother never paid for his crimes."

Pela sighed, realising there would be no changing his mind. "And what about Marianne?"

There was a pause before Ruebyn answered. "She is loved by the people, like her father before her, but my own family is somewhat less trusting. They fear the Plorseans have corrupted her, that she might be a snake in devil's clothing."

"On that at least, we can agree," Pela chuckled.

They let the conversation fall quiet for a while then, concentrating on the way ahead. The canyon walls grew narrow around them and the ground sloped upwards, making the going difficult. Several times they stumbled into the blackberry brambles Pela had spotted the night before. The thorns tore at their clothes and skin, but at least they were able to collect berries as they walked. The fruit was dried by the long summer, but it was the first food they'd found since emerging from the cave.

Another hour passed and Pela started to wonder at something Ruebyn had said earlier, about differing philosophies within the Order. But hundreds had come to Malevolent Cove to witness the Great Sacrifice—surely such an event could not have gone unnoticed by others, even by someone as sheltered as Ruebyn.

"Ruebyn, what do you know of the Great Sacrifice?" she asked finally.

A frown creased her companion's forehead. "It has occurred on the night of the solstice, every ten years since Alana's sacrifice. But it is a secret of our Order—how do you know of it?"

Pela snorted. "Because I *was* it," she said, her heart sinking. Ruebyn had claimed to disbelieve the more violent tendencies of the Order, but his actions said otherwise. "They tried to burn my mother and me alive, to please your *dear* Saviour."

"What?" Ruebyn gaped. "That's…not possible. The Great Sacrifice is not a person, but an act, a gathering of the faithful to send our strength to the Saviour. Only the most faithful, the most devout, are allowed to attend."

Coming to a stop, Pela turned to stare at him. He seemed earnest, but then perhaps that was all part of the lie. The Order would protect its secrets at all costs, and she could not dismiss the thought Ruebyn was lying.

Then the face of the Elder Lewis flickered into her mind. He'd been rigid in his own way, but he'd believed her, and had condemned the Order's cruelty. Perhaps she could give Ruebyn the benefit of the doubt as well.

They continued, the ground rising steeply now, and each

footstep grew more difficult than the last. They had lost altitude in the caverns, but Pela sensed they had already made that up—and then some. Her lungs burned and no matter how deeply she inhaled, she could not seem to catch her breath. A pounding began in her head as they twisted their way up the canyon, taking turns at random whenever the way ahead split.

At times the stream vanished, its waters disappearing into hidden holes in the earth—then reappearing seemingly from nothing, bubbling up between the stones to continue its inevitable journey from mountains to ocean. They paused more often now, as the air grew colder and Pela's headache became a constant. Ruebyn said nothing, just kept on with his head down, eyes on the treacherous path.

Eventually they staggered to a stop. Ruebyn slumped against a boulder and slid to the ground, his head falling to his knees. A groan whispered from his chest as he toppled sideways.

Frowning, Pela stumbled across to where he lay. A tingle of concern passed down her spine as she gripped him by the shoulder and found him cold to the touch. He moaned again as she turned his head to study his face.

"I'm okay," he croaked. "Just…so…cold." His teeth began to chatter and a great shiver wracked him.

Pela cursed. They hadn't made it half as far into the maze as she wanted. And she was sure they'd left enough tracks for even a passable hunter to follow. But it was clear Ruebyn was in no state to go on. She stood and moved back down the path, scanning their backtrail. The canyon remained dark—no sign of their followers yet. Perhaps they'd missed where Pela and Ruebyn had left the river. She could only hope.

Returning to Ruebyn, she studied him a moment. He lay huddled on the ground with his arms wrapped around his chest. Every so often a shudder shook him and his teeth would chatter again. She might have left him there and continued alone, but after coming so far, Pela could not even contemplate the thought.

There was no help for it. Lying down beside him, she held out her arms.

"What…are you…doing?" he stammered, the cold making his speech difficult.

"It's the only way to warm you," she snapped, suddenly angry.

Why was she doing this? The boy was only slowing her down, putting her at risk of being captured. He was so cold she began to shiver herself. It only fed her anger. Why hadn't he said something sooner?

They lay there in the darkness as the minutes ticked by. Wedged between the boulder and the canyon wall, they were protected from the wind, and sharing one another's heat, they began to warm. Slowly the anger left Pela. Ruebyn had no idea what he was doing out here, had never even been in the mountains. It was a miracle he'd made it this far without exposure and the altitude striking him down.

Eventually Ruebyn ceased shaking and his eyes slid closed. Knowing she could not afford to do the same, Pela studied their surroundings. The walls of the canyon were steeper now, falling from above in shelves rather than a slope. Ledges had been formed in the sandstone, creating vertical steps every thirty feet.

An idea came to her. The rough sandstone would not be difficult to climb, even for a novice. With the ledges they could rest and recover between sections of cliff. She gauged the distance. It was maybe two hundred feet to the top. A tough climb, but if they could escape the canyon without leaving trace of their passage, they would leave their hunters clueless.

Deciding they'd rested enough, Pela rose and approached the wall for a better look. There was no question it would be dangerous. Despite the shelves, a single slip might still send them tumbling the entire way to the bottom. They could not afford mistakes. She didn't need to ask Ruebyn to know he'd never climbed a cliff before.

Even so, she continued her inspection. The ledges ran horizontal to one another, but looking back the way they'd come, she realised they were not in line with the valley floor. The ground fell away steeply from where she stood, so that the height of each ledge grew greater relative to the path.

Her heart lifted as a new plan came to her. Maybe they didn't need to climb all the way to the top. Each ledge was only a few feet wide, but it was enough to negotiate if they were careful. They might be able to backtrack down the canyon using one of the ledges, while their hunters passed unknowing below.

Ruebyn was just waking when Pela walked back to where he lay. A smile touched his lips when he saw her, but it quickly vanished when she explained her plan.

"You can't be serious?"

❧ 23 ❧

"We can't outrun them," Pela snapped at Ruebyn, "not before daybreak."

She didn't like the plan any more than he did. Heights were not one of her many fears, but she had no desire to die falling from one of those fragile ledges. But she could see no other alternatives. There were only a few hours of darkness left. Even in the shadows of the canyon, she would not last long in the day, if it proved as bright as yesterday.

The stone would leave no trace of their passage, but once they were further down the canyon, they would have to be as silent as mice. If their pursuers heard them, Pela and Ruebyn would have nowhere left to go.

"Come on," Pela said quickly, before she lost her nerve. "If we can get to the third shelf, I think we'll be okay. It looks the widest. You go first, and I'll help your feet find the holds from below."

Ruebyn's wide eyes stared at her, but the time for hesitation was over. At least the moon was bright enough for them to see. He approached the wall as though it were his mortal enemy and took hold of the rock. The thirty feet to the first ledge were the easiest, the cliff sloping slightly away from them, so they barely had to use their arms to make the climb. It still cost precious time though, as they had to take care not to leave any scuffs or broken rocks that might give them away.

Reaching the first ledge, they took a moment to gather their strength. But with time in short supply, they soon pressed on. Here the wall was steeper, but the sandstone was well-worn, offering plenty of holds if you knew where to look for them. Unfortunately, they might as well have been invisible to Ruebyn. Pela was no expert herself, but she did her best to direct him to each new perch. She could do nothing to help with his hands, but she braced his feet with her palms each time he moved, ensuring his boots did not slip.

Even so, Ruebyn was panting hard by the time they reached the second ledge. One look at his pale face and Pela knew he would not make it to the third. He was too exhausted, too inexperienced. If they attempted it, he would fall.

She glanced down the canyon, but in the gloom there was no telling whether they were high enough to pass unnoticed by their pursuers. It would depend on how many torches the hunters had, whether they looked up.

It was going to be a mighty gamble.

"Come on," she murmured, drawing Ruebyn carefully to his feet. "This will have to do."

Ruebyn nodded, though he knew she'd been hoping to make the third shelf. Pela took the lead, heading back the way they'd come but now some sixty feet above the canyon floor. The ledge was narrower than the one above and she had to take care with each step, lest her crumbling boots slip from the sandstone. Ahead she glimpsed the distant flicker of torchlight. She was terrified of knocking loose a rock at the wrong moment.

They followed the ledge through the darkness, their way lit only by the cold light of the moon. It hung in the sky like a silver shield, their only hope of safely navigating the tiny shelf. But as the orange glow of flames drew nearer, Pela realised it might also be their doom. They were some hundred feet above the ground now, but if anyone looked up the two climbers would be clearly visible in the moonlight.

A glance at the cliff-face above revealed it was just as sheer in this section of the canyon. She could probably have managed it, but not Ruebyn. Only closer to where they had entered the canyon had the rain and wind eroded the rock enough that they might both climb it. They needed to wait for their pursuers to pass below before they could get that far.

She could do nothing to help Ruebyn now, for the ledge was too narrow for her to turn around. Pela had told him to place his feet where she did, but it would only take one mistake to send him plunging to the canyon floor.

Fear touched Pela as the brilliance of a torch appeared around the next bend in the canyon. Her heart jilted to a stop and she gripped the cliff-face with one hand, waving for Ruebyn to stop. His eyes were glued to his feet and he did not notice the gesture. Their pursuers were just fifty yards away now—any movement would be sure to draw their attention.

"*Stop!*" Pela hissed as quietly as she could.

Ruebyn's head jerked up, his eyes widening as he finally saw the orange glow. He froze, his hand shooting out to grasp at the cliff-face. But the rocks here were slick and the ledge narrow, and he missed by an inch. Panicked, he staggered another step, trying to catch his balance. Pela held her breath as his foot slid perilously close to the edge, but the Gods or his Saviour must have blessed them, and Ruebyn managed to finally catch himself.

The breath whistled between Pela's teeth as she crouched, gesturing for Ruebyn to do the same. The moon still shone in all its brilliance; there was not a cloud in the sky. They must be as small as possible, and hope their pursuers did not look up.

Ruebyn offered a shaky smile and crouched where he stood, not daring to move any closer to the cliff-face in case he slipped. Pela was glad. If he fell, it would be over for both of them.

The flickering glow marched steadily up the canyon. Squinting against the glare, Pela made out a dozen shadows beneath half as many torches. Too many to stand a chance against, even if they'd been armed and in any shape for a fight. Only their wits could save them from so many. Pela closed her eyes and prayed to whatever deity remained to watch over them.

The soft *crunch* of boots on stone echoed from the cliffs as their pursuers neared. Voices whispered in the darkness, though she could not make out what was being said. Pela guessed none of them were too pleased to be in the mountains at night, with all the perils that entailed. There weren't many Baronians in these parts, but she still hadn't forgotten the animal tracks they'd crossed earlier.

They belonged to a Feline, or maybe a Raptor—either could tear a man in two. Even those below would struggle to defeat such a beast, let alone herself and the unskilled Ruebyn. She doubted he'd ever even held a sword—not that she'd been any better before starting this journey.

Then again, maybe his noble parents had trained him in the martial arts. Pela knew next to nothing about his youth, other than his story about the courtyard. Was there anything else to know? Sadness touched her at the thought of such a closeted existence. She'd roamed the walls and hillslopes of Skystead at will. A life spent surrounded by walls must have been almost as much a prison as the one she'd just escaped.

Well…not quite.

Flames glinted off steel armour as the hunters passed below. There was no doubt now—it was the Knight that had come for her in the mines. She could not understand how they'd been tracked so easily. Was that another skill the Lonians had developed with their strange engineers? She swallowed, the collar pressing hard against her throat, and she touched a finger to it. Could it be helping them to find her? She prayed not, for she'd already tried to crack it open with a rock—to no avail.

Pela held her breath as the group passed below, but not a soul looked up. Slowly the hunters continued through the canyon past them. Letting out a heavy sigh, Pela was about to stand, when a sharp *crack* rang from the rockface. She swung around in time to watch cracks spiderweb outwards from where Ruebyn crouched.

There was another *crack*, then abruptly the ledge gave way. Ruebyn leapt for the wall but in the darkness his fingers missed the holds, and crying out, he tumbled back. It seemed he would fall all the way to the bottom—but at the last moment his hand flashed out, catching a jagged edge. A scream tore the night as the rocks sliced his flesh, but he did not let go.

Pela stood frozen, too shocked to act. Shout echoed around them, followed by the crash of boots against gravel. Their pursuers were returning, racing down the gorge towards them. There was no way they would miss Pela standing on the ledge this time, nor the young man clinging to the cliff-face for dear life.

With an effort Pela would not have thought him capable of, Ruebyn almost managed to haul himself back up to safety. But at the last moment his strength gave in and he slumped back, only an elbow propped over the lip holding him in place. His terrified eyes searched the darkness, finding Pela standing across the gap the landslide had left.

"Pela!" he gasped.

A tremor shook her. She looked from him to the cliff-face above their heads. It would be an easy climb for her. She could be over the top before the Knight and his followers reached them. Without Ruebyn to slow her down, she might just get away. She gathered herself, trying to summon the courage to make the leap.

Ruebyn must have seen the look on her face. His mouth fell open, as though to beg her not to leave him. But no words came out, and after a second he pressed his lips tight together again. Tears shone in his eyes as he glanced down.

Pela followed his gaze. Shouts echoed up from below. The hackles rose on her neck as she caught the pungent scent of their oil lanterns. The light hurt her eyes, but she could see the frantic gestures the hunters made as they reached the bottom of the cliff. Even if she saved him, there was no way they could both get away.

Their eyes met and Ruebyn clenched his jaw. "Go," he said. "I'll say you held me against my will."

Pela didn't need to point out the absurdity of the idea. She had no weapons and in her half-starved state, Ruebyn had a good forty pounds on her. And even if she had beat him in a fight, there was no way she could have forced him to come.

"*Go!*" he said again.

Another tremor shook Pela. She put a hand to the cliff-face, readying herself for the climb. The shouts grew louder, the glow brightening to illuminate the scarlet of the sandstone. Within minutes they would scale the cliff and take him. Then Ruebyn's life would be worth less than the lowliest of slaves. They would not let him die easily, not so long as she was free.

The breath left her in a rush. Without giving Ruebyn a chance to object, she leapt across the gap in the ledge. His mouth dropped as she landed beside him, but wisely he said nothing. Grasping him by the back of his shirt, Pela mustered her strength and heaved. With much scrambling of boots and puffing, she hauled him up, until they were both crouched on the ledge again.

"Why did you do that?" Ruebyn gasped. "Now they're—"

"Don't say it," Pela croaked, closing her eyes.

Her chest swelled as she drew in a breath. She struggled to keep the terror from her face, but her legs were shaking so badly that if she stood, Pela was sure she would have tumbled over the edge.

The scuffing of shoes on stone whispered from below as

the hunters began to climb. A shudder raced down Pela's spine as she imagined their knives, the pain they would inflict for her defiance. She had killed an Elder—and a Knight—and they would ensure her death was a long time coming. Or maybe they would simply lock her up as a slave again, with a new overseer to inflict his daily cruelty, for the lack of food and strength and light to slowly waste her away.

Pela stood suddenly, teetering on the edge. A shrill keening came from her throat, her every hair standing on end. She would not go back, not now or ever. What madness had made her go back for Ruebyn? Now it was too late to flee. She could see the hunters, just a few feet below, their eyes aglow in the light of their lanterns. Even if Pela ran, in her weakened state, she would be overhauled within a mile.

"Pela, what are you doing?" Ruebyn gasped.

Ignoring him, Pela stared down at the sheer drop. The first of the hunters were drawing close. Thickly-muscled and dressed in leather armour, the man was no Knight, but then he didn't need to be to doom Pela. He was climbing away to their right, so that they could not keep him from gaining the ledge. Others were just a few feet behind, moving to cut them off from either direction.

Another shudder shook Pela as she fixed her gaze on the canyon floor. Dotted with boulders, it was some hundred feet below. A dozen watchers looked back at her, and she closed her eyes. It was high enough to kill her, if she…

Pela swallowed, not wanting to finish the thought, to think about what she was about to do. Letting out her breath, she released the wall, and swayed on the edge.

"Pela!" a voice carried from below.

Her eyes snapped open and she stared down at the silhouetted figures, searching, seeking…

Genevieve's face appeared amongst the hunters, lantern held high. Her eyes were wide, pleading.

"Stop!"

✣ 24 ✣

Caledan shivered as he stepped into the queen's apartments, the cold of the dungeons still clinging to him. Rubbing his wrists, he crossed the room and stepped out onto the marble balcony. Sunlight greeted him and he closed his eyes, savouring the feeling of the sun on his face. It was almost enough to banish the creeping horror he'd felt below. Almost.

Footsteps came from behind him as Marianne stepped out into the light. She joined him, leaning against the marble baluster and looking out across the city. The granite and marble rooftops of Ardath spread out below. Many of the mansions still sported the gold and silver enamelling from ages past, when the wealth of Trolan and Lonian trade had flowed through Plorsea's borders. For others, time and neglect had left the marble tarnished, and the precious furnishings had long since been pawned off to see their owners through the hard times.

Yet despite such efforts, many buildings now stood empty, their doors and windows boarded up, the owners fled in search of greener pastures. For Caledan, the sight of Ardath's degradation was yet another reminder of Braidon's failures.

"I still don't understand," he said finally, turning to the queen. "What do you want from me?"

Marianne's eyes were fixed on some distant point, far out beyond the walls of Ardath and across the great lake, but at his voice she blinked, slowly focusing on him.

"Servo spoke the truth—I am alone here," she murmured. "I knew before the…event in the dungeons that the Elders had betrayed me, but I needed to know the extent of their duplicity. I cannot trust my Queen's Guard, cannot trust anyone—not with the life of my son. So I would have you serve me."

It took a moment for the woman's words to sink in. Caledan blinked, then started to laugh. "You think you can trust *me*? After I tried to kill you?"

The queen's cheeks crinkled as she shared a conspiring smile. "I am not mad, I promise you!"

Caledan's laughter faded as he realised she was serious. "Why would I serve you?"

Marianne shrugged. Returning to the apartment, she pulled a bell beside her desk. A servant appeared as she faced Caledan. "You must be hungry?"

Caledan's stomach gave an audible rumble. He hadn't eaten for more than a day. The queen laughed and waved for the servant to bring food and drink. As the man departed, she wandered across to the sofa and seated herself. She patted the cushion beside her, but occupied by his hunger, Caledan ignored the gesture.

"I believe you are a simple man, Caledan," Marianne said then. "Despite your claims of friends and loyalty, you have abandoned Braidon, in what is surely his time of greatest need. In the end you are still a sellsword, your loyalty given to whoever offers the most gold. And I would pay handsomely indeed."

Caledan's head jerked up. He stared at the queen, turning her words over in his mind. Perhaps what she'd said had once been true, though even in his youth that one over-arching goal had driven his every decision. He had accumulated wealth and skills, a reputation as a formidable foe, but always he was plotting to achieve his own ends. If not for the peace treaty between Lonia and Plorsea, he might have gotten close to Braidon and had his revenge long ago. Without a war to fight, a sellsword had had little chance of coming within a hundred yards of Braidon.

"You're wrong," he said finally. "My motives have never been simple."

"Oh?" Marianne gave a knowing smile. "Pray tell me, I am intrigued."

"It was a means to an end," he admitted. Taking the seat beside her, he looked her in the eye. "You are not the only one with a grudge against the *good* King Braidon."

Marianne arched one thin eyebrow, but when she said nothing, Caledan continued:

"I have loathed him for thirty years, since the day his sister stole the magic from this world, and doomed my mother to death. Alana destroyed my family, while her brother inherited a kingdom." He found himself staring into Marianne's sapphire eyes, seeking to pierce the carefully constructed veil she held about herself. "I made it my life's undertaking to set the balance right."

"A noble cause, revenge." Marianne pursed her lips. "Perhaps you are a more complicated man than I first thought. But why then do you align yourself against me? Why save Braidon's life, when I could have taken revenge for both of us?"

A spark lit in her eyes as she spoke of her husband, and for just a moment Caledan saw her hatred, a mirror of his own. He swallowed, but before he could respond, the door cracked open and the servant reappeared, a silver platter in hand. Crossing the room, he set it down on the coffee table beside the sofa, bowed, and vanished back outside.

Another rumble came from Caledan's stomach as he eyed the spread laid out on the platter. There were a half a dozen different cheeses—some streaked with blue veins, others soft and creamy, and still more dotted with nuts and sliced fruits. Saltines and olives and pickled peppers had been laid around the edge of the board. A second plate held enough cakes to satisfy even the worst sweet tooth.

Chuckling, Marianne lifted the pot of tea and poured them each a cup, then gestured to Caledan. "Help yourself, sellsword," she said. "I hope it might balance my lack of hospitality earlier. I wanted your imprisonment to be convincing."

It was convincing enough for me, Caledan thought with a shudder, remembering the rat watching him from the shadows.

But he said nothing and did as she bid, combining a piece of blue with one of the fruit cheeses. Caledan would have preferred a steak, but he was too hungry to be fussy, and the rich flavours of the cheeses were pleasant enough. The hot tea finally helped to banish the last of the cold from the dungeons.

"So, you were about to explain why my husband still

lives?" Marianne said when he finally sat back, the worst of his hunger sated.

Caledan sighed. "Because Devon bade me protect him."

"Despite your hatred for the man?"

Caledan looked away. "Ay. Despite everything. But Devon was my friend. I could not refuse him."

"A true friend would not have asked such a thing of you."

"He believed Braidon was a good man, that he could stop you—and the Order—from taking over Plorsea."

Marianne's laughter peeled like a bell. "Then the hammerman was more a fool than I thought." Her eyes narrowed. "But what do you believe, Caledan? You have travelled with Braidon, fought beside him, saved him from my blade. What do you think of the man?"

This queen's words recalled memories of Dragon Country, and Caledan saw again Braidon on his knees, begging for Caledan to end his suffering. Just thinking of the fallen king filled Caledan with disgust. How had he ever thought Braidon a worthy enemy? The man was a worm, and Caledan should have put him down there and then, before his incompetence brought more misery to the Three Nations.

"He does not deserve to live," Marianne murmured. Edging closer to him on the sofa, she placed a hand on Caledan's knee. "You know that is the truth."

Caledan sighed. "On that, at least, we agree." He glanced at the queen, his lips tightening. "But I cannot go against Devon's final wishes."

"Devon was wrong. Perhaps Braidon was noble once, but he lost his way long ago."

"And what about you?" Caledan hissed, leaning away

from her. "Whatever evil Braidon did against you, however much you hate him for your arranged marriage, you cannot say the same for Devon. He was a good man, who lived his life in the light. You killed him for it."

To his surprise, Marianne could not meet his gaze. "You cannot understand how long I had waited for that moment in the Cove," she whispered. "To cast off the role of loyal wife, of obedient daughter. How I hated my father for sending me away, and Braidon for taking me. Then, in my moment of triumph, the *hero* sought to stand in my way."

"You tried to murder his daughter, his *granddaughter*, everyone he ever loved."

Marianne stood suddenly at that. She walked to the desk and leaned against it. Her hands turned white, she clutched the wood so tightly. "I told you I regretted that decision, but it had to be made. The Elders wanted their Great Sacrifice, and you have seen how little control I have over them. Besides, I needed that power to free myself from their control."

"Even at the expense of innocent lives?" Caledan asked. He rose and approached her, their eyes meeting across the desk.

"What are a few innocent lives to the future of our nations?" Marianne asked, though there was a haunted look to her face.

"*Everything*," Caledan whispered, remembering Devon's conversation with Braidon, how the hammerman had pleaded for the king to help save his daughter. At least there was one honourable deed in Braidon's murky past.

Marianne slumped into her chair. "What would you have had me do?" she whispered. "I could not save them, once Servo and his fellows took them. I would only have succeeded in making myself powerless, ensured I was never more than a pawn in someone else's game."

"You are still a pawn," Caledan snapped. "You cannot even stop their Knights from slaughtering your citizens."

"Then *help* me!" Marianne hissed, coming to her feet. The scent of her filled his nostrils and she stepped in close, eyes aglow. "Help me stand against Servo. Help me free this city from his Knights." She hesitated, her eyes softening. "Help me protect my son."

Caledan stared down at the woman, wondering again why he was there, why he had been spared while so many others had been doomed. Even now he might have reached out and throttled the life from her. Almost unbidden, his hand rose, but she made no move to stop him now, only stood in silence as he wrapped his fingers around her pale throat.

She swallowed, the slightest shimmer of fear appearing in her eyes, but still she did not oppose him. Perhaps her powers had been spent in the conflict with Servo. Caledan did not know, but he sensed in that moment she was in his power, that this was his opportunity to free Plorsea from her evil.

Then he thought again of Servo, of his words in the dungeons. If Marianne died, who would take her place? Did Braidon have the steel to take control of Plorsea again? It was a foolish thought, immediately dismissed. So who then?

It would be the boy, their son. The Elders would lift him to the kingship and rule in his place. Then there would be no one to stand against their vile plans. All Caledan would succeed in doing was to replace one evil with something far worse.

Letting out a long sigh, he released Marianne.

"Well, sellsword?" she whispered. "Will you be the Queen's Champion?"

A shiver lifted the hairs on Caledan's neck. His mother's words whispered from the past, telling him of their family's history, of an ancestor who had once stood beside the Plorsean King. He was said to have been the greatest swordsman ever seen, had served as the King's Champion for nigh a decade. But the coming of the Tsar had cast their family low, and by Caledan's time, the story was just that—a fiction of the past, an imagination, for all he knew.

Yet as a child, he had dreamed of following in his ancestor's footsteps, of lifting his family back into the ranks of nobility. Those dreams had died with his mother, but now they rose unbidden, resurrected by the queen's words—if only he had the courage to take what Marianne offered.

He dropped to one knee before her, bowing his head. "I will be your Champion, My Queen."

Stepping in close, Marianne traced her fingers across his stumbled chin, lifting him back to his feet. "You need never kneel before me, Caledan."

He stood there in silence as her sapphire eyes inspected him, as though only now wondering whether he could truly be trusted. Then her face softened and the queen smiled, the mask falling away to reveal the woman beneath the façade.

"Thank you," she whispered.

25

Red seared across Pela's vision as the steel boot descended, catching her in the side of the head and sending her tumbling across the jagged stones. A cry tore from Pela's lips as her tormentor laughed, then came after her, driving another blow into her ribcage.

The breath exploded between Pela's teeth and she collapsed, choking, to the ground. A groan rattled from her throat. She dug her fingers into the stones and tried to drag herself away, but there was no escape. Her scream echoed from the cliffs as the Knight grabbed her by the hair and pulled her up.

"Filthy witch!" he snarled.

Pela lashed out with a fist, but the blow bounced harmlessly off of the Knight's armour. He laughed in her face.

"You thought I would let you escape?" he growled. "That after you murdered my brother, I would not stop until I had your cold, dead body lying at my feet?

He didn't wait for Pela to reply. Instead, he hurled her at a nearby boulder. Pela's hands windmilled but there was nothing to slow her flight, and she struck the rock with an awful *thud*. Something tore inside her, agony stealing away her breath. She managed only the faintest moan as she slid to the ground.

Struggling to her knees, Pela looked for her attacker, but the Knight had found another victim. She flinched as Ruebyn's voice echoed her earlier scream. She could see no sign of Genevieve, but the woman was here, somewhere.

Why had the huntress stopped Pela from jumping? She could have been free of this torment, free of everything. All she'd needed to do was hurl herself from that ledge…but instead Gen's voice had brought her fear rushing back, and Pela had stood frozen as the hunters climbed, submitting meekly with Ruebyn when they reached the ledge.

Pela prayed Genevieve had a plan; otherwise she was doomed. Her mind whirled, wondering at her fate. Would they sacrifice her to the altar of Alana, or sentence her to toil again in the darkness for weeks or months or years? The thought made Pela shake with fear and her eyes flashed around the canyon, seeking out the huntress.

Ruebyn's screams broke off as the Knight hammered an iron fist into his face. He fell to the stones like a dead weight. The Knight towered over him, his shoulders heaving from the exertion, while Ruebyn lay still. Pela's heart lurched and for a moment she thought the boy was dead, that she had gone back for nothing. Then his chest moved and his eyelids flickered, and she realised he was only unconscious.

Pela quickly lowered her eyes, not wanting to draw the Knight's attention, but she was too late. Metallic laughter rattled from the helmet as he approached and crouched alongside her.

"I should slay you now," he murmured, "but the Elders

have marked you for the Saviour. You and your mother. Where is she?"

"I don't know," Pela croaked truthfully. She stared into the hateful helmet, wondering who hid behind it. The Knights never removed them amongst strangers, but she could just make out the beady eyes beyond the visor. The sight offered no hope though, and she swallowed. "We were separated in the Cove."

"Pity," the Knight replied, straightening. "I would have been richly rewarded. No matter; the witch will come for her daughter."

Pela's stomach churned at the thought of her mother walking into a trap. She cursed herself again, and Genevieve too. If only she'd chosen to escape, or fallen to her death, Pela could have at least spared Kryssa. The Knight was right—her mother would come the second she heard Pela was held by the Order.

"Slave!" the Knight bellowed. A figure stepped from the crowd. Pela's stomach twisted into knots. It was Genevieve. "Secure them. The rest of you, set the camp. We'll rest here until midday. I am tired of walking."

"Yes, sir," Genevieve said meekly, her head bowed.

The rest of the party moved quickly, hauling off their packs and dragging out canvas tents to pitch. The slope was uneven and the stones jagged, a poor place for a camp, but not a soul objected to the Knight's command. He alone wore the steel armour of the Order—the rest were mere followers, squires in training and retainers, waiting for their chance to ascend the holy ranks.

Stones were swept from the flattest section of the valley floor and a larger tent set using ropes and metal poles. The

Knight sat watching from a boulder until it was ready, then rose and disappeared within.

Genevieve approached them, her face a careful mask, and took a loop of rope from her shoulder. "Hold out your arms," she said, her voice as blank as her face.

Pela swallowed, but did as she was told. As Genevieve went to work binding their arms and legs, she stared into the woman's eyes, wondering what game the huntress was playing.

"How did you find us?" Pela asked finally, when she was sure the others were occupied. Despite her efforts, she could not keep the anger from her voice. "I thought we were free."

The slightest flicker in Genevieve's eyes revealed her irritation. "You left tracks any imbecile could follow." She scowled. "You didn't think they'd check the cavern? Once we found where you'd left the pool, they could have followed you, even without me. Don't worry though, I'll think of something."

Pela's heart lurched. "*What?*" she hissed, struggling to keep her voice low.

Genevieve's eyes widened at Pela's anger. "I said I'll think of something to save you."

Pela couldn't believe her ears—Genevieve didn't have a plan at all. Now *she* would suffer for it, would be beaten and tortured and slaughtered like an animal, all because she'd put her trust in this woman. There would be no escaping this place. Even without their bindings, they were surrounded by the Knight's loyal followers. The anger bubbled up inside her as she stared at Gen, all the rage and frustration of the past weeks, the hopelessness.

"I knew I should not have trusted you," she said coldly.

"I don't know what my mother sees in you. It must be that you're both such great liars. I never even suspected you were her lover."

Gen rocked back on her haunches as though struck. Her mouth hung open but no words came out. Pela spoke into the silence.

"Lesson learned. Go away, Genevieve. We don't need you. We never did."

For a moment it seemed the huntress would refuse. She crouched, staring at Pela, eyes shining, lips curled downwards in agonised indecision. Then her eyes slid closed, and she turned away.

Pela watched Genevieve walk away, immediately regretting what she'd said. But she could not bring herself to call the woman back, to apologise. After all, her words had been the truth. The woman had spent weeks in Pela's company without ever mentioning her relationship with Kryssa.

Even so, her heart ached with the sudden loneliness. For a second, Genevieve's presence had been a comfort, the last hope to which she could cling. But Pela could not afford such fantasies now, not with the cold reality of the Knight looming over them.

Ruebyn still lay unconscious beside her, but Genevieve had bound him as securely as Pela. She felt a pang of guilt for having dragged him with her, for convincing him of her mountaineering skills, then failing so gravely. Now he would die alongside her, or perhaps sooner, once the Knight realised he did not need to keep Ruebyn alive.

Crouching beside her companion, Pela turned him on his side, wishing he would wake. As though bidden by her thoughts, Ruebyn's eyelids flickered and he groaned.

"Quiet," Pela hissed, putting her lips to his ear. "Don't draw any attention to us."

"What's happening?" Ruebyn croaked.

"I failed," Pela whispered, unable to keep the despair from her voice. "I'm sorry I brought you into this mess, Ruebyn, truly I am."

Ruebyn must have been terrified, but to his credit, it did not show. He glanced around before sitting up. "Where's the Knight?" he asked.

"In his tent."

Nodding, Ruebyn rubbed his jaw where the man had struck him. "So what do we do now?"

The other hunters had set up makeshift shelters of their own, though theirs were only pieces of canvas tied to boulders or the cliff-face. They would provide some semblance of protection against the elements, although not in the face of a storm. Unfortunately, the sky remained clear. A guard had been set to watch either end of the canyon.

Stones crunched as a man approached them. Pela shrank away, but he said nothing, only sat on a nearby boulder. Eyes fixed on the two prisoners, he pulled out a knife and whetstone, and started sharpening the weapon.

Pela shuffled back against the boulder. They were in the centre of the camp—no chance of sneaking away with the three guards.

"Nothing," she finally said in answer to Ruebyn's question. A tremor slid down her spine as the wind whistled through the canyon. It had changed direction and now seemed to be funnelling directly between the cliffs. "I'm cold, come here," she added without thinking.

Ruebyn obeyed, shuffling closer until their arms pressed together. Pela shivered again, though this time it was at his touch, from his warmth. Suddenly she was glad he was there. She didn't want to face what came next alone.

They sat there together, watching the guard watch them, the shrill grinding of steel on whetstone setting their nerves on end. Pela longed for her father's sword, if only to die with it in hand, but it had been lost in Malevolent Cove.

Despair touched her. Who was she kidding? She couldn't have even taken on the single watchman. After all, who was she but an inexperienced child? Who had she ever beaten in a fair fight?

She sobbed as the pain from her beating redoubled. Pulling her legs to her chest, she sank her head into her knees to keep Ruebyn from seeing the tears. He noticed anyway, awkwardly giving her shoulder a squeeze. She was relieved he did not speak. His words could offer no solace. She had doomed them both.

The night grew late, the first rays of sunlight catching on the distant peaks. Her eyes began to water, but the pain was not half as bad as the day before. She stared at the orange glow, willing her eyes to adjust. She did not want to miss a single second of the sunrise, not if she was doomed to return to the darkness. The collar grew tight around her throat. Pela wished she'd at least been able to remove it. It chafed her skin with every movement, a constant reminder of her fate.

Ruebyn's breathing deepened as he drifted into sleep, but exhausted as she was, Pela resisted the call. Snuggling closer to his warmth, her gaze roamed the canyon. The twisted cliffs turned a brilliant scarlet as the sun rose higher, and the soft gurgling of the stream mingled with the whistling of the wind. The rest of the camp slept. Pela could almost imagine the two of them alone on the mountainside, the rest of the world a distant memory.

A flicker of movement from the cliffs drew her attention, but she could see nothing against the red rock. She frowned, scanning the ledges, sure it had been *something*. Perhaps a bird or a rodent come to investigate the smells of the camp.

Nothing.

Pela was about to look away when the flicker came again. Her heart lurched in her chest—then crashed to an abrupt halt as she saw the shadow amidst the rocks. Her mouth opened but terror robbed her of voice. Lifting one trembling hand, she pointed a finger.

The guard saw and cast a quick glance back, but he could not see the camouflaged beast. Scowling, he faced her.

"What are you doing?" he snarled.

Pela's mouth opened and closed, but still no sound came out. Ruebyn had slumped alongside her but now he stirred, his eyes flickering open. A smile touched his lips, but seeing her outstretched arm, his gaze followed to where she pointed.

"Feline!" The word exploded from him.

The scream broke the spell. They staggered to their feet, but the bindings on their ankles and hands almost sent them crashing down again. Panicked voices came from around the camp as others heard Ruebyn's scream, but the guard would not be fooled. He took a step towards them, dagger raised.

"You little ba—"

An almighty *roar* cut him off. It echoed through the canyon like an avalanche, silencing even the loudest screams. Pela watched with detached horror as the Feline leapt from its ledge, the enormous body rippling with sheer muscle. The scarlet fur shifted, changing from red to yellow like quicksilver.

One of the camp followers had just emerged from his makeshift shelter when the beast landed beside him. He barely had time to scream before it was on him. One swat of a giant paw smashed the man to the ground. Groaning, his leg twisted at a terrible angle, he scrambled desperately for the hilt of his sword. The Feline lunged, its awful jaws stretching wide to close around his head.

There followed a sickening *crunch*, like a melon splitting on the rocks—then silence. A rotten stench filled the canyon and the man lay still, but the beast was not satisfied. It swung around, yellow eyes aglow in the morning sun, seeking out a fresh victim. Pela cried out as the twin globes fell on her. She tried to stumble back, but her bindings caught on a rock and sent her crashing to the dirt.

Screams came from across the camp as two retainers drew their swords and charged. Distracted, the Feline turned to meet them. Moving faster than thought, it leapt. One second the men were racing towards it, the next, a yellowed blur smashed the leader from his feet. A scream pierced the air as fangs sank into flesh, followed by the sharp *crack* of breaking bones.

Horrified, the second warrior staggered back, sword clutched before him. The Feline tore another chunk from its victim, then spun as the man's foot knocked loose a rock. The golden eyes followed the stone as it tumbled down the canyon, then flicked back to the man. He cried out, thrusting at it with his blade. The Feline batted aside his blows, then tore out his throat with a single swipe of its claws.

Blood gushed down the man's chest as he stumbled away, clutching at the wound. His eyes were wide, filled with fear, but he did not have long to live. With a roar, the Feline was upon him, jaws descending, blood and bone and flesh devoured.

Pela watched the events unfold in horror, unable to think, to move. This was a creature of death, a beast from the days of Archon, that even powerful Magickers had once feared to battle. What chance did any of them have against such a creature?

"Quickly!" A cry drew Pela's attention back to her surroundings. Genevieve had appeared beside their guard, longbow in hand. She grabbed their guard by the shoulder and thrust him at the beast. "While it's distracted!"

The huntress nocked an arrow as the guard glanced back, terrified. The sight of the longbow seemed to reassure him though, and turning, he rushed at the beast. Other attendants were also converging on the creature now, but their leather armour meant little before its ferocity.

As soon as the man turned away, Genevieve dropped her bow and drew a knife from her boot. She slashed Pela's bindings, then Ruebyn's. Retrieving her weapon, she glanced at the Feline. Another retainer lay dead already, his face replaced by a mangled caricature of a man.

"Come on," Gen hissed, tossing a pack down beside them. "*Quickly!*"

"Gen!" Pela gasped, lost for words. She stared at the woman, mouth hanging open, wanting to say so many things, to grab her and hug her and repent her horrible words. But there was no time for any of that, and swallowing her fear, she managed only, "*Thank you!*"

Gen's jaw clenched and she nodded, though Pela could

still see the hurt in the woman's eyes. She prayed there would be time for apologies later. Sweeping up the pack, she pushed Ruebyn ahead of her.

"Where?" he cried, his face white with fear.

"Up the canyon," Genevieve snapped. "Now, before…"

She didn't need to finish the sentence. Not ten yards from where they stood a desperate battle was taking place between beast and man. Whether the Feline emerged victorious, or the hunters, neither would hold any qualms about finishing off Pela and her friends.

A roar came from the Knight's tent as he emerged fully armoured, broadsword in hand. The Feline swatted aside another retainer and turned to watch him come, yellow eyes aglow. Its jaws opened wide and its roar sent men stumbling backwards. It leapt to meet the Knight.

Pela turned away as a crash echoed up the valley, Knight and beast coming together. A dead man lay nearby and her eyes caught on his sword. She swept it up and immediately felt better with the weapon in hand. Genevieve was already moving off, arrow still nocked to her bow, and they hurried to keep up. The guard at the top of the camp had abandoned his post to fight the beast, and the three of them passed by unnoticed.

Another roar came from behind. Pela looked back and saw the Knight go down, Feline atop him. Its claws raked his chest with a squeal of metal, but could not pierce the heavy steel. His fist came up, still clutching the broadsword, and drove the blade through the beast's chest. An awful scream echoed up the canyon but the Feline did not fall. It renewed its attack, rending and tearing with claw and tooth.

Pela looked away and sent up a prayer to the Three Gods that the two would kill one another. She could not imagine the Knight surviving such an encounter, but nor did she savour the thought of the Feline stalking them through the mountains. The sounds of battle followed them up the narrow canyon.

Only when they were a mile from the camp did silence finally return to the dawn.

❧   26   ❧

Pela, Genevieve and Ruebyn walked for the rest of the day in silence, each too exhausted, too shocked by the violence of the morning to speak. Pela's mind kept returning to the slaughter, repeating again and again the image of a man's chest being torn open, the *crunch* of his skull as those awful jaws closed around it. In her exhausted state, she imagined the beast stalking them, a dark presence brooding in the back of her mind that would not go away.

She thanked the Gods for Genevieve, for acting so quickly, for scooping up a discarded pack and spiriting them away. If not for the huntress, they would all have been dead by now. Pela had seen the fierce intelligence in the eyes of the Feline, its hunger, its hatred. It would have slaughtered them all.

All the worse then, what Pela had said to the woman. In her anger and despair she had lashed out, and now she could not take back the words. There was a chasm between herself and Genevieve now, a distance created by hurt and mistrust, one Pela did not know how to heal.

Ruebyn said little either. Pela wondered what he thought of this fresh turn of events. He trudged along beside her, eyes fixed to the ground, uncomplaining though he must have been at the end of his strength.

In the aftermath of the slaughter, Pela had at least one thing to celebrate. The sun now hung bright above the clifftops, and while her eyes were aching, the pain was bearable. She could see! The relief was so great she might have cried, if she had not spent so many of the last few days in tears.

For hours they followed Genevieve through the winding canyon. She seemed to have a six sense when it came to the myriad of corridors, unerringly choosing the turns as they came to them. Not once did they encounter a dead end, and finally they emerged back out into the open, finding themselves in another broad valley bounded by rocky cliffs.

A braided river threaded its way across the plain, its path broken and twisted by the giant boulders littering the valley floor. A few yards downriver, an enormous mound of earth spanned the gulley, barring half the rivers path and diverting several of the channels down the canyon from which they'd emerged. They stood on a gentle slope, though behind them the pitch increased, eventually becoming a cliff-face that stretched five hundred feet above their heads.

"It's a glacial valley," Ruebyn said suddenly. When they only stared at him blankly, he smiled guiltily and went on. "My teachers say great rivers of ice once flowed through these mountains. Their weight carved broad avenues through the rock, then later when the glaciers retreated, they left these valleys."

"And how does this help us?" Gen snapped.

Ruebyn's mouth opened and closed, before he managed to stammer. "It…doesn't?"

Genevieve snorted. Her eyes turned on Pela. "And where were we going?"

Pela swallowed. "I…Trola," she said shortly.

"Terrible plan," Genevieve replied. Ruebyn looked like he was going to agree, but the huntress went on. "But probably the best we've got at this point."

Without offering another word, she set off up the valley. Pela offered Ruebyn an apologetic glance. She had created this problem; now she needed to fix it. Squaring her shoulders, she chased after Gen, leaving Ruebyn to catch up.

"Gen," she said, drawing alongside the huntress. "I… I'm sorry, okay? I didn't mean what I said."

"You did," Gen replied sharply, her eyes fixed on the path ahead. The gravels were larger here, shifting unexpectedly beneath their weight, and they had to take care where they stepped the unstable ground send them tumbling into the river.

Pela sighed. "I suppose I did, in a way," she murmured, "but my anger wasn't meant for you. It's…my mother kept so much from me! How my father died, that they were both members of the King's Guard, *you*. And in Malevolent Cove…I never had a chance to yell at her."

"So you yelled at me," Genevieve sighed, finally glancing at Pela. "You were right to be angry. Kryssa kept her secrets close."

"You too," Pela said, though this time a smile touched her lips. "All those weeks, and I never guessed you were dating my mother!"

"Am I?" Genevieve asked, eyes wide with innocence.

Pela raised an eyebrow and the huntress chuckled. "Okay, I suppose I am."

"You didn't think to tell me that, back when we set off from Skystead?"

Genevieve wore a knowing smile now. "It wasn't my story to tell. It never sat right with me, but you are Kryssa's daughter, it was her decision to make."

Pela snorted. "I don't suppose you have any thoughts on why she kept it from me?"

"At first…well, we weren't sure *what* it was between us. I've always enjoyed my own company, but with Kryssa…" They shared a glance, and Pela was surprised to see the hint of a blush on Gen's cheeks. "She's…special," the huntress finished.

"How did you meet?" Pela asked, smiling despite herself.

"We were just friends…at first, taking coffee together, walking the mountain paths. A few times Kryssa joined me for a day hunt, when the inn was quiet and you were out roaming the town. At some point…we realised something had grown between us. Then we became—"

"Okay!" Pela gasped. "That's enough, I don't need the details!"

A grin tugged at Genevieve's lips. "I am sorry I kept it from you. Kryssa is a very private person."

"So I've discovered! Did *you* know she served in the King's Guard?"

Genevieve laughed. "No, that was as much of a surprise for me as it was for you. Though, she was always good with a blade. I once saw her strike a hare with her knife from twenty paces away. I couldn't have matched that shot if I practiced for a year."

Pela smiled, recognising the warmth in Gen's voice. It

was good to finally speak about her mother. For so long in the darkness, she'd barely had the strength to worry for herself. Now that she was finally free, might finally have a future, her thoughts returned to the fate of those she loved.

Then she remembered Townirwin, and the pain of thinking her mother had been killed. Her heart throbbed as she realised Genevieve had suffered that agony alone.

"You should have said something," Pela murmured, placing a hand on Genevieve's shoulder. "It can't have been easy, fearing for Mum all that time, and not being able to speak of it."

"I've been alone most of my life," Genevieve replied. "I'm used to it."

Sadness touched Pela, as she saw Gen with fresh eyes. "But you're not alone now. You have me, and Kryssa and…" She trailed off, remembering Devon's death, the uncertain fate of her mother and the others. A lump lodged in her throat. "Do you think…they survived?"

"I don't know," Gen replied. "I hope so, though…" Her eyes were drawn to some point over Pela's shoulder.

Pela glanced around. A smattering of vegetation grew amongst the branches of the river, some just a few feet from where they walked. Pela's heart beat faster as she glimpsed movement within the shadows. She reached for her sword, but before she could draw it the creature burst from the bushes.

A shrill cry echoed from the cliffs as the young deer bounded nimbly up the river and ducked behind a cluster of boulders. An arrow flashed from the rocks a second after it vanished. Genevieve swore and nocked another, but the creature was already gone. After a moment she returned the arrow to its quiver.

"Wishful thinking," the huntress murmured.

Pela's stomach gave an answering growl. "I'd settle for a rabbit, let alone a deer!" she agreed.

"That was a tahr," Ruebyn said as he caught them, then flicked an apologetic glance at Genevieve.

This time the huntress only smiled. "You're right; a young one, too. Keep an eye out, there might be more."

Ruebyn cast an uneasy glance behind them. "We should keep going," he said, shuddering visibly. "That Knight won't give up until his brother is avenged."

Genevieve waved a hand. "That Knight is *dead*, and good riddance. Hopefully he managed to do one good deed and take that cursed beast with him."

A frown twisted Ruebyn's lips. "I don't think so. Monstrous as it was, the Feline couldn't get through his armour."

Pela was surprised. She'd sensed Ruebyn's fear as they walked, but had thought it was the beast that frightened him. It certainly terrified her. But she'd hardly given the Knight another thought since their escape.

Silence had fallen at his words, but finally Pela shook her head, determined to put the fear from her mind. "The beast had him, we all saw it. Even if he managed to survive, they won't be in any condition to come after us…surely." Pela said the words with conviction, but somehow she failed to convince even herself.

Neither of her companions replied, but after a brief rest for water, they set off once more. Exhaustion weighed on Pela and eventually she traded the pack to Ruebyn—though he looked little better than she felt. She had checked its contents earlier and had been relieved to find a fur-lined jacket, a block of flint, some kindling, and a waterskin. No food, though.

Her stomach rumbled again, and she looked ahead, alert for fresh prey. Genevieve was better prepared than either of them, having her own pack and jacket, along with the bow and quiver.

They walked on until the sun began to set. By then, Pela was so tired she could do nothing but put one foot in front of the other. Her eyes ached and the pain of her body had driven all thought of deer and rabbits from her mind. There was only the next step, the next boulder to climb, the next stream to ford.

Here and there banks of soil formed along the edges of the valley, allowing vegetation to take root. Where they could they walked through these areas, finding the way easier on dirt than the gravels that constantly shifted beneath their boots.

Slowly the twilight slipped away, the light of the sun giving way to the faint glow of the rising moon. It seemed an age had passed since they'd emerged from the caves, but the brilliance of the near-to-full moon proved it had only been a few days.

Still they kept on, pressing themselves to the ends of their endurance. Ruebyn's words about the Knight became a promise, a threat that ate at the back of their minds, refusing to rest. Pela watched the moon as they walked, wondering if her mother still looked upon the silver orb each night. The Knight had not thought Kryssa captured, but then they had not realised Pela's identity either. Could the same have happened to Kryssa?

No, Pela insisted to herself. *Mum is free, and the king, and Caledan. They have to be.*

How Pela longed to find a way back to them. But with every step she took they drew further away, leaving behind the lands of the east, marching into the unknown. No one knew what had become of Trola since the fall of the Tsar— no one was *allowed* to know. Under normal circumstances it meant death to cross the border, but surely the Trolans would understand? They were desperate, could not survive much longer in these harsh mountains, even with the new supplies.

Trola was their only hope.

Finally they reached a break in the valley. Another great mound of earth lay across their path, rising almost two hundred feet above their heads. Twisted trees sprouted from the slope, while away to their right the river roared over a cascade of interlocked boulders to crash upon the rocks below. Thankfully the way was not sheer, but it would still make for an exhausting climb.

"It's a moraine," Ruebyn said unhelpfully, "sediment left behind when the glaciers melted."

"Let's just reach the top and make camp," Genevieve said.

They started up, eager for a view of what they would face on the morrow, and to finally rest. Pela's stomach rumbled as they climbed, and she prayed Genevieve's pack might have a little food. Despite her trepidation, the going was easy, the trees providing plenty of holds with which to pull themselves up. Even Ruebyn was able to make the climb unaided.

Only towards the top did the way become more perilous. The stones were loose in the soil and there were fewer trees. Pela and Ruebyn slowed, forced to take care with each foot and handhold, while Genevieve forged ahead, disappearing into the darkness. Pela hoped she'd gone ahead to set camp, but a few minutes later a cry carried to them from above.

Heart racing, Pela picked up the pace and soon the huntress reappeared. She was still on her feet, but moving slowly now, and her right foot no longer appeared able to take her weight.

"Twisted my ankle," Gen explained with a curse as Pela drew level. "Bloody rock shifted under me."

"Almost there," Pela said, giving her a reassuring pat on the shoulder.

The huntress offered a wan smile. She made it the last few dozen feet at a limp, and though she kept her complaints to herself, Pela could see the pain in the lines of her face.

Finally they emerged from the sparse trees onto an open flat at the top of the moraine. There, Genevieve sat herself on the ground and stretched out her leg, a scowl on her lips.

"That was stupid," she muttered to herself. Her eyes flickered around them, and the anger faded. "Least the view was worth it."

Only then did Pela look up. A gasp slipped from her as she saw the way ahead. Below, the ground dropped a hundred feet to a lake. Its crystal waters stretched up the valley as far as they could see, the stark snow-capped peaks rising all around. In the moonlight, the water seemed aglow, as though it had absorbed the day's sun and now cast it back at them. Barren slopes surrounded the lake, rising a thousand feet in every direction—except one tiny notch Pela glimpsed in the far distance. There, the ground rose only fifty feet before falling away to who knew what. Pela glimpsed stars beyond, and hoped it meant they might have finally found a pass through to Trola.

But they would have to navigate the lake first. It was massive, at least fifteen miles long and three hundred feet wide, filling the whole valley with its alien glow. The going would be tough on the steep slopes, especially with Gen's injured ankle.

A cold wind blew across the waters, reminding Pela of her aching eyes. Shivering, she turned her attention to Genevieve.

"Let's get this elevated," she said. "No more walking tonight, or you'll struggle tomorrow."

Genevieve smiled grimly. "I'll do my best. Can you manage a fire?"

Pela grunted. "I'm not entirely useless. Do you think it's wise though?"

"Depends if either of our enemies survived," Gen replied. "It could be useful, if that beast is stalking us, but if it's the Knight—"

"I don't think we should," Ruebyn croaked, moving up beside them.

Pela caught the heavy tang of fear on his voice. The hackles on her neck rose as she looked back the way they'd come, out across the scraggly trees, to the shadows of the glacial valley. A long way off, a single light glinted amongst the darkness.

"It wasn't the Feline that survived," Ruebyn whispered.

☙ 27 ❧

The crowd pressed against Kryssa as they marched through the winding streets of Chole, their voices echoing loudly against the narrow walls. Many carried makeshift weapons they had collected along the way—clubs and hatchets and pitchforks, whatever came to hand. But while they must outnumber the enemy twenty to one, she was apprehensive for the coming confrontation. The Knights had the advantage with their plate mail and broadswords, to say nothing of the Castle walls they could hide behind.

In contrast, Braidon's forces were woefully unprepared for a battle. But his call to arms had caught her off-guard and the king had been lost amongst the crowd before Kryssa could reach him. Now as she struggled to catch up, she wondered what madness had taken Braidon. The Knights would see them coming a mile off. What would his ragtag army do when they found the Castle gates barred?

Shoving bodies from her path, she threaded her way to the side of the street, and the press lessened. Her sword slapped against her leg and she had to take care not to trip in the chaos. Braidon was somewhere ahead, leading the mob. She needed to reach him before this went any further.

Amongst the lighter crowds, Kryssa moved faster, dodging in and out of the slow-moving citizens. Even so, the walls of the Castle were looming overhead by the time she finally reached the king. Dominic marched alongside him, a broad grin on his bearded face. As she approached, he faced the crowd and roared, his spear pointing to the way ahead.

"Braidon!" Kryssa gasped, slipping past Dominic and grabbing the king by the arm.

"There you are!" Braidon grinned when he saw her. "You finally decided to join the party?"

"I'm not sure I'd call this a party," she muttered. "How are you planning on getting inside?"

They had just turned the final corner before the Castle. It rose above the single-storey buildings lining the street, its granite walls topped by thick crenulations. Just as she'd suspected, the gates were barred and armoured men stood atop the ramparts, crossbows in hand. Kryssa shuddered at the sight, remembering the damage they had wrought against the Red Dragons. She feared to think what the weapons would do to a human.

"We're just here to talk," Braidon replied lightly. He seemed to be enjoying his sudden turn of fate. The only sign left of his exhaustion were the shadows beneath his eyes.

"Are you sure *they* know that?" Kryssa asked, gesturing at the mob.

Braidon shrugged but he did not reply. They continued their march down the street until a voice bellowed from the ramparts.

"Come no closer!" A man in flowing green robes

appeared atop the ramparts, arms outstretched. He called again, his voice like thunder in the street. "Or we will be forced to defend ourselves."

"Halt!" Braidon shouted, raising his arms to his followers.

The men and women at the front obeyed, but those further back continued forward, and it took several minutes for the king to calm the chaos. Even then they were not cowed, and Kryssa could sense the tension building amidst the mob. Braidon had stoked their anger at the Knights and their Order. Now hundreds were crowded into the narrow street, cramped and jostling one another, stocking their rage. Braidon needed to act fast if he wanted to avoid a riot.

She shared a glance with the king and he nodded his understanding. They strode forward together, Dominic one step behind, until they stood halfway between the Castle and the mob. A cold wind blew across the street, sending a tremor down Kryssa's spine. She felt a foreboding, as some sixth sense screamed that they should turn back. But it was already too late for that.

"Come out, Elder!" Braidon called, his voice as loud as the man in the Castle. "I must speak with you."

A strained silence hung over the street, though the whispers of the crowd were rising. The man atop the wall did not move, but after a moment his words carried down to them.

"And who are you to command an Elder of the Order?"

"I am Braidon, rightful King of Plorsea!" he bellowed.

"I see no king," came the Elder's reply. "Only a violent mob intent on murder."

"These are faithful of the Three, loyal citizens all,"

Braidon replied. "They will do you no harm, Elder. You have my word."

There was a long pause. "Very well," the Elder said finally.

He disappeared from the crenulations. A few minutes later the gates of the Castle cracked open and the man stepped out. Kryssa and Braidon shared an astonished look, while Dominic edged up to the king's other side. The crowd fell silent as the Elder approached. His face was lined with age and his robes were faded, though there was a strength in his gaze as he came to a stop before them.

"Very well, you who claim to be king," he said softly, his tone resigned. "What would you say to me?"

For a moment Braidon looked lost for words, but he shook himself and straightened. "Your Knights attacked the Temple of Antonia, threatened innocent citizens. Your kind are no longer welcome in my city."

"I have lived in this city ten years," the Elder snapped, but then his face softened. "That deed was not by command. Those Knights came from Lonia."

"And yet they have taken refuge within your walls."

"They were attacked, but by your own magic, if I'm not mistaken," the Elder snapped. "And they are not the only ones who have taken refuge within my walls. *My kind* are afraid. Can peace not prevail here? Already a Knight lies dead, his soul forever joined with the Saviour—"

"My sister be damned," Braidon snarled, taking a step towards the man. "The man came to my city intent on murder. I'll not grieve him, nor will I stop until his fellows are held to account."

"I have already stripped them of their ra—"

"*I* will be their judge," Braidon interrupted. "They

broke the king's peace; now they must answer to my justice. Open up your gates so the guilty can be judged."

"This is a sanctuary," the Elder replied. "As I said, many have come to us these last hours, fearing the rumours, fearing for their lives. I will not allow any harm to come to them."

"My friends and I won't be leaving without the guilty," Braidon retorted.

"And who are the guilty?" the Elder hissed. "There are those who would hold *you* to account, My King, for killing a man with magic. A man who had no means to defend himself against such an attack."

"The Knight put himself in my path," Braidon said. "I gave him fair warning. Had he left my people alone, there would have been no need for his death."

"Is that what you intend for all of us then?" the Elder asked. "To burn all you find within these walls, because they sought refuge in their faith?"

"No!" Braidon gasped, seeming taken aback by the Elder's words. "I only want those responsible. Your Knights will be imprisoned, and banished back to Lonia when the battle is won. All others will go unharmed, you have my word."

"But only the Lonian Knights were present at the temple."

"Perhaps," Braidon murmured, "but how could we know? Their helmets covered their faces."

"I will bring the ones who attacked you," the Elder insisted.

For moment Braidon seemed to consider it, but finally he shook his head. "I am sorry," he said, sounding genuine.

"I cannot take the risk. There is a war coming and I cannot allow your Knights to stand against me."

The Elder's face hardened and Kryssa thought he was about to refuse the king's demands. But then his shoulders slumped and his eyes fell to the cobbles.

"Very well," he whispered.

His chest rose as he sucked in a breath, then stepped forward and lifted a hand. Kryssa tensed, reaching for her sword hilt—but the hand was empty. On Braidon's other side, Dominic did not hesitate. His spear flashed down, bringing the Elder up short.

"Halt!" he snapped.

The Elder stumbled back, unharmed but taken by surprise. Braidon frowned and turned on the guard, a scowl on his face. Atop the wall, a shout came from Knights gathered there, followed by a sharp *twang.* The hackles on Kryssa's neck rose and without thinking, she hurled herself at Braidon. They slammed together and crashed to the ground.

Pain slashed her arm as the crossbow bolt tore past and buried itself in the cobbles. Collapsing alongside Braidon, Kryssa stared at the thing. It stood quivering beside them, the steel point embedded an entire inch into a cobblestone.

Her head snapped up as a roar came from down the street. The mob surged forwards, weapons raised as they rushed to avenge their fallen king. Kryssa stared in horror as the Elder fled, while atop the walls the Knights turned their weapons on the crowd. Screams pierced the air as bolts tore through flesh and bone, but they could not stop the mob.

Men and women raced around Kryssa and streamed after the Elder. He moved faster than Kryssa would have thought the old man capable, but he still only reached the gates with mere moments to spare. He slipped inside and the heavy wood slammed closed. A second later the hatchets of the mob were hammering at the door.

Beside her, Braidon groaned. There was blood on his shirt and for a second Kryssa thought he'd been struck after all. He shook his head as though to answer her unspoken question.

"Opened my wound," he murmured, hauling himself to his feet. "Thank you, though. That was too close." He offered his hand.

Kryssa accepted it and rose beside him. Her heart sank as she watched the chaos unfolding beneath the walls of the Castle. Dozens had already fallen to the Knight's weapons, their blood staining the granite cobbles. Most of the mob had passed them now, and Kryssa saw a young woman lying nearby, pinned to the cobbles by one of the great bolts. She was clawing at the arrow as though to pull it free.

A lump lodged in Kryssa's throat and she staggered over to help. A great shudder shook the woman, air hissed from her throat, and then she lay still. Kryssa stopped and stood over the dead woman. She was barely older than Pela. Tears stung Kryssa's eyes as she forced herself to look away.

Her gaze travelled up the street, taking in the carnage. Everywhere men and women lay dying, while above, the Knights still fired into the milling crowd. The fight was already going from Braidon's followers, though those at the front continued to hammer at the timbers of the gate.

Kryssa swallowed. "We have to stop this."

"We have to stop *them*," Braidon said. He stepped past her, eyes aflame. "We have to end this."

$$\mathbf{\text{❧}} \quad 28 \quad \mathbf{\text{❧}}$$

A child's laughter echoed from an open doorway in the hallway ahead, and Caledan slowed his approach, wondering for the thousandth time if he was doing the right thing. But it too late to change his mind now; the opportunity to dispose of the mad queen had passed. Swallowing his hesitation, he stepped through the entrance to Marianne's apartment.

The queen was out, and he closed the panelled doors behind him. They were thin and would not hold longer than a few seconds, but at least they would warn of an enemy's approach. In the centre of the room, the boy Calybe looked up. Caledan wore a light chainmail vest and his sword at his side, and the boy's eyes widened at the sight.

"Who are you?" he asked.

He sat on a rug at the foot of Marianne's bed, a cube of some sort in his hands. Caledan crossed to the double doors leading out onto a balcony. He checked it was unoccupied before returning and addressing the boy's question.

"Your mother sent me to look after you."

A youthful frown wrinkled the boy's forehead. "I saw you," he murmured. "With my mother, when she was working."

Caledan nodded. "She and I are friends."

The announcement bought a smile to the child's face. "That is good! She doesn't have many friends…not now… Father is gone."

"I was sorry to hear about your father," Caledan said, and seeing the sadness in the boy's eyes, was surprised to find he meant it. Whatever his opinion of Braidon, it was obvious the man was loved by his son. "And I am glad to be your mother's friend."

The boy smiled and turned his attention back to the strange cube. Each side sported nine squares painted in different colours, but they moved as the boy twisted the object, shifting the colours into rows.

"What have you got there?" Caledan asked finally, squatting beside the boy for a better look.

Calybe held the toy up to the lantern light. One side was now all the same colour, but the others remained mismatched.

"You can make them all the same," he explained, his lips twisted in a frown, "but this is as far as I can get," he finished sadly.

Caledan smiled. "Perhaps it is a trick, and it is not possible at all?"

"No," Calybe replied, "my mother showed me, but she would not tell me the trick! She said it was for me to figure out."

"Your mother is very wise—" Caledan started, but a sudden *boom* cut him off. The floor shook as an answering explosion followed.

The boy's eyes widened and Caledan rose and went back to the balcony. Leaning out over the banister, he looked across the sloping rooftops of the citadel. Smoke rose from where he guessed was the throne room, thick acrid stuff that stained the pale sky. He closed the doors and strode to where Calybe still sat.

"What was that?" the boy asked.

Caledan said nothing. His mind was in the throne room, wondering what fate had become Marianne. She claimed to have mastered the strange power wielded by the Elders, to have enough strength to force Servo from her city. Now she had finally taken the battle against the Elder and his followers.

But the queen's magic was limited. She could not be everywhere at once, could not trust anyone with the protection of her son. Only him.

And so here he was, his sword the only thing standing between an innocent boy and the Knights of Alana. The thought did not fill him with confidence.

"I think we'd better be going," he said. The plan had been to stay and wait for Marianne's victory, but she had entrusted Calybe's safety to him. And the more he thought about it, better they run than stay and fight. "Let's take a trip down to the lake," he finished.

The boy stared at him and then rose with a nod. He took Caledan's offered hand, but as they started for the door, something heavy slammed against it from outside, splintering the wood. A great *crack* followed as a second blow struck, and an axeblade appeared through the thin panelling.

"Under the bed!" Caledan hissed, spinning and shoving Calybe away from him. "*Quickly!*"

The boy obeyed without question this time. Caledan faced the door in time to see the latch disintegrate under a third blow. The doors crashed open and two Knights stepped inside, three of the Queen's Guard close behind. Seeing Caledan they hesitated, confusion in their eyes.

"Who are you?" the leader bellowed. "Where is the boy?"

"I am your death," Caledan hissed, drawing his sword. "And the boy is gone."

The Knight scanned the room, his eyes settling on Calybe's hiding place. "Under the bed." Sword already drawn, he started towards the young prince, ignoring Caledan.

Irritated by the show of disrespect, Caledan leapt, his boot flashing out to catch the Knight in the side of the head. The blow staggered the man and he stumbled back into the arms of his comrades. Snarling, the Knight recovered. The group spread out in a half-circle, arranged against him.

"That's better," Caledan laughed. "Come and meet your Saviour, boys."

Shifting his feet, he drew a heavy hunting knife from his belt and waited, sword raised high, knife low. His foes were wary now, unsure of this strange warrior who stood against them. Another *boom* echoed from below. The sound seemed to spur them into action, and with a roar, the leader charged.

Caledan leapt to the side and the Knight's broadsword cut empty air. Driving his hunting knife low, he thrust it at the gap between the Knight's backplate and steel leggings. His aim was true and the blade sank to the hilt, severing the man's spine. An awful scream rent the air as he fell forward, dragging the knife from Caledan's grasp.

Taking a double-handed grip of his sword, Caledan thrust up to block a swing from the second Knight. Sparks flashed as the Knight's broadsword ricocheted sideways, almost slamming into the shoulder of the Guard coming up beside him. Unable to drag back his sword in time for a blow, Caledan drove his shoulder into the Knight's breastplate.

Off-balance, the man hurtled backwards into another of the Queen's Guard. The two went down with a crash of metal. Before the other Guards could close on him, Caledan spun and retrieved his knife. The fallen Knight screamed as he tore the blade loose, but made no move to stand. His sobs echoed pitifully from the marble walls as Caledan leapt at the two Queen's Guard still on their feet.

Wearing only chainmail, the Guards moved quickly, though it was clear their confidence had been sapped by the fall of their leader. They retreated before his blows, until a bellow from the remaining Knight brought them up short. Behind them, the two fallen men struggled back to their feet.

Screaming an obscenity, one of the Guards leapt at Caledan, but his comrade hung back, waiting for the others to re-join the fight. At the last moment, Caledan's foe realised he was alone and tried to pull back, but it was already too late for him. Caledan's short sword took him in the throat, the razor-sharp blade tearing through the thin steel of his gorget.

Grinning, Caledan started for the remaining three, but a sharp pain tore through his leg, bringing him up short. He glanced down and cursed, surprised to find a dagger protruding from his thigh. Releasing his blade, the Knight on the floor collapsed, the last of his energy spent.

Caledan gasped as the strength went from his leg. He almost fell, but with an effort of will forced himself to remain upright. Raising dagger and sword, he looked at his three remaining opponents, and laughed.

"Ready, boys?" he asked with false bravado.

They came at him in silence. Unable to match their speed, Caledan let them approach. The two remaining Guards reached him first, one of their blades hacking for Caledan's head. But it was a clumsy blow and Caledan's sword flicked up, turning aside the attack and then lancing at his foe's helmet. The Guard's helmet lacked the full visor of the Knights', and Caledan's blade slid through the eye slot with a sickening *crunch*.

Screaming, the Guard dropped his blade and stumbled away, blood pouring from his helmet. Caledan leapt to finish him, but pain seared through his injured leg and instead he found himself retreating. Ignoring their injured comrade, his remaining foes parted and came at him from either side, seeking to divide his attention.

Caledan lunged at the Guard, his blade feinting for the man's helmet, then spun to deflect a blow from the Knight. The man shouted in surprise, almost losing his grip on his sword when their weapons connected, but he leapt back before Caledan could counter.

Stepping after him, Caledan's leg almost gave way. He cursed, tried to straighten, and heard the tread of the Guard approaching. Spinning, he thrust his sword up in a block—but this time the man had put all his weight behind the blow. Their swords came together with a screech of metal, then the weapon was jarred from Caledan's hand.

He dove to retrieve it, but a painful *thump* from the Guard's broadsword hammered into his ribs, bringing him up short. Caledan staged back as something went *crack* in his chest. His vision spun, but he sensed the chainmail had done its job. The power in the blow had broken bones, but the blade had not penetrated.

The Guard laughed and stepped in close, readying himself for the final blow. Baring his teeth, Caledan stepped in to meet him, driving his hunting knife up into the man's armpit. The laughter ceased as the blade sank deep into unprotected flesh, replaced by a terrible gurgling as blood gushed into the man's lungs.

An answering scream came from the last Knight as he charged. Caledan tried to face his foe, but a wave of pain overwhelmed him and he could not raise his dagger in time. A sword speared for his chest, and this time the chainmail could not withstand the blow. The metal links shrieked as they snapped, and the blade sank deep into Caledan's chest.

A gasp tore from Caledan as he slumped against the cold steel. Suddenly he felt as though he were drowning. His mouth opened and closed as he tried to breathe, but the air did not seem to reach his lungs. Blood bubbled on his lips and he slumped to his knees.

With a wrench, the Knight tore his blade loose. Caledan toppled forward, but the Knight caught him by the shoulder and held him there.

"Foul blasphemer," he spat. "It is an honour to cleanse your kind from our world. Your life, and the lives of my brothers, now serve the Saviour. As will the boy, in his death."

A great weakness was sweeping over Caledan, a yearning to sleep, to embrace the darkness, to flee the pain.

But with the man's final words he saw again the fear in Marianne's eyes, the innocence on Calybe's face. The black mask of the Knight's helmet watched him and Caledan opened his mouth, struggling to find words.

"What's that, blasphemer?" the Knight cackled, leaning closer. "Do you still plea for your Gods to save you?"

Caledan could barely lift his head, but as the Knight neared, he thrust up with the dagger. The blade slid low, catching the gap in the armour near the man's groin, and sank to the hilt. The pressure on Caledan's shoulder tightened momentarily, then vanished as the Knight fell back.

Gasping, the man within the iron shell clambered to his feet. Blood pumped down his leg to pool on the tile floor, but by an effort of will he stumbled towards the bed. A roar echoed from the darkness of his helmet. He hurled the bed aside. A scream rent the air…

Caledan did not see what happened next. He found himself suddenly on his side, the cold stone pressing into his face, numbness spreading through his body. The light faded from his vision and he imagined himself back in the dungeons, his only light a candle in the darkness.

As he watched, it flickered low…

❧ 29 ❧

P ela and Ruebyn stood atop the moraine, watching the distant torchlight. It was still miles off, back where they'd first left the canyon, she guessed, but there was no mistaking it, no avoiding the truth. Someone had survived the Feline. Someone was coming after them. And they were still at least a day's march from Trola. Exhausted, injured, at the end of their endurance, they could never make it in time.

"Go," Genevieve said, sitting up.

"We can't," Pela wailed. "Your leg!"

"No, *you* go," Genevieve hissed.

She pushed herself up and hobbled to a boulder on the edge of the moraine. Taking a seat, she swung her bow from her shoulders and laid her quiver alongside her.

"What are you doing?" Pela asked, taking a hesitant step towards her.

"She's going to fight," Ruebyn whispered, his eyes wide.

"*No,*" Pela snapped. She held out a hand to Gen, as though to pull her back from the edge.

Gen only smiled. "There's some beef jerky in my pack. You'd better take it." Her eyes turned to the distant light. "I'll do my best to stop them. There can't be many left. They'll be out in the open climbing this slope—I should be able to pick off a few."

Pela straightened her shoulders. "Then we should stay," she announced, dropping a hand to her sword. "We can help."

"No," Genevieve said. "You have to go, in case I…fail. If I can deal with them, I'll catch up."

A lump lodged in Pela's throat as she caught Genevieve's eye and saw the truth there. Her quiver had only six arrows. If even half the Knight's entourage had been slain by the Feline, she would have to make every shot. Then there was the Knights' armour. Gen had only hunting arrows—the wooden points could not pierce solid steel.

Pela swallowed, struggling to find the words. "We…we can help you."

"No, Pela," Genevieve said, offering a sad smile. "Kryssa can't lose us both. And she would never forgive me if I let something happen to you."

"I told you, I can look after myself!" Pela insisted. She knelt beside her friend and took Genevieve's hand in hers. "Please don't do this."

Genevieve touched her other hand to Pela's head. "It's already done," she whispered. "Now *go*." Her eyes flickered to the sky behind Pela. "Before the storm arrives."

Twisting where she crouched, Pela saw that Genevieve spoke the truth. Lightning flashed above the distant peaks and the sky had darkened, the stars vanishing behind unseen clouds. Even as she stood, the rumble of thunder carried to their lonely perch.

Pela closed her eyes, unable to bear the thought of leaving her friend behind. But she had already faced this choice, had already opted to stay rather than allow Ruebyn to fall to his death. Remembering the awful fear, the despair of her capture, she knew she could not do it again, not for anyone. Genevieve had offered her a way out, and for better or worse, Pela had to take it.

Exhaling, she stood. They shared another glance, she and Gen, but there was nothing left to be said. They were all exhausted, weary beyond belief, but they had to push on, had to continue or be lost.

Biting her lip, Pela nodded to Genevieve and turned away before the tears could spill. Walking past Ruebyn, she took his hand and drew him away, stopping only to collect her pack and take the food from Genevieve's. There was a thin animal trail along the edge of the lake and she started along it without looking back. Pela prayed it would lead them to safety.

The darkness pressed down as they began the long journey around the lake. Soon the clouds overtook the moon, but the midnight waters still glowed with that unearthly light and they continued unhindered. The lake became a presence of its own, a strange, haunting thing. There was a sadness about the place, as though a great tragedy had taken place here in ages past.

Pela imagined the glow must come from the souls of the long dead, trapped within the icy waters, forever longing for freedom. She wondered if that was to be their fate, to die upon these windswept slopes, their lives stolen by the unforgiven mountains—or the Knight that pursued them.

Jagged gullies crisscrossed their path and as they climbed the broken slope, and the ground to their right fell away, becoming a cliff that plummeted down to the lakeshore.

Soon Pela's legs began to shake. Every movement became an effort of will, her knees so weak they threatened to collapse with every step. In all her life, Pela had never pressed herself so hard, had never come so close to utter exhaustion.

On they marched, clambering over boulders and shuffling along narrow ledges, the way lit by the flickering glow from far below. Several times they were forced to rest, clinging to each other in their desperation to keep warm. The winds grew stronger, howling across the lake with a terrible fury, while a threatening darkness stole the sky.

The weather closed in, the icy gales slicing through their thin cloaks. They took turns wearing the jacket from the pack, until Ruebyn's face lost all colour and Pela left it with him. Boulders dotted the slope, offering scarce shelter. An ache began in the base of Pela's skull, and despite the extra layer of clothing, Ruebyn started to lag, forcing her to slow.

Lungs burning, they continued, for without shelter they could not stop. Then with a roar, the skies opened, and sleet fell down to lash the mountainside. Pela gasped as it struck like a frozen wave. She was drenched within moments, so cold the breath was stolen from her lungs. No matter how hard they walked, they would never warm themselves now.

They could go no further. They would freeze on the shores of this lake if they did not find shelter. There were no trees here, only stark stone and water, but surely there must be a cave, something, anything that might protect them. They had enough kindling for a small fire, but it would never light in these conditions.

Her eyes caught on a dark patch above, set back in the cliffs. It might have been nothing, a twist in the rock or darker stone, but there was no choice. They staggered towards it, ice seeping into their bones, their strength fading with every step. Pela knew if she was wrong, they would die.

By the time they reached the cliffs, the sleet was so thick that Pela could barely see a foot in front of her. The cold stung her eyes and she had lost all feeling in her face. Ice-laden water rushed across the ground, soaking their boots. A deep ache had begun in her hands and feet, and she feared frostbite would soon follow.

For a second, Pela could see only blank stone. Blood pounded in her skull as she stumbled up to the cliff-face and placed her hands to the rock, feeling for what she had seen so easily just moments before. Could her instincts have been wrong?

She almost fell as the cliff gave way suddenly to a cave. Turning, she grasped Ruebyn by the arm and dragged them both inside. The cave hardly went ten yards into the mountain, but the respite from the wind and sleet was instant. Pela's relief was so great that she almost fell to her knees. But there was no time to rest, not yet.

Tearing off her pack, she dragged out the pile of kindling. It was barely enough for an hour of fire, but it might still prove the difference between life and death. She dumped it in a pile while Ruebyn stood dumbly in the entrance, his face so pale he might have passed for a ghost himself.

"Stack the wood!" Pela cried, her teeth chattering.

The ache in her extremities was growing worse. A tremor shook her and she cursed as the pack slipped from her frozen fingers. Ruebyn staggered over and started sorting through the wood, doing his best to prepare it for a fire.

It took long minutes for Pela to find the flint. By then Ruebyn was ready, though she had to rearrange several pieces of wood to give the fire room to breathe. Her hands were shaking so badly she could barely strike the flint. It took several attempts before she produced even a single spark. The flames died quickly on the damp earth, but she persisted until finally a soft glow caught amongst the tinder she'd placed in the centre of the wood.

Pela fanned the tiny flame, only sitting back when she was sure it would not go out. Another tremor ran from her scalp to her toes. They'd lit the fire right at the back of the cave, where the stone would reflect its heat back at them. Even so, she could barely feel its warmth against the icy storm.

Water from her hair tricked down her back. Pela cursed. They would die of hypothermia in their drenched clothes before the tiny flame did anything to help them. She dragged the jacket from her back and slung it across a nearby rock to dry. Ruebyn stared as her pants and shirt followed, until she wore only her filthy underclothes.

"What are you doing?" he cried.

"Take off your clothes," she snapped, unable to muster the energy to explain. "Before you freeze."

Ruebyn hesitated, but with a glare from her, he obeyed. The oilskin jacket they'd shared was soaked through and he laid it alongside hers. He removed his shirt next, revealing the pale skin of his chest. There he hesitated, casting a glance in her direction.

"Pants too," she said, unable to keep the grin from her lips. "They're soaked."

Understanding showed in his eyes and Pela couldn't help but giggle at his naivety. He laid his pants as near to the fire as he dared then stood in his underwear, hands extended to the flames. A shiver rippled through him, the hairs on his arms standing on end.

"I'm *freezing!*" he gasped.

"Be thankful we found the cave," Pela replied, "or we'd already be dead."

Ruebyn nodded. Seating himself alongside her, he wrapped his arms around his chest. "Do you think your friend is okay?"

Pela swallowed. For half a second she'd forgotten Genevieve in their own desperate fight to survive. What would she do with this storm approaching? But then, she was better clothed than them, and there were trees on the moraine that could provide shelter.

"Gen used to hunt in the mountains of Golden Ridge," Pela answered finally. "She knows what to do in a storm."

"I hope she can stop them," Ruebyn said.

Remembering the last look Genevieve had given her, Pela did not answer. A cold breeze whistled through the cave, sending the firelight flickering across the stones. Pela shuddered, though whether it was from the cold or dread, she could not have said. Her chest ached with an awful loneliness, with the realisation she had lost her last connection with Skystead. She edged closer to the fire, basking in its heat, but it did nothing for the hole in her heart.

"Come here," she said suddenly to Ruebyn. "I'm cold as well."

"What?"

"Just come here," she gasped.

Her teeth were chattering, the awful emptiness swelled within her chest. A shrill keening began in the back of her throat and she felt as though she must explode, that the terror and despair and desolation must all come bursting from her, must tear her apart.

Then Ruebyn was there. She shivered as his arms went around her waist. He was as cold as she was but he held her tight, and the pressure within lessened, if only a touch. She closed her eyes, relaxing into his embrace. Her heartbeat slowed, her mind drifting.

How had it come to this, the two of them alone against the Knights of Alana? Just a week ago she had loathed Ruebyn, could not have even tolerated his touch. His cold indifference had been anathema to her, his rigid subservience to the rules a cold cruelty she could not bear.

Absently, Pela touched a hand to her cheek, tracing the thin line of the scar Ruebyn's whip had left on his first day. It was only one of many, and yet it was everything, a cold reminder of their reality. She started to pull away from him, then flinched as his hand touched hers. Her eyes snapped open to find him watching her.

"I'm so sorry, Pela," he whispered. His hazel eyes shone in the firelight.

Pela stared at Ruebyn, wondering whether she could trust him. For the first time since their escape, she really looked at him, seeing how his face had changed. The plumpness had melted from his cheeks and there was no fear in his eyes now, no uncertainty. The last few days had changed him utterly, burning away the child she had met in the mines. She wondered who he was now.

Almost without realising it, Pela entwined her fingers in his and leaned her head against his shoulder. She moved his hand to her ear. It still ached from the blow he had struck before their escape, the flesh torn and broken.

"What about this?" she murmured.

He shivered, cupping the side of her face. His fingers were cool and she sighed as they stole away some of the pain. Pela burrowed her head into his chest, catching the rich, earthy scent of him. After so long with the awful dust and the stench of burning coal, his smell was surprisingly pleasant.

"So, so sorry," he croaked. Pela was surprised to hear his voice break.

She lifted her head and watched the tears spill down his cheeks. She wiped them away.

"No more tears," she said.

He swallowed, his head bobbing up and down. "I wish I could take it back."

"You can't," Pela whispered.

"What can I do?"

"I'm still cold," she replied.

She took his head between her hands then, turning her face to the side. For once, Ruebyn knew what to do. A tingle ran down Pela's spine as he pressed his lips to her ear, a shudder that went right through her. He pulled her closer, his chest a burning warmth against her flesh.

Turning again, she stared into his eyes, then drew him to her cheek. His lips caressed the line of her scar and her eyes fluttered closed, her breath quickening. Her hand slid down his back, savouring the softness of his skin, so unlike her own, made rough by the long days in the sun, beaten by the torture of the mines.

Finally Pela could wait no longer. With the hand still on his cheek, she turned his head so their lips brushed gently together. Then they were kissing, his body pressing hard against hers, drawing her down. And suddenly the cave was no longer quite so cold, quite so lonely.

$$\text{\ff} \quad 3\,0 \quad \text{\ff}$$

Kryssa watched as Braidon pushed his way through the crowd and lifted a hand. The gates gave way with a horrible *crack* and Braidon staggered, but the mob was already surging through the opening. She gave Braidon her shoulder and they stumbled after them, weapons in hand.

The *twang* of crossbows greeted them as they stepped through the gates into a courtyard. Ahead, a dozen of Braidon's followers went down. Those still on their feet charged at the enemy.

The Knights of Alana tossed aside their crossbows and drew swords. They stood barring the entrance to the inner keep, a large doorway closed at their backs. Shouts came from overhead as those still atop the wall fired down into the courtyard.

Braidon shouted at those crowding around him, gesturing to a nearby staircase that led up to the ramparts. Part of the mob split off, weapons at the ready, and a minute later the sound of fighting carried down from above.

Kryssa and Braidon turned their attention to the more immediate threat. The mob was hurling themselves at the line of Knights, but their makeshift weapons were little use against steel armour and heavy broadswords. Even as she watched, a club bounced from a Knight's breastplate before its wielder was cut down.

A growl hissed from Braidon as he straightened and shrugged off her aid. Hefting his sword, he leapt to join the melee. Kryssa cursed and raced after him. The king still had not recovered from the confrontation at the temple, and who knew how much energy he had used busting open the Castle gates.

Ahead, the tide was already turning in the Knights' favour. Using their weight, they pushed the crowd back, swords rising and falling in bloody fashion. Fear showed in the faces nearest Kryssa. If they broke, it would be a massacre.

A gap opened in the press of bodies facing the Knights. Braidon leapt to fill it, his sword flashing at the first Knight to stand against him. Steel grated on steel as his blade struck the man's armour, but Braidon dragged it upwards so that the point slammed into the gorget protecting his opponent's throat. The thin iron crumbled beneath the blow and the Knight staggered away, dropping his sword.

Another iron-clad warrior stepped up to take his place. Braidon ducked a blow from his sword and Kryssa joined the fray, her blade slamming into the Knight's wrist. Steel crunched and the broadsword tumbled harmlessly to the ground. Seeing the man was unarmed, another of Braidon's followers leapt on him and bore him to the ground. Others piled on, clubs and axes hammering at the man's armour. Inevitably, they found their mark.

Roaring at their comrade's death, the Knights attacked with renewed fury. Braidon parried a blow, but the Knight's momentum carried him on. He slammed into the king, hurling Braidon from his feet. Kryssa charged to intercept the silver warriors before they could strike a mortal blow, her sword flashing furiously to keep them back.

Then Braidon was up again. Joining Kryssa, he attacked with a cold fury, struggling to hold back the iron tide. Lacking the skill and arms, those around them died by the dozens. Only Braidon and Kryssa could hold their own, while Dominic had disappeared in the first minutes of the siege. Kryssa could sense the mood of Braidon's followers turning, their rage giving way to fear. If something didn't tip the scales…

Bellowing, Braidon leapt at the nearest Knight. His shoulder caught the man in the chest and hurled him from his feet. But now Braidon stood alone, isolated from his allies. Two Knights moved to intercept him, their swords held at the ready.

Braidon's lips twisted in a snarl and he roared again. Kryssa struggled to go to his aid, but a third Knight attacked, forcing her to defend herself. The king's blade lanced out to meet the first of his foes. Their weapons came together with a *shriek,* but instead of deflecting the blow, Braidon's sword carved straight through the Knight's. A shriek came from the ironclad warrior as the king's blade continued its path, slicing through his breastplate like a knife through cheese.

Dragging back his weapon, Braidon spun to meet the second Knight, but the man had frozen at the fate of his comrade. Braidon cut him down before he could recover. Others fell back as well, fearful of the king's power. Armies and mobs these men could face without a hint of fear, but the sight of magic unnerved them above all else.

Braidon strode forward, and with a cry of terror, one of the Knights dropped his sword and turned to flee. Seeing their opportunity, the mob chased after him. One hurled a club that slammed into the Knight's knee, sending him crashing to the ground. Then they were upon him.

Kryssa looked away in time to see the other Knights turning to run. The battle suddenly became a rout, the terrified Knights fleeing for their lives—only to be brought up short by the barred doors of the inner keep. Her heart thudded painfully in her chest as she staggered over to Braidon.

"Are you okay?" she croaked. His face was hard, but she could see the exhaustion behind his eyes. She wondered how much of his own life force he had used in the past few minutes.

"I'll manage," he replied, then gestured to the giant oak doors. "Let's get these open."

"Do we need to?" Kryssa asked as men and women leapt to obey. She gestured at the dead lying around the cobbled courtyard. "Wasn't this enough?"

Axes crashed into the wood, sending splinters across the yard. She could still hear the sound of fighting from the ramparts, but there had only been a few Knights atop the wall by the time the gates had fallen. Even so, she spied a crossbow lying nearby and swept it up. Taking a quiver of bolts from a dead Knight, she loaded the weapon and then eyed the battlements, in case anyone attempted another attack on the king.

"There could still be Knights inside," Braidon

murmured. He leaned against the courtyard wall, looking wan. "I want to be sure."

"What about what the Elder said? There could be innocent people hiding inside."

"What choice do we have, Kryssa?" Braidon asked. "If we leave them, it's only a matter of time before they're reinforced. Then they'll strike again. We need to put an end to this plague while they're still weak."

A chill blew across Kryssa's neck, but she said nothing. There was no more time to argue. A great *crack* came from the timbers of the door and then those too were crashing open. Braidon bellowed an order and the crowd parted for him. Kryssa followed the king as he led the way inside.

Within, the hallways were unlit. Braidon shouted for torches to be brought. No one wanted to be stumbling around in darkness, with the crossbows the Knights wielded. A calm fell over the crowd as burning brands were lit and passed around. Many had taken swords and armour from the fallen Knights, and a few like Kryssa now wielded the heavy crossbows.

Silence hung over the Castle as they crept through the dark corridors. Kryssa scanned the shadows, seeking out danger, wondering if all the Knights had fallen on the doorstep.

It wasn't long before she was proven wrong. They came screaming from a side corridor, attacking the group from the flanks. Braidon spun to meet them, sword in hand. A crossbow discharged, sending a bolt straight through the breastplate of a Knight and stopping him dead. He fell back against his comrades, slowing their charge, and Braidon's followers fell upon them.

Kryssa watched in shock as the carnage played out.

There had been only five Knights in this group; they were horribly outnumbered. With the impetus of their charge ruined, they didn't stand a chance, and they fell within minutes. Braidon led the crowd down the corridor from which they'd emerged, leaving Kryssa alone in the dark.

Swallowing, she made to go after them, but something gave her pause. The last attack did not sit right with her. Braidon still had over a hundred followers with him—the five Knights could not have possibly thought to win. Why had they thrown their lives away?

It had to be a distraction. Drawing her sword, Kryssa continued down the corridor in the direction they'd originally been heading. She did not know what to expect, but she encountered no one in the long hallways, not a soul in any of the rooms branching off the main corridor. After a while she began to think she'd been wrong, but still she did not turn back. Finally she turned a corner and realised where she'd been heading.

In Townirwin, there had been a holy pantheon in the centre of the Castle, a great chamber dedicated to the sacrifice of the Saviour. The corridor ahead was painted with the same murals as the ones outside that Caste. Kryssa hesitated. If the Elder had spoken the truth, if innocents had taken refuge inside the Castle walls, she would find them here.

She started towards the twin iron doors that waited at the end of the corridor. Shadows clung to the floor, the only light coming from the open windows high above. When she was halfway to the end, movement came from ahead. Kryssa acted instantly, the crossbow coming up, but she hesitated when a lantern was unshuttered.

The Elder who had spoken with them outside the gates stood barring her path.

"Put down your weapon, sister," he murmured.

Kryssa tightened her grip on the crossbow. "Step aside, Elder. I have no wish to harm an unarmed man."

She started towards the man, but the air grew dense, until it was as though she were wading through thick mud. Within a couple of steps Kryssa found she could not move forward at all. An invisible barrier stood between her and the Elder.

"I need no weapon but my mind," he murmured, "but I wish no harm to you either."

Kryssa took a step back and the pressure eased. "You have power."

"I do."

"You cannot stop us all," Kryssa replied. "Braidon told me how your new magic works. You are limited by the strength of your own life force."

"I fear I have power enough to stop you all," the Elder replied sadly. "I have drunk the lives of the sacrificed, as have all the Elders of the Order. It is a strength I am loathe to use, but I will not hesitate to protect my people."

Kryssa's stomach churned. "What sacrifices?"

"You know very well, Kryssa. You may have escaped my brothers, but you were not the first to go beneath their blades. I left that darkness behind when I came to Plorsea, but all these years the power I collected has lain dormant."

"You're a murderer," Kryssa whispered, her hands shaking.

"I am," the Elder replied, bowing his head.

Anger boiled up within Kryssa. She started towards him again, but the barrier brought her up short. Her fist slammed against it. "You took me from my home!" she snarled. "You tried to burn my daughter alive!"

"I took no part in your Great Sacrifice," the Elder replied. His voice was barely a whisper now. "But to my shame, I once performed cleansings, once believed our two kinds could not live side by side."

Kryssa ignored him. "So you lied! It *was* you who sent those Knights out into the city, to slaughter our priests and burn our temple." Teeth bared, she pointed the crossbow and fired.

The bolt slashed the air, but it only managed a few feet before it slowed to nothing and clattered harmlessly to the floor. Growling, she tore another from the quiver and reloaded the weapon.

"I did not lie!" the Elder tried, but Kryssa barely heard him.

She turned her mind inwards, anger driving her to action. Three times now she had seen Braidon tap into that unknown power. Recalling their discussion, Kryssa sought to do the same. Drawing in a deep breath, she stared at the Elder, but she no longer really saw him.

Her consciousness was elsewhere, plunging inwards with each inhalation, following the passage of breath to her core. She needed no schooling in meditation. Kryssa had been practicing since the first day Selina had taken her off the streets of Ardath. It was a skill valued by the followers of the Old Gods, a way to control their emotions and themselves.

The practice helped to cool her anger and calm Kryssa's racing heart. But she knew now Braidon had been right. This man had confirmed as much. The Elders had a terrible advantage with the power they had collected. They needed to be stopped, to pay for what they had done to her and Pela and so many others. Kryssa would make them regret choosing her for their Great Sacrifice. She was a helpless prisoner no longer. She intended to show this Elder as much.

Slowly the rest of the world dissolved away, until only darkness remained, the empty void of her inner mind. This was where Magickers had once found their power, but now that infinite black was empty. She had never encountered the power Braidon had discovered before, but then, she had not been looking for it, had not needed it.

Now she did.

Kryssa searched the void, seeking the flickering of power, but finding only darkness. Drifting through nothingness, she wondered what she was doing wrong, why the power would not come. Braidon had said this new magic belonged to all…so why, then, could she not reach it?

Cursing, her control slipped. Her mind retreated, but as the darkness faded she caught a flicker of light in her spirit eyes. Hope touched her and drawing another breath, she centred herself. The void returned—and the glow vanished.

What am I doing wrong?

She could not understand it. The power was her own life force, it should be here, it was part of her…

A part of me!

In a rush, Kryssa spun in the dark, turning her eyes upon herself, and saw the brilliance at her centre. Braidon had been right—the power *was* her, but she'd been so concentrated on finding some outside force, she'd missed it.

Fear touched her now. The flame was a tiny, pale thing, surrounded by an infinite void. Surely it could not hold the power she needed, not enough to stand against the Elder.

He had claimed the lives of so many—what could her little candle do against him?

But perhaps she could catch him by surprise. Kryssa's resolve tightened, and gripping the flame with her spirit fingers, she opened her eyes. Power surged through her but she held it in check, not yet ready to act. The crossbow was heavy in her hand. She started to wind back the crank.

"You cannot pass, Kryssa," the Elder said sadly. "You cannot harm me."

"Like hell," Kryssa snarled.

"I understand your hate," the Elder continued, "but I will not let you harm those inside."

"I don't care about the people inside, it's you I want!" Kryssa snapped.

She took hold of her power and sent it questing out beyond her. There was a strange, disorientating sensation, as though her mind had separated from her body, and then she *was* beyond her body. Drifting between herself and the Elder, suddenly the barrier became visible, flickering before her like a wall of mist.

Time slowed to a crawl as she examined the swirling white. At first it seemed impenetrable, but as the fog flowed, she began to see gaps, weaker points through which she caught glimpses of the Elder beyond. She focused her energies on one of these, tugging and pulling with her mind, feeling the energy draining from her with each touch. Braidon had been right about their limits. Working against her was the strength of who knew how many innocent lives.

The thought restored her anger, and baring her teeth, Kryssa kept on. Finally, with a cry of triumph, she stabbed through. An answering cry came from the Elder as an inch-wide hole opened in the mists. In her mind's eye she saw him stagger, then thrust out his hands. Power streamed from him, burning and churning reality, but Kryssa's arm was already sweeping up.

The crossbow *thumped* backwards in her grip as she fired. The bolt hissed down the corridor, passing freely through the hole in the barrier, and buried itself in the Elder's chest. His eyes widened and his mouth fell open. The barrier blinked out as though it had never been.

Then the power he had summoned slammed into Kryssa, picking her up and driving her into the wall. Her head smashed against the marble and she collapsed to the floor. Stars danced across her vision and she had to close her eyes to keep herself from throwing up.

When she finally opened them again, the Elder was gone.

31

Pela woke to the warmth of sunlight on her face. Her eyes flickered open. For a second, she was surprised to find herself lying naked in Ruebyn's arms. Then her memories of the night came rushing back and her cheeks grew hot. In the grips of the storm, she had not been cold.

She sat up quickly, disentangling herself from Ruebyn. He gave a quiet moan and rolled over, his arms curling around her waist. Still drowsy from lack of sleep, Pela examined their little cave in the daylight. The fire had burned out long ago but the storm had broken, and now light streamed in from the crooked entrance…

Cursing, Pela leapt to her feet. Her heart was suddenly racing. For the sun to reach them here, it must already be well above the mountain peaks. They had slept too long!

"Wake up!" she gasped, grabbing Ruebyn by the shoulders and shaking him. "We have to go."

"Wha…?" he groaned, blinking in confusion. A frown touched his forehead as he saw her standing over him. Then a handsome smile crossed his lips. "Good morning."

Pela paused, her cheeks warming as she recalled the night…before her sense of urgency came rushing back. She threw off his arm.

"We can…discuss what happened later!" she said. "The sun's up. We have to go. Unless you want that Knight to catch us."

At the mention of their foe, Ruebyn's senses returned. He leapt to his feet and they scrambled for their clothes, mostly dried from the fire's heat, tugged them on, and gathered their gear. Ruebyn swung the pack onto his back while Pela strapped the sword to her waist, and together they stumbled outside.

Pela's gaze was drawn down to the slopes behind them. She searched the dark rocks surrounding the lake, looking for their pursuers, but there was no sign of movement. She let out a long sigh and turned to continue their march.

"Good morning, young lovers."

The words froze them in their tracks. Pela's mouth fell open as she saw the Knight sitting alone on a boulder, sword resting across his iron legs. Sunlight danced from his visor as he rose, his armour squealing with the movement. An arrow protruded from his shoulder, where it had torn through a joint in the steel, and the Feline had left great gashes across his breastplate. Even his sword was nicked and twisted, as though some weight had put it under great strain.

"You led a merry chase," he growled, taking a step towards them. The blade was in his left hand, though he had wielded it right-handed against the beast. "But it is over now."

Pela struggled to breathe. Panic rose to choke her, but there was no time to lose control. She scanned the slopes around them, but there was no sign of anyone else. The Knight was alone.

"Where is Genevieve?" she growled, returning her gaze to the Knight.

The Knight laughed, the sound echoing awfully from his helmet. "The slave fought well, but I killed her all the same. Her strength now serves the Saviour."

The news staggered Pela, and if not for Ruebyn's hand on her back, she would have fallen. She thought she'd accepted Gen's death the night before, but now she realised that that had been a lie. Somehow, she'd still expected the wily huntress to win. Now the truth stood before them, cold and implacable, and there was nowhere left to run.

But there was no time to mourn now. The Knight might have been injured, but with his broadsword and armour, they were still outmatched. She dragged the sword from her belt.

"I'm glad she took your friends with her," Ruebyn spat. He swung the bag from his back and dragged out a dagger.

Their foe only laughed. "My retainers wait for me below. This is Trolan land, and it means death to be caught here. A sacrifice I alone am willing to make, to ensure there is justice for my brother's murder."

He swung a practice blow with his sword. It was twice the length of Pela's blade. He would cut her down before she could get anywhere near him. Ruebyn edged closer to her, dagger in hand.

"I hope you know how to use that," she muttered as the Knight started forward.

Ruebyn flashed a regretful smile. "I think you know the answer to that, Pela."

Pela sighed, but there was no changing things now.

"Keep away from his sword. Aim for the joints in his armour, if you can."

She slid sideways across the slope, seeking to draw the Knight after her. Her feet spread instinctively into the fighting stance Caledan had taught her, improving her balance on the uneven surface. Dotted with rocks and loose gravel, the slope ran fifty feet towards the lake before plunging over the cliff, down another hundred feet to the water.

The Knight's armour squealed as he followed her. He had seen them back in the canyon, and must have known that Ruebyn was no threat. All the better—maybe Ruebyn would have a chance to attack him from behind. If he had the courage.

"Come on then," Pela hissed, brandishing the short sword, trying to raise him to anger. "Come die like your brother."

Her words had the desired effect, as with a roar, the Knight lunged. He moved faster than Pela had expected, given his injuries, and she barely managed to avoid the first swing of his sword. The blade hissed dangerously close to her throat as she staggered back, only the weeks of Caledan's training keeping her upright.

The man obviously wasn't going to take prisoners this time. That was fine with Pela—she didn't intend to be taken alive anyway. Setting her shoulders, she thrust the sword out in front of her and waited for the next attack.

This time when it came, she was ready. His sword flashed down in an overhanded blow. Pela skipped to the side and the blade carried past, striking rock and jarring violently sideways. Seeing the opening, she stepped in, her blade flashing for his midriff. But her blow was off and she missed the fine gap between the armour under his arm. The point of her sword scraped off solid steel, leaving a long scratch in the metal.

He felt the blow though, and roaring, he swung out his injured arm, catching Pela in the shoulder. There wasn't much power in the blow, but it knocked her back. Recovering her balance, she retreated another step as the deadly broadsword carved an arc where she had stood.

Beyond the Knight, Ruebyn darted to and fro, his face an agony of uncertainty. He didn't know how to help, how to find the weak spots in the Knight's armour. In a sudden premonition, Pela realised he could only get himself killed in this fight.

"Stay back, Ruebyn!" she screamed, then leapt at the Knight again.

His sword rose to meet her, but it was an awkward blow and she easily caught it with the hilt of her sword, sending his blade slamming into the ground. Then she stabbed out, aiming for his throat. The point of her sword slashed his gorget, but he turned aside and the blow only dented the lighter steel.

Pela retreated a step, drawing back her sword, and the Knight's gorget fell loose. She had sliced through its bindings and now his throat was exposed. A smile crossed her lips as she faced her iron foe. He must be growing weary by now, his energy sapped by the forced march to catch them —whereas sleep had restored some of Pela's strength. And he was clearly not skilled with his left hand.

She sent up thanks to Genevieve for her final act, and a prayer for the Old Gods to bless the huntress. Genevieve had suffered so much for Pela and her mother—she deserved to rest now.

Tightening her grip on the sword, Pela beckoned the Knight forward.

Stones crunched as he came for her. Ruebyn hung back and Pela hoped he would listen, would not interfere. She could not stand to see him die for nothing, to be left alone on this stark mountainside. Snarling, she hurled herself at the Knight.

His sword rose to meet her, but he was lagging now, weighed down by pain and exhaustion. In a fair fight they could never have matched this armoured man, but Genevieve had given them a chance, and Pela was more than happy to take advantage.

Their weapons came together with a crash, but as she swung again the Knight slipped in the loose stones, and her sword drove beneath his guard. The blade crunched into his wrist, leaving a dent in the steel and forcing him back. Tasting victory, Pela chased after him—but his wound was not as bad as she'd thought, and his broadsword flashed for her face.

Only instinct saved her. Stones scattered in all directions as she threw herself at the ground. The hackles rose on her neck as the blade passed overhead, but before could regain her feet, the Knight's foot flashed for her face. She rolled desperately and the steel-shod boot collided with her shoulder. A cry tore from her lips as she flung herself back, sword raised to defend herself.

Their weapons came together with a crash, but the impact tore the blade from Pela's hands. Her foe gave a cry of triumph as Pela's weapon skittered across the ground and struck a rock, snapping in two. The broken blade flew off down the slope, disappearing over the cliff, leaving the hilt discarded amongst the gravel.

Fear froze Pela in place. Lifting her chin, she looked at the Knight, waiting for the end to come. He raised his sword, so close Pela could not avoid the blow. Then roar came from above them, and Ruebyn charged. He was on the Knight before their foe could react, slamming into his armoured back and hurling them both from their feet. Their weapons went flying as they crashed down the slope, coming to rest several feet below.

Groaning, Ruebyn struggled to his hands and knees. But the Knight had been protected by his armour, and was the faster to recover. With a shriek of twisted steel, he tackled the young overseer, slamming him into the ground. Pinning Ruebyn beneath his weight, the Knight reached with iron hands for his throat.

"No!"

Sweeping up the broken sword hilt, Pela came to her feet and hurtled down the slope. The stones shifted beneath her weight, almost toppling her, but she recovered and leapt again. Ruebyn was beating at the iron arms but he could do nothing to dislodge his tormentor. His face was turning pale, suffocated by the unyielding strength of their foe.

Fixated on Ruebyn, the Knight did not see Pela coming. She slammed into him with the force of a small avalanche, tearing him loose from the overseer. Her momentum carried them on, and out of control, she and the Knight flew down the slope. Each time they struck the ground, sharp gravel flew in all directions. Pela cried out as stones sliced her flesh.

Clutching a hand to her face, she glimpsed the lake— and the cliff rising quickly to meet them. It was a hundred foot drop into the icy waters. Even if she somehow survived the fall, the cold would kill her before she found a way out.

She slammed into the mountainside again, driving the

last of the air from her lungs, but this time she lashed out, stabbing the broken end of her sword into the earth. There was only an inch of blade left and she prayed it would not break. Steel shrieked on stone as she clung to the hilt, her weight almost dragging her arms from their sockets.

Stones rained down around Pela as she slowed, then ground to a stop. Gasping, she slumped against the dirt. Her shoulders shrieked, the muscles torn and bruised from the effort it had taken to stop her downwards plunge.

She could not rest yet, not until she knew they were safe. Gathering her strength, Pela pulled herself to her hands and knees, an awful groan slipping from her in a sigh.

But as she made to stand, a hard weight struck her, driving her backwards into the gravel. The broken dagger spun from her hands. Stars flashed across her vision as her head was slammed into a rock. Her groan turned to a scream as she found the mottled face of the Knight just an inch from her own.

He must have lost his helmet in the fall, for now she saw him in all his terrible truth. His nose had been crushed sometime in the past, leaving it flattened and purple with broken blood vessels. Bloody eyes bulged from their sockets as he bared his teeth and clasped his iron fingers around her throat, silencing Pela's scream.

She gasped as the iron collar was crushed against her windpipe. Only the slightest whisper of air made it to her lungs. Then not even that was possible as he leaned closer. She beat at his twisted breastplate, but all she achieved were bruises on her knuckles. Changing tact, she searched for the gap in his armour.

Finding a crack, she shoved her hand through, stabbing at his flesh with her nails, pinching, scratching, whatever she could do to hurt him. His face twisted and momentarily his grip loosened. She sucked in a desperate breath, and the darkness retreated slightly. He twisted, one hand still gripping her throat, the other knocking aside her questing fingers.

Then he lifted her up and slammed her head back down into the rocks. The strength left Pela in a rush. She slumped against the ground, watching as a grin warped that awful face. He crouched over her, both hands at her throat again.

"May the Saviour condemn you to a fiery pit," he snarled, goblets of spit spraying her face.

Pela's lungs screamed for air. Her whole body throbbed, her skull pounding like a drum. A great weariness crept over her. She felt the darkness calling, an open void crying out for her. In her mind's eye, she turned towards it, saw something flicker, reached for it.

The light was only the tiniest of candles amidst the dark. A strong breeze would blow it out, but when Pela touched it she felt a rush to her spirit, a renewed will to live. The flame flickered, shrinking, as though the act of restoring her will had lessoned it. Fear touched Pela, an understanding that the light was her, that she was the light.

If it died, so did she.

But it was not yet extinguished. She had strength enough for one last, desperate act. She touched the light again.

Back on the mountainside, her eyes snapped open. The Knight's face loomed above. His laughter rang distantly in her ears and there was a joy in his eyes, a sickly ecstasy at his power over life and death. It fed her desperation, and drawing on the light, she willed him to release her, to fall back, to fly.

It was as though some invisible power struck the Knight. Little more than a tap, but his position was unstable on the mountainside, and it was enough to push him back from her. He reared up, his feet slipping on the loose stones, arms windmilling. But he could not regain his balance, and with a cry he tumbled backwards. His armour added momentum to the fall and he bounced twice on the treacherous slope.

That was all it took.

One second the Knight was there, the next he was over the cliff, disappearing as though he had never been.

Pela stared at the space where he had vanished for a long second, and then fell back against the gravel. Her eyes fluttered closed. She was suddenly so weary she lacked the strength to move. In her mind's eye, the candle was reduced to an ember, its glow surrounded by the frigid void.

"Pela!"

Warm fingers touched her cheek. Her eyes cracked open to find Ruebyn crouched beside her.

"Hey," she croaked.

"You did it!" he gasped. "You beat him."

Pela smiled, but could not find the strength to reply. Her eyes slid closed again. "So…tired."

"Hey, stay with me, okay?" Ruebyn cried.

His arms went around her as he lifted her up. She gasped, feeling then the damage the Knight had dealt to the back of her skull, the pain in her shoulder, in her entire body. He shifted her carefully, resting her head against his shoulder.

"I've got you!" he cried.

Pela did not reply. Her head shrieked with every step they took. Several times Ruebyn staggered, and she gasped, but each time he managed to recover and continue. She would never know where he found the strength, but somehow he carried her all the way up the long slope to their cave.

She let out a long breath as he laid her down, feeling the sun's warmth shining down. She wanted desperately to open her eyes and look upon the lake in daylight, to see its beauty, but could not find the will. Ruebyn's arms were warm around her and she sighed, secure in the knowledge she was finally safe, that they had defeated all their enemies.

That she could rest.

$$\mathbf{32}$$

Braidon found Kryssa sitting slumped on the floor outside the pantheon. He and his followers had encountered several more groups of Knights throughout the Castle, and had only realised she was missing half an hour earlier. His gaze caught on the pool of blood staining the floor nearby her. Thinking she was badly injured, he rushed to her side. Her head lifted at the sound of movement and seeing his approach, she rose unsteadily to her feet.

"Are you okay?" he asked, offering his hand.

His men gathered behind him in the corridor, Dominic at their head. He'd lost the guard in the melee outside the gates, but he'd reappeared not long after they'd entered the Castle. Braidon planned to have words with the man later, but for now he was just happy to have another trained sword at his side.

"I'm fine," she replied. "The Elder got away."

Braidon breathed out a sigh when he saw her clothes were unstained, though a large bruise now marked her forehead. His eyes returned to the blood.

"His?"

She nodded. "I thought the wound was mortal, but obviously not."

"Our people have secured the exits. He won't get far." He hesitated. "Though if he has power, it had better be me who confronts him."

"I'll come," Kryssa said, straightening. Their eyes met. "Though he's stronger than both of us."

Braidon clenched his jaw, understanding her meaning. He looked from the blood to the corridors leading off the main hallway. It didn't take long to find what he was looking for. In his haste to flee, the Elder had left a trail of blood leading away from the pantheon.

"Let's go find him," he said grimly.

"Wait," Kryssa said, "what about his people?"

"What?" Braidon asked, his chest tightening.

"Inside the pantheon," Kryssa said wearily.

Her feet still slightly unsteady, she strode to the giant double doors and pushed them open. Braidon followed her inside and was met by a hundred pairs of eyes watching from the shadows of the hall. Men and women shoved children behind them at the sight of Braidon. They had stacked the wooden pews between themselves and the door, but it was little barrier against attack. Their eyes were filled with fear, and too late Braidon realised his clothes were covered in blood. He must have appeared a fearsome sight. But there was not a weapon between the crowd, and letting out a long breath, Braidon retreated into the corridor, Kryssa a step behind. They closed the doors and shared a glance.

"So he was telling the truth," Braidon murmured.

"About some things," she replied, her eyes shining. "He also spoke of cleansings and the Great Sacrifice."

Braidon nodded grimly and faced Dominic and the others. They had come to form the core of his fighting force since entering the Castle, but there were still other groups roaming the hallway. If any of them stumbled upon the pantheon, Braidon feared what they might do in their righteous anger. The innocents within needed to be protected.

"Dominic," he said. The man could be trusted with guard duty, at least. "You and the others stay here. Make sure no one leaves or enters this room. I trust you can take care of these people?"

Dominic looked from the iron doors to Braidon. "Are you sure, Your Majesty? What of the Elder?"

"We will take care of him," Braidon replied curtly. "I leave this responsibility to you."

With that, Braidon turned away, drawing Kryssa with him. They followed the trail of blood their quarry had left through the twisting corridors, then up a spiral staircase to the upper floors of the Castle. Braidon had not yet explored these parts, and now they slowed, fearful of ambush. Kryssa and Braidon were both nearing the end of their strength, worn down by injuries and the expenditure of energy, but they could not rest while the task remained unfinished.

Braidon scanned the way ahead, cautious for any sudden attack. Kryssa's warning about the Elder's power rang in his ears. He still wasn't sure how they could counter the man if he had stolen the lifeforce of others.

At least Kryssa had injured him. She still carried the crossbow—maybe they could get off another lucky shot.

Sunlight lit the upper levels of the Castle, streaming in through broad windows and half-raised shutters. Marching down another corridor, Braidon caught glimpses of the courtyard outside and heard the distant cries of his followers. Worry touched him as he leaned out a window and saw them waving torches. If someone was careless, they might burn the whole place to the ground.

Movement came from ahead. Braidon spun as the Elder stepped from an alcove. Blood stained his satin robes and he seemed to have aged since their meeting outside the gates, his face even more lined, his skin sallow.

"Braidon, Kryssa," he greeted them calmly, as though they were two passing visitors and not his mortal enemies.

Braidon gripped his sword tightly in one hand. "Surrender, Elder," he said. "Kryssa told me about your past. You too must answer for your crimes."

The Elder's eyes fell on Braidon's blade. "You will not need that, King," he murmured. "I am no threat to you. Your faithful servant saw to that."

Kryssa scowled. "I am no one's servant," she snapped, gesturing with the crossbow. "Now, are you going to surrender peacefully, or do I need to put another bolt in you?"

"Surrender?" the Elder asked, his voice sad. "So you can slaughter me like my faithful Knights? Or will it be prison, a comfortable cell to wile away my final days? Which is it, my dear king, that you would doom me to for a past I left behind long ago?"

"Your choice," Braidon snapped, hefting his sword. "I will not allow your kind to rule us."

"My brothers and I said the same about Magickers, long before the Saviour freed us of their curse. Why do you think we worked so hard to keep the secret knowledge from this world? Why we sought to squash the practice of meditation?"

"Because you wanted the power for yourselves!" Braidon snapped.

The Elder sighed. "I fear it has become so. Too many of my brother Elders have given themselves to conceit, allowed avarice to outweigh the greater good. I had thought my efforts here in Chole might bring balance, might begin the Order anew, but alas, it has all been in vain."

"You speak in riddles, but your guilt is clear. You attacked Kryssa with your power."

The Elder's head bowed lower. "In my fear, I lashed out," he whispered. His chin came up and he caught Kryssa's eye. "I am glad you are okay."

"I thought I killed you," Kryssa said coldly.

A smile creased the Elder's face. "You struck me a mortal blow." His face fell. "Coward that I am, I used the last of my power to heal it."

"I don't believe—"

A great boom came from behind them, cutting Braidon off. Braidon spun towards the window as screams came from the courtyard. His people were fleeing towards the open gates. He spun back to the Elder.

"What treachery is this?" he cried. "You were biding your time, distracting us from the last of your Knights!"

"No—"

As the Elder opened his mouth, Braidon lunged, seeking to strike him down before he brought his power to bear. The Elder's hand came up and Braidon felt a moment's resistance. Summoning his own strength, the king forged on, concentrating that energy into the point of his blade, cutting through the Elder's assault. A cry tore from his enemy and Braidon glimpsed despair in the old man's eyes—then his blade plunged home.

A sigh whispered from the Elder's lips as he slumped against the blow. Eyes wide, he stared at Braidon, mouth opening and closing. Blood bubbled from his nostrils as he struggled to speak.

"Please…" came his whisper. "The…pantheon."

There was a long hiss of expelling air as his lungs emptied, and then he was dead.

Braidon carefully lowered the man to the floor and retrieved his blade. Standing over the lifeless body, he felt inexplicably sad, as though lessened by the man's death. The quiet *drip-drip* of blood from his sword sounded loudly in the corridor. He scrunched his eyes closed.

"*Braidon!*" Kryssa screamed.

He leapt back, expecting to see the Elder rising again, but instead saw Kryssa at the window, a hand to her mouth. Braidon quickly crossed to where she stood, his heart beating hard in his chest. Smoke was pouring from the rooftops of the citadel, the first tongues of flame just beginning to appear through the slate tiles.

"The pantheon," she whispered.

To his horror, Braidon saw she was right.

They ran the whole way, but it made no difference. It was already too late.

Gasping, Braidon staggered up to the great iron door. Dominic still stood at his post, his face impassive as he watched Braidon's approach. He did not seem to notice the smoke pouring from beneath the doors, nor the distant crackling of flames, the fading screams. His other companions wore identical expressions.

"*What are you doing?*" Braidon screamed.

Dominic blinked. "We took care of them, Your Majesty," he said simply.

Braidon blanked, his stomach spasming in horror. He shoved Dominic aside and staggered forward, hauling at the locking bar set across the pantheon's entrance. Heat radiated from the steel doors, burning his face, but he would not retreat. The bar slid free and he reached for the knob.

With a roar, the doors flew open, unleashing a wave of heat that struck Braidon in the chest and hurled him back. He screamed as his beard caught flame, the fire searing at his skin. Holding up a hand to shelter his face, he squinted through the inferno, desperate to reach the pantheon, to do something, anything to help those trapped within. A desperate wail rose above the crackling, though Braidon could no longer tell whether it was real or imagined, the souls within or his own, or Kryssa's, the long dead Gods or his own sister, crying out for the innocent.

He sank to his knees and slammed a fist into the stone tiles. His scream shook the walls, filled with the torment of regret, of pain and guilt and the awful knowledge that he had done this. It had been his words that had stoked the crowd, that had given them their rage, fed their hatred.

Braidon scrunched his eyes closed against the heat, unwilling to retreat, to turn away. His mind reached out towards the flames, but there was nothing he could do to extinguish them. Such a feat was beyond his feeble power.

But as his mind quested out, Braidon sensed something else, something terrible and remarkable and brilliant. In his mind's eye, the pantheon was aglow—not with the inferno, but a swirling, shining whirlpool of energy. It hung in the air before him, almost tangible in its power, as though he might reach out and touch it like the currents of a river.

The hairs on Braidon's scalp stood on end as he realised this was the power released by the dead within the pantheon. Fire and smoke had stolen their lives, casting their spirits into the void and releasing their life force into the world.

It hung before him, a burning, raging force that none could stand against. Braidon's heartbeat quickened as he realized it was everything he'd prayed for, everything he needed to stand against Marianne, to free his people from the tyranny of the Knights of Alana.

Could he truly do such a thing? But what was the alternative? If he let this opportunity pass, he would face Marianne unarmed, his feeble life force a shade before her own power. He would lose, and Plorsea would be left to suffer her wrath…

No.

Whatever the consequences, Marianne must be defeated. It was too late to save those within, to protect them as he should have. But he could ensure their lives were not wasted. Their deaths might still help restore peace to the Three Nation, if only Braidon had the courage to grasp the opportunity.

And so Braidon reached for the shimmering vortex, and drew the power to him.

33

"Caledan, wake up!"

Light flashed across the darkness. Caledan cried out as the agony of his body suddenly came rushing back. He gasped, fresh air filling his lungs, and a fiery warmth swept through him. Glowing lights swirled across his vision as he opened his eyes. Panicked, he tried to sit up, but his limbs refused to obey and he slumped back to the floor.

"What…?" he croaked.

"You're alive!"

This time Caledan recognised Marianne's voice. Drums hammered at his skull, making it difficult to think. The queen's face swirled overhead. He could feel her hands on his chest. Slowly the spinning slowed and he saw she was smiling—then the image split in two and it was all Caledan could do to keep from throwing up. He closed his eyes again and it helped…somewhat.

"What happened?" he asked when the sensation had passed. "Is the boy okay?"

"He's safe," Marianne replied, though her voice was faint. "Thanks to you."

"And the Elders?"

"Gone!" she gasped. Her fingers tightened on his chest as she continued. "Though I barely…had the strength…"

Caledan's eyes snapped open as her voice faded away. Her head thumped into his chest. His arms went around her before she slid to the floor. Forcing himself up, he held Marianne in place. Fading light streamed in from the balcony and he realised it was already sunset. Marianne was still awake, though exhaustion hung heavy in her sapphire eyes.

Only then did he remember his own injuries. He placed a hand to his chest, feeling the tear in his shirt, the blood soaking his tunic—but the skin beneath was whole. He stared at the queen.

"What did you do?"

A smile creased her cheeks. "Could…hardly let you…die," she murmured. Her eyes slid closed as she continued. "You saved…Calybe."

"What's wrong with you?" he asked.

"Used…too much energy…against Servo," she croaked. "Had to use…my own life force…for you."

"Why would you do that?"

"Why not?" she whispered. "Think…I'm going to sleep…awhile now."

Caledan smiled despite himself. Lifting her in his arms, he stood and carried her to the bed. Calybe lay asleep beneath the covers. He laid her down beside her son, then sat on the edge of the bed and took Marianne's pulse, reassuring himself she would live.

Then he stood as realisation came to him. Servo and his Knights were gone. The city was free. And now the evil queen lay sleeping, defenceless. He stared at her, remembering that night in Malevolent Cove, how she had struck down Devon and tried to burn Kryssa and Pela alive.

This was the opportunity he had come to Ardath for, to rid the Three Nations of Marianne's evil, to avenge Devon's death. Without the Order pulling the strings of the capital, someone true could be lifted to the kingship, until Calybe came of age.

Beside Marianne, the boy stirred. Reaching out in his sleep, Calybe pulled himself closer to his mother. Caledan's heart hammered in his chest as he watched them sleep. His hand drifted to his chest, feeling again the smooth skin where the Knight had torn him open. He'd been dying, would already be dead if not for Marianne. She had given the last of her strength to save him.

Recalling the cold, calculating woman of Malevolent Cove, the hate-filled monster that had come for Braidon, he could not reconcile the two. There was no reason for Marianne to have healed him. She had won her battle, her son was safe—why then take such a risk, weakening herself at the moment of her victory?

He could not understand it.

Finally he let out a long sigh and sank onto the bed. The boy's eyes flickered open at the movement. Seeing Caledan sitting beside them, he smiled and hugged his mother tight.

"Thank you for helping us," he whispered. Then he looked at his mother, a frown touching his forehead. "Is Mum okay?"

"She's fine," Caledan murmured. "She's just tired."

A smile lit the boy's face. "I'll keep her safe!" he said, cuddling beneath his mother's chin.

Caledan smiled as the boy closed his eyes. A knock came from the door. Rising, he collected his sword from where it had fallen. The Knights and Queens Guard still lay where they had died. Crossing the room, he found the ruined doors half-propped up in the frame. He hauled them open, weapon at the ready.

A frightened man jumped back, hands raised in surrender. "Please, no!" he yelped.

Caledan hesitated. "What do you want?"

"Sir, the queen, I have news for her?"

"The queen is currently indisposed," Caledan growled, then wondered at the man's words. "I speak for her, at this moment. What is the news?"

The messenger hesitated, trying to see into the room, but Caledan barred the way. The man's shoulders slumped and he shrugged. "What does it matter? It will be common knowledge within the hour."

"Out with it then, man!" Caledan barked.

"It's the king!" the messenger gasped, then seeming to realise the statement needed more explanation: "King Braidon has risen from the dead. He has proclaimed Queen Marianne a traitor and led an uprising in Chole, claiming the city for his own."

Caledan stared at the man, stunned. "Truly?"

"Of cou—"

The sellsword slammed the broken door in the messenger's face. Half the panelling fell out with the movement, but taking the hint, the man turned and scuttled off down the corridor.

Caledan stood staring at the wood. He could not believe

it. Braidon, leading an uprising? Thinking of the miserable mess he had left behind in Dragon Country, it was inconceivable. How had this happened?

Returning to the bed, Caledan sank onto the mattress alongside Marianne. This changed everything. This meant he had to choose a side—the rightful king, the man Devon had begged him to protect, or the woman who had usurped his crown. The woman who had murdered his friend.

Marianne stirred beside him, her eyes sliding open again. "What was that about?" she whispered.

"Braidon lives," Caledan murmured. "He has taken Chole."

He watched her, trying to gauge her reaction, but she only smiled. "Of course he has."

"I'm serious."

The queen pushed herself up on one elbow, though he could see it took her an effort of will. "So am I," she said. "My dear husband comes from a line of heroes—and villains. No doubt he hates me now as much as I him. He has nothing left but that, and so he will not stop, not until I lie dead at his feet."

Caledan's chest tightened. "I should have done my duty in Dragon Country," he said. "He begged me to do it then."

"The mistake is made, my Champion," Marianne replied. Her hands found his wrist, squeezed. "And so the question becomes: will you do your duty now, even against your rightful king, even against your friends? Will you kill Braidon for me?"

Caledan stared into the queen's sapphire eyes. Her face was a mask of beauty, untouched by flaws, her auburn hair tumbling around her shoulders, as perfect as though she had just bathed. She was the most beautiful woman he had ever seen, more intelligent than Servo and all the Order's scheming, more powerful than Braidon, a Magicker of old. Who else could rule Plorsea, but this woman before him? He let out a long breath.

"I will, My Queen."

EPILOGUE

Servo's horse was breathing hard by the time he galloped through the gates of Sheffield. He had ridden all day and night to reach the southernmost bastion of Lonia, a retinue of Knights and retainers stretched out far behind him. Yet even with their support, he could not be sure of his safety.

How far did the queen's power truly extend? She had taken the Lonian capital without a fight, cowing the council with her power. And despite Servo's efforts, Ardath had fallen into her hands. The news would travel the land within days.

Marianne was now the undisputed queen of two nations.

He could not understand where she had found the power. How many souls had the woman slaughtered without his knowing, to wield such strength against the Order? A dozen Knights had died in the throne room—and a dozen more of Servo's loyal Queen's Guard—and still he had barely escaped with his life.

It was inconceivable. Servo had spent the better part of ten years collecting power, ever since he'd discovered the secrets of the Elders and joined their ranks. He had manipulated kings and councils and even his fellow Elders, all to achieve one end—to make the Order supreme ruler across the Three Nations.

But Marianne had picked his plans apart, piece by piece, until they lay unravelled for the world to see.

He would not stand for it.

"Sir?"

With an effort of will, Servo returned his thoughts to the present. They had reached the central plaza of Sheffield and his escort had drawn up around him. They numbered some fifty Knights and twice as many retainers—enough for what he planned. Darkness still clung to the dusty streets of the mining town and there was no one else in sight.

"Take the town hall, empty the guard barracks, wake the citizens of Sheffield. They are to be the first to hear the new words of the Saviour."

Within an hour, it was done. Sheffield was a small town, without walls or a standing army, but it would do for now as his safehold. First though, he had to be sure of its citizen's loyalty. He could no longer afford mercy—the blasphemous must be uncovered and cleansed, lest their treachery wake the Gods from their slumber.

No, with the sunrise, a new day would dawn. Let Marianne think him defeated, but the Order would rise again, and soon. His Knights had planted their seeds across Plorsea—Braidon's people could not turn from it now. They had murdered their neighbours in the name of the Saviour and seen the truth.

Close to a thousand men and women had been packed into the town square, many still in their bedclothes, so hurriedly had they been forced from their homes. Servo sneered at their weakness. Sheep—that was all they were, these people, livestock to be used and discarded at their master's will. Had they the strength, they might have fought off the Knights. Instead they cowered, defeated before the fight had ever begun.

Exhaustion weighed heavily on Servo's shoulders. He had wasted too much power in his battle with the queen. But it mattered little now, with the sheep gathered. He had only to sort the loyal from the blasphemous—and he still had power enough for that.

"My people!" he bellowed. He stood in the centre of the square, surrounded by Knights, but his voice carried out over the heads of the crowd. "She who would be our queen has betrayed us!"

Whispers spread through the crowd. Servo let them grow for a moment and then clapped his hands. Thunder boomed across the square—a simple illusion—and silence returned.

"Marianne serves not the Order, nor our mighty Lonia. She cares only for power, and has made a deal with the False Gods to raise herself above her fellow mortals. She intends to enslave us all with their magic."

Now there was terror in the voices in the crowd. They jostled back and forth, as though the False Gods walked amongst them even now, preparing to strike them down.

"But fear not, my people!" Servo bellowed, enhancing his voice with a touch of power. "The Saviour has armed her Elders with weapons of our own." He threw out his arms, and with a *whoosh* fire leapt from his hands. Gasps came from the crowd at the illusion, and Servo suppressed a smile.

"The Knights of Alana will stand against the dark queen, but we cannot stand alone. So I ask you, my people, are you with us?" His voice dropped to a whisper. "Or are you against us?"

As he spoke, Servo released a wave of power. The day was proving costly, but he still had enough—or so he prayed. He should have done this long ago, but the other Elders were old, limited by the past. They had forbidden such uses of power, for fear of what might follow.

But Servo would no longer be constrained. He knew what was needed. In one stroke, he would restore his power and destroy his enemies amongst the crowd.

A collective cry rang out as Servo's power touched each of the gathered townsfolk. A thousand fists lifted skyward—but not all. As one, a hundred men and women fell to their knees. Their voices no longer lifted in agreement, but dissent.

"No! Never! No!"

His power had given their true nature voice—their rejection of the Order, of the Saviour, of Servo.

Still smiling, Servo let the power ebb. Horror contorted the faces of the blasphemous as they realised what had happened. Servo wanted them to know, to realise the consequences of their failure.

"The blasphemous lie revealed before us," he called. "Let us cleanse them in the name of the Saviour!"

He did not even need his power now. A roar rose from the crowd as they fell upon the traitors. With foot and fist his loyal soldiers knocked their enemies to the ground and tore away their lives, one by one. Servo wandered amongst the slaughter, hands—and mind—extended, drawing the departing souls to him. His heart raced with the thrill of it, with the intoxicating power of their life force.

He should have done this long ago, should have walked amongst the cities of Lonia, through the streets of Ardath, culling the blasphemous. Instead he had bided his time, given people time to change their ways, to join the Order of their own free will. He had put up with Ashoka and his mechanisms, with Braidon's resistance to his own sister's call, with the Trolan blockade.

But no more.

From this day forth, he could afford no weakness. He would gather the faithful and destroy all who stood against him. None could conceal their treachery from him now.

The sun lit the distant peaks by the time the slaughter was done. By then, Servo felt better than he had in weeks, his power restored. He might have moved against the queen immediately, but without knowing the true source of her strength, he dared not act so recklessly. He would take no chances this time. When the time came he would attack with overwhelming force, and Marianne would be swept away like a leaf before the storm.

"Elder!"

Servo turned as a voice called from the back of the crowd. A group of several men and a woman stood there, their clothes tattered and torn, faces dirt-streaked and hair unkept. It looked like they had just spent a week in the wilderness. They must have just arrived in Sheffield, and missed his ceremony.

Unwilling to take any chances, Servo sent a sliver of power through the group, demanding their loyalty. None wavered, but for the woman. She cried out and fell to her knees. The men took a collective step back from her, surprised by her cry.

"What have we here?" Servo asked as he approached. Closer, he saw that the woman wore the collar of a slave. Little wonder she was unfaithful.

"An escaped slave," one of the group said, stepping forward to address Servo. "One of two who escaped the mines this past week. The other crossed the border into Trola, but she won't get far. She killed a Knight—and apparently an Elder. Sir Isyc went after her alone. He won't stop until she's dead."

A scream came from the ground. Leaping to her feet, the woman charged the speaker. Servo flicked a hand and she staggered to a stop. Eyes wild, she clawed at her throat, mouth opening and closing like a fish out of water.

Chuckling, Servo stepped in close. "Feisty, isn't she? You said she was a slave? Best not kill her too quickly then. An example must be made for the others. What was the punishment for a runaway slave again?" He paused for effect. "Oh, of course!"

He snapped his fingers and a sharp *crack* came from the slave's legs. At the same time, he released the power from her throat. Screaming, she fell to the ground clutching her ruined shinbones. Servo stood over her, savouring the screams, before finally making to turn away. But something her captors had said gave him pause.

"What did you say of the other slave? That she had killed an Elder?" he asked.

The leader nodded quickly. "Yes, sir. In Townirwin—at least that's what Sir Isyc claimed."

It couldn't be.

"What was the girl's name?" Servo asked quickly.

"Pela, sir!"

It was! One of those who had caused so much chaos in Malevolent Cove. And she'd escaped with this woman. He looked at the slave again. Her face was contorted in agony and she no longer seemed to know where she was, what was happening. He studied her features, but it was not the mother. But he recalled there had been another woman in the amphitheatre.

"I know you," he murmured. "You were with the sell-sword, and the king. What was it they called you?"

The woman only moaned, writhing in the dirt, clutching her ruined legs. One bone had broken so badly it now stabbed through her flesh. Servo sighed. He would get nothing from her in this state. Touching a finger to her forehead, he took the pain from her—if only for the moment.

She collapsed sobbing to the ground, incoherent words tumbling from her mouth. Impatient, Servo grasped her by the hair and pulled her head up.

"I asked you a question," he snarled.

Her pupils constricted as they concentrated on Servo, seeing him for the first time. "I know you."

Servo struck her hard across the face. "And I you," he snapped. "What is your name, woman?"

"Genevieve!" she gasped.

Servo smiled. "Was that so ha—?" He broke off, staring at the woman.

She scowled, locking eyes with him. "What, lost your tongue, butcher?"

"It can't be," he murmured, ignoring the taunt.

He grasped the woman by the chin thrust her head to the side, exposing the iron collar. She tried to fight him, but a trickle of power was all it took for Servo to hold her. He had taken the pain from her legs, but she still could not stand. There was nowhere she could go, no way she could escape him.

Staring at the collar, Servo struggled to believe what he was seeing. So this was why Marianne had gone to Lon. He should have realised the experiments had not truly failed. That had been the last news he'd received from the engineers in the capital, that a mechanism to synthon a victim's life force from afar was impossible to create.

But here was the truth laid bare. A jet-black jewel had been set into the centre of the iron collar, a channel through which the woman's life force would be conveyed upon her death. Sure, a slave's life force might have dwindled by the time of their death, but there were thousands of them working in the mountains and fields of Lonia. More than enough power for one woman.

Rage touched Servo, that Marianne had realised this opportunity while he had been blind. No wonder she'd wanted to halt the Order's cleansings. She no longer needed them. The woman could sit on her throne and gather enough power to conquer the Three Nations, without ever getting a drop of blood on her hands.

Growling, Servo gripped the collar between his fingers. A sharp *shriek* followed as the iron cracked in two and fell to the ground. He raised a fist, readying himself to strike the woman dead, but something gave him pause.

This woman had been with the sellsword Marianne had recruited to her cause. She knew the man, had travelled with him—King Braidon and the woman Kryssa as well. All had proven to be wily foes, but this Genevieve could be a weapon against them.

Perhaps the slave might yet prove useful.

———

FIND OUT WHAT HAPPENS NEXT IN CROWN OF CHAOS, AND don't forget to leave a review if you enjoyed the story.

NOTE FROM THE AUTHOR

Well well well, I've certainly got a few loose ends to tie up in the last book don't I! Braidon, Marianne, Servo seem destined to clash and there's still Pela, lost in the mountains of Trola. How does she fit in the big picture? Sadly you're going to have to wait until I suspect almost December to find that one out! But let's just say, there's a reason Trola hasn't featured until now. I'm excited to show you why… I'm also excited to figure out just exactly who is the good guy (or girl) in this series now Devon's guiding light is gone. Aren't you? ;-) In the meantime though, you can always join to my mailing list for updates, specials, and a free copy of my two novels Stormwielder and Oathbreaker!

FOLLOW AARON HODGES

Join Aaron Hodges on his newsletter to **receive TWO FREE novels and a short story!**

https://aaronhodgesauthor.com/newsletter

ALSO BY AARON HODGES

The Sword of Light

Book 1: Stormwielder

Book 2: Firestorm

Book 3: Soul Blade

The Legend of the Gods

Book 1: Oathbreaker

Book 2: Shield of Winter

Book 3: Dawn of War

The Knights of Alana

Book 1: Daughter of Fate

Book 2: Queen of Vengeance

Book 3: Crown of Chaos

The Evolution Gene

Book 1: Reborn

Book 2: Havoc

Book 3: Carnage

Descendants of the Fall

Book 1: Warbringer

Book 2: Wrath of the Forgotten

Book 3: Age of Gods

Book 4: Dreams of Fury

The Alfurian Chronicles

Book 1: Defiant

Book 2: Guardian

Book 3: Conquest

The Swords of Heaven and Hell

Book 1: <u>Darkstrider</u>

The Four Circles

Book 1: Help! My Wizard Mentor Had A Heart Attack And Now
I'm Being Chased By A Horde Of Giant Spiders!

The Untamed Isles

The Path Awakens

www.ingramcontent.com/pod-product-compliance
Lightning Source LLC
Chambersburg PA
CBHW061011120726
47910CB00006B/1881